COUNTING *on* LOVE

RL BURGESS

BELLA
B O O K S
2019

Acknowledgments

To my darlings Sam and George, thank you eternally for keeping the lights on while I followed these characters around.

Thank you to Ann for your insightful suggestions, guidance and teachings through the editing process. I will never look at an exclamation mark the same way.

Thank you to Bella Books for opening your doors to me, and so many others, who love to get lost in a fictional world that reflects our realities.

And to everyone who reads this story, thank you for doing so, it makes me and the characters very happy.

About the Author

RL Burgess is a musician, writer, lover, mother, best friend, dog owner, slave to two cats and decaf coffee drinker. She writes mostly when other people are sleeping, before six a.m. and after nine p.m., spending her days playing music and working with community groups. Rosie lives on the beach side of Melbourne, in Australia.

Dedication

To Sam, George, Ruby, Pep and Fred. We are a motley crew but the love could not shine brighter.

CHAPTER ONE

Zoe (Monday a.m.)

"Ahem."

"Ouch," Zoe cursed, knocking her head on the desk as she shifted beneath it.

"May I ask what you're doing under there?" came the voice of Mel, Zoe's workmate and best friend of twenty years.

"I'm fixing…" Zoe grunted with effort, scrabbling with her fingers blindly around the back of the computer stack, "…my computer. What does it look like?"

"Hmm. It looks like you're trying to hide under your desk," Mel replied, a laugh in her voice.

"Well I'm not. My screen's packed it in. And right when I was knee deep in the McFarlane audit, but I'm sure," she paused to catch her breath as she tried to stretch further toward the back of the computer, "I can fix it if I can just change out this cable."

"Well that does sound tricky. Have you considered calling IT?"

"Mel. As if!" Zoe shuffled herself out from under the desk and stood up, rolling the tension out of her shoulders. Her cheeks felt warm with effort and her brunette hair, normally so carefully attended to, had slipped out of its usual simple clip. It fell around her face in dishevelled waves. "I'd have more luck getting them to bring me a coffee than fixing my computer."

"Harsh."

"But true. What are you doing this far down the hallway, anyway?"

"I'm bringing up the business cards for your team. We designed them with the new logo so they look pretty schmick."

Zoe took the box Mel was waving, glancing at the new design. Hers read, *Zoe Cavendish, New Business Specialist, Azoulay House*. A miniature of her own face stared at her from the corner of the card, hair pulled back in a ponytail, acorn-coloured eyes, her crisp white shirt blending in with the linen on the card.

She snorted. "Was the picture necessary?"

"Yeah, everyone has their face on nowadays. It adds a sense of authenticity and trust."

"Right. Well, thanks." Zoe tossed the box on her desk. "I've got to get this bloody computer sorted."

"Seriously. Let me call IT. Desperate times," Mel replied with a smirk, flashing her dimples. She was dressed straight out of the 80s today, sporting a woollen grey suit with oversized shoulder pads and matching high-waisted trousers. That was the benefit of working in the marketing department, Zoe thought, tucking in her own shirt, which had come adrift while she was under the desk. There was a certain creative licence allowed in that department.

Mel changed her hair colour every other month and no one seemed to mind. Lately she had been going for a *Desperately Seeking Susan* look, her hair a tangle of bleached blond and dark roots, a style that appeared haphazard but Zoe knew was carefully crafted. Not something Zoe could get away with as a New Business Specialist. She was expected to meet the corporate expectations of a high-flying financial adviser with snappy business suits and a well-manicured look. She actually enjoyed dressing the part, but every now and then she was a little jealous of the creative freedom Mel had with her wardrobe. Not that she wanted to come to work looking like Madonna, but the occasional day in her track pants wouldn't be so bad.

"I am actually desperate. I've got to finalise this audit by lunchtime." Zoe paused, chewing her bottom lip anxiously. Her eyes lit upon her laptop, tucked into its bag under her desk and she crowed triumphantly. "But not desperate enough to sit around waiting all day for some lecherous slimeball from IT to come and breathe their coffee breath all over me. I'll just go and take this little guy to the tea room and work from there."

"Good idea. And in the meantime, I'll pop in an IT help desk for you."

"Don't you dare," Zoe warned, scooping up her laptop and and stalking out of her cubicle past Mel. She swiped a wayward lock of hair out of her face as she went, feeling like a bear on the warpath.

"Pop in to see you in the tea room if we need you today then, yes?" Mel asked sweetly, trotting after Zoe down the corridor.

"That's where I'll be," Zoe said, her tone self-righteous. "And don't be interrupting me with endless cups of coffee. I have much to do." And with that she turned abruptly into the tea room, running straight into the CEO who was exiting the room with a brimming cup of hot tea.

"Oh god, Reyna, I'm sorry." Zoe exclaimed, as tea slopped over the edge of the cup, spilling onto Zoe's laptop and scalding the CEO's hand. Reyna yelped in pain. "Quickly, run it under cold water," Zoe instructed, grabbing the dripping cup and manoeuvring her boss to the sink. She flipped the tap open and blasted the cold water, holding Reyna's hand firmly under the stream.

"Are you burned too?" Reyna asked.

"No, just you I think," she replied, her eyes wide with concern. "God, I'm so sorry."

"It's fine, I believe I can manage from here. Thanks, Zoe," Reyna said, gently extracting her hand from Zoe's grasp. "It's just a little scalded."

trademark goofy grin, resting his lanky great arms around them all. They were younger, fresher versions of themselves now. The photo had been taken just after their university graduation—how long ago was that? She mentally counted forward from her twenty-third birthday and realised this November would be the tenth anniversary of that photo. She was lucky to have such a solid group of friends.

But Mel was her rock. She had scraped Zoe off the floor after her first big breakup and helped her find her own apartment. They had pounded the pavements together after uni looking for work. She had been there when Zoe's mother had died unexpectedly a year and a half ago, always ready to lend an ear, a hand, or a shoulder—anything, anywhere. In fact it had been Mel, working in the marketing department of Azoulay House, who had shown Zoe the job advertisement for the position she currently held.

Zoe searched for the file she had been working on, scanning through the list of auto-saved documents, relieved to find it was there and intact, just where she had left off when her screen had fizzed out. When this was done she would organise a digital presentation for McFarlane's management team, with the outcomes of her audit and a little extra for them, some handy tips on how to restructure their tax burden to enhance cash flow for the business. She knew they would be impressed with her work. That was one of her career mottos and she worked hard to nail it on every brief: never miss an opportunity to impress.

Zoe flashed back to Reyna's dark, almond-shaped eyes as she asked Reyna to let go of her hand in the tea room. She flushed with embarrassment at the memory. Definitely not her most impressive moment. But then, Reyna Azoulay was hard to impress. She would stop to chat for a moment or two if Zoe bumped into her in the tea room, but she never really divulged anything about herself.

And yet nothing escaped her attention. She had sent flowers to Zoe's home when her mother had passed away. At the time, Zoe had only been with the company six months. Now that she thought about it, most likely Reyna's PA had purchased those flowers. Still, it represented the ethos of the company under Reyna's leadership.

Zoe was also a fan of Reyna's dry humour and quick intellect, often evident at staff meetings. Not to mention the fact that she was drop-dead gorgeous. Her strong dark Middle Eastern features reminded Zoe of a more delicate Frida Kahlo, shining black hair lightly curling over her shoulders, flawlessly smooth, tan skin and a body that curved and stretched in all the right places. She had heard that Reyna was fluent in both Arabic and Hebrew, a fact that was supported by their strongly diverse client base.

Yes, Reyna was in a league of her own, and Zoe had been the head cheerleader for Team Reyna since she had started with the firm two years earlier. In fact, if it weren't for the issue of Thomus, Zoe would have said Reyna could literally do no wrong. For some reason Reyna continued to support him, even when it seemed to Zoe the whole world must see his incompetence, but somehow it seemed to have escaped Reyna's notice. Oh well, you couldn't be perfect on every level, she thought, dreamily chewing on the end of her pen, but Reyna was as darn near close as could be.

"I've called IT for you," Mel said, sticking her head into the cubicle. "But you stay there. I'll work at your desk when they're done. Better to finish your train of thought."

Zoe swivelled around to face her. "Thanks," she said, her gaze still far away.

"No problem," Mel replied. "Er, why are you looking at me like that?"

"Like what?"

"Like you've turned into some kind of liquid chocolate and you want to be eaten up."

Zoe coloured, snapping out of her Reyna daydream. "I'm not. I was just thinking… Anyway, thanks for letting me use your computer."

"It's fine," Mel said slowly, drawing out the words suspiciously. "Take your time. Have it for the rest of the day. I'll just be over at your desk." She backed out of the cubicle.

"Thanks Mel. You're a good friend."

"Yes, yes. Get over it. I'm going to sign you up for an online dating account if you don't snap out of it."

Zoe sat up straight and glared at her friend. "You will not."

"That's better. I don't know what you were thinking about but that was weird. Don't do that again, okay?"

Zoe laughed, feeling guilty. "Fine, whatever. Let me get on with this now."

"Good idea," Mel said, retreating from her cubicle. "I'm gone," she called. "I don't know why you're even still trying to talk to me. Get on with it already."

Zoe laughed and turned back to the computer. The clock at the bottom of the screen read 10:45 a.m. She didn't have long to go. She really would have to concentrate now if she was going to get this wrapped up on time. Definitely no more time for daydreaming about Reyna Azoulay.

CHAPTER TWO

Reyna (Monday p.m.)

Reyna stared at the tousled black curls protruding from the top of the thick, quilted blanket. For some reason he liked to sleep with his face under the doona. She worried he wouldn't be able to breathe properly and gently slipped it down from his face, like she had every night so far, admiring the sweet curve of his nose and the perfect rose of his lips. He looked so much younger than eight when he slept. Undoubtedly he would pull the blanket back up again before the night was done. His face was slightly flushed and she touched his forehead with the back of her hand. Warm and damp. She lifted the edge of the blanket, fanning him lightly, wondering if he would wake up and be confused. He was actually an exceptionally deep sleeper. Reyna joked that she could have a band play in his room and he would sleep right through it, but then again, the nightmares still woke him up quite regularly. The result of the trauma, the child psychologist had said.

Reyna searched his sleeping face for evidence of her sister, a habit she had fallen into over the last six months. His father's solid features had left little room for her sister's delicate lines, but there were subtle similarities. There was the curve of his chin, the length of his eyelashes. Other features were vastly different. Sarit's nose had been straight and thin, inherited from their Israeli mother, and his was wider, softer. Reyna knew his face would change as he aged, but it was difficult to picture it now. He had their father's thick Egyptian brow and when he opened his eyes, the dark irises of a long line of Middle Eastern ancestors. Asleep, he looked impossibly young, even for his brief eight years.

She took a long sip from her frosted glass, enjoying the burn of the whiskey as it slid down her throat. It had been a long day. Meeting after meeting after meeting. Her hand still ached from the burn she'd received in the tea room this morning and she pressed it absentmindedly against the cold glass. Zoe Cavendish was flying high as a financial adviser, a real rising star for the firm, but she was possibly a bit of a klutz.

Holden shifted, whimpering slightly as he turned to face the wall. He had decorated it with posters lifted carefully out of the kids' magazines she sometimes bought him at the supermarket. An array of footballers, soccer stars, and comic figures stared down from the walls, brightening up the space. She supposed these were his heroes. A far cry from the movie stars and ponies she had put on her own walls as a child.

He frowned in his sleep, a quick furrow of his brow, almost a flinch. Soft black curls fell across his face and Reyna reached out and lightly smoothed them away. Was he dreaming of them—his mother and father, her sister, now forever out of reach? Reyna's throat ached and her eyes welled with tears. He was doing well, but god it was hard. She had watched him struggle against the weight of his inner demons day after day, trying to fit in at the new school, doing his best to embrace this strange new life. She had seen shadows of pain pass over his face when he stared out the window on a rainy day. Occasionally he would break down, sobbing until he was hoarse, and she would hold him while his little body wracked and trembled in her arms. They had only talked a little; he wasn't so big on talking. The psychologist had said this was normal. She still felt guilty for moving him back to Australia, but what else could she have done? There had been no one left to care for him in England after his parents had died. One fiery car crash had taken away his whole life.

Kissing him lightly on his forehead, she adjusted his blanket again and headed back to the kitchen to sort through the detritus of their evening meal. A stray pair of Lego men lay on the floor under his chair, locked in suspended battle. Reyna picked them up, tossing them into the toy box in the corner by the TV. He certainly was a whirlwind. It was impossible to keep up with the chaos that seemed to follow him from room to room, a tornado of toys and books.

She had been touched by the support her friends had shown when she had first brought him home, supplying her with much needed Legos and stuffed toys, books about superheroes she hadn't even known existed (seriously, Ant Man?), and action figures. She had bought a few things as well, but there really had been little need. Even his clothing had been taken care of, with bags of small, bright T-shirts and pants arriving in the arms of friends, whenever they visited. They had organised it all while she had been over in London collecting him. She had only just held it together when she had arrived home, jetlagged and heartbroken, a small sleeping boy resting his head on her shoulder in the back of her parents' car.

Her closest friends, Samira and John, had been on the doorstep to usher them in, casserole in the oven, a glass of wine poured, and a bed made up for him in her spare room. When everyone had finally left, she had sat outside his room and cried herself to sleep. The room had been so bare back then, just plain white walls and the guest futon that doubled as a couch, one small bookshelf with some treasured items and a lamp. They had redecorated it together after a trip to Ikea. Holden wanted yellow, so they bought a sunny yellow desk and a burnt yellow bedspread. They painted the walls a warm and friendly dandelion, fetching the ladder to stick a set of glow stars on the ceiling. But that first night had been hard and strange. For both of them. She had woken on the cold wooden floorboards outside of his room, stiff necked and heart sore, with Holden standing in front of her looking anxious.

"Aunty Rey, I need to pee," he'd said. "Where do I go?"

Somehow they had made it through the last six months, intact. Her parents had been a godsend, picking him up from school each day and helping him with his homework until Reyna could make it back from the office. Most nights she made it home in time for dinner. Juggling the demands of her role as CEO of Azoulay House with this new responsibility of raising a child had been quite the challenge.

Single at thirty-eight, she hadn't exactly given up on the idea of having children, but in truth, she also hadn't really thought about it much. Friends joked that her career was her baby. And in a way it was. Seven years ago she had started Azoulay House, and since then, through long hours and dedicated hard work, she had taken the company from a respectable, but small accountancy firm, to a nationally sought-after industry leader and corporate business partner of the highest calibre. It had been hard work, but it had been worth it.

With the arrival of Holden, things had shifted. When she wasn't in the office, she was learning to be the parent of a thoroughly grief-stricken, utterly beautiful eight-year-old boy. He required all her attention. There was no more casual dating, no more lazy Sunday mornings drinking coffee and reading the paper, many fewer bottles of wine with friends. She kept her business trips to a minimum. She was Skyping more with her national offices, conducting more of her work from her computer screen, rather than face-to-face. She had considered selling the firm or stepping down from her role as CEO, but with her parents' support, she had allowed herself the luxury of maintaining her job. These days, though, she worked a lot from home in the evenings, finishing off the day's emails and juggling the workload she would normally have fit into long days at the office when Holden was asleep.

Her mobile phone buzzed, snapping her out of her reverie. She dried her hands on her jeans and fished it out of her pocket. A message from Samira. *Sunday night dinner?*

Sure, we'd love to.

Her phone buzzed again. Smiley face. *Come early. Boys can play.* For the hundredth time she felt lucky to have such supportive friends as Samira and John. It had been Samira's idea for Holden to try out for the local soccer club with their boys.

"It'll be a great way for him to make some friends," she had said as Reyna hauled herself across a freezing, muddy field at eight a.m. on a Saturday morning. And he had really seemed to come alive. He had played soccer back in London, he had told her, half wistfully, half excited. His favourite position was goalie. She had gasped with shock when he had fallen, taking a hard ball to the stomach, but he had nodded at her stoically and set himself back on his feet, his little body rigid with determination. And so, with her shoes entirely ruined, she had resolved to buy herself a pair of gumboots and a much warmer jacket, and sign him up for the team.

We're doing okay, she thought as she pulled out his lunchbox and started to prepare his sandwich for school the next day. Her heart gave a painful little kick. We're doing okay, she silently told her sister.

CHAPTER THREE

Zoe (Tuesday p.m.)

Zoe's intercom crackled.

"Could you come to my office, please," a familiar voice sing-songed. Her team leader Thomus (Thom-arse to his team behind closed doors) was a fan of buzzing people in to his office. He never came to their desks if he could help it. It was one of his many power plays.

"Sure," Zoe replied, sighing as she saved her work and gathered up her notebook and pen.

Thomus was not renowned for being quick. He loved to theorise and digress, expounding his ideas mercilessly as he leaned back in his oversized swivel chair, hands linked behind his thinning, blond ponytail. By three o'clock he would have pronounced sweat patches under each armpit, and his room would be pungent with the mix of his man-scented deodorant and his heavy body odour. An afternoon meeting with Thomus was not something to look forward to. At least he tries to do something about it, Zoe thought charitably as she made her way to his office.

True to form, Thomus was not just leaning back in his oversized, black leather office chair, he actually had his shiny, brown brogues propped up on the large mahogany desk, ankles crossed.

"Zoe, come in, come in," he sang at her as he twirled a pencil with his right hand, his mobile tucked between his shoulder and his ear. "I'll just be a sec."

Which he was not. Ten minutes later she was feeling far less charitable as she fidgeted in her seat, waiting for him to wrap up his call, his self-important tone grating on her nerves.

"Sorry, darl," he said eventually, dropping his feet from the desk and tossing his mobile onto a pile of paperwork in front of him. "I had to take that." He tipped himself forward in the overbearing chair, leaning his elbows on the desk. "The McFarlane audit," he said, giving her a meaningful look. His black-rimmed eyes were small and rounded, sitting closely together in his thin, pale face, on top of a pair of large dark shows, almost racoon-like.

"Er, yes," she replied, unsure where he was going with this. "I submitted the report yesterday at lunchtime as requested."

"And what did you put in there?" From his tone, one could have concluded that Zoe had packaged up the final report with a handful of cockroaches included.

She spread open her palms, as if to say, just the usual. "Results of the audit, tax implications and future projections. Just everything the team has been working on for the last few months."

"And?" He pressed his fingertips together, clearly probing for something in particular. She was at a loss to know where he was going.

"Cover page? Contact details?"

"I don't suppose you included any advice in your report? No little suggestions for improvements?"

"There may have been a couple of small suggestions." She tried not to look guilty. "But nothing beyond the scope of my role. I saw a way they could structure their tax burden slightly differently in the future and included it as a pathway for their consideration. That is perfectly within my scope."

Thomus sighed, his thin eyebrows drawn together in disapproval. Slugs, she thought. His eyebrows looked like silvery slugs, creeping across his forehead. She would not be intimidated by him. She had done nothing wrong.

"You like to be a high flyer, don't you, Zoe Cavendish?"

"Excuse me?"

"Not everything we do has to be pushed to the nth degree, you know. Sometimes we can just meet the brief and move on. We don't need to strive for industry recognition with every client." His sarcasm clearly referenced the award she had won the previous year for Victorian Advisor of the Year.

Zoe pursed her lips, a slight flare of her nostrils the only indication that she was angry. "I'm just trying to do my job."

"Well, they want to meet with us and explore this option further."

Ah, so that was it! She blew out a short breath. Thomus hated field trips. He hated any reason to leave his pretentious office and potentially have to do extra work.

"Would you like me to go on my own?" she suggested, knowing he wouldn't be able to accept. If there was any chance McFarlane's wanted to take up her suggestions, Thomus would need to be there to claim the credit.

"No, no." He waved his hand, brushing aside her suggestion. Suddenly his brow cleared. "I will invite them here."

"Great." She closed her notebook and pushed back her chair, hoping their meeting was done. The centrally heated air was thick with his smell and she was starting to feel lightheaded.

"Book us a meeting room and arrange this into a prospectus. If we're going to assist them with this restructure, we should really take over the account entirely. You can organise a little morning tea for them or something. I like those biscuits with the shortbread and chocolate."

"Right," she said, knowing it would be useless to argue that booking meeting rooms and organising morning teas was hardly her role. "I'll organise it. Have you spoken with them?"

"Not yet, just had the email. You can call them and get them in."

She stood. "Anything else?"

"Try to stick to the script next time, Zoe. We don't need to be fishing for extra business everywhere we look."

She nodded briefly, and left the office, taking a deep breath of fresh air as she tried to calm herself. What an arsehole he was. Surely a manager was supposed to be pleased when a client was so impressed with your work they wanted to talk further. Wasn't that what they were supposed to be doing? Building up business for the firm. Reyna had been banging that drum consistently since Zoe had joined the firm. "We offer an holistic service." Zoe could clearly hear Reyna's voice quietly driving the point home at their staff meetings. We aim to be corporate partners with the businesses we serve, not just tax agents, not just accountants, not just financial advisers. *Their investment is our investment,*" Reyna intoned.

Zoe knew the drill by heart. Thomus was possibly the laziest manager she had ever had. Why the firm put up with him, she did not know.

She stepped into the bathroom to freshen up, pausing at the mirror to check her face. She splashed some water on a paper towel and pressed it against her flushed cheeks. For some reason it always felt ten degrees hotter in his man cave.

The face she examined in the bathroom mirror looked reasonably well put together, given the hours she had put in this week. Long lashes framed her light brown eyes, slight shadows beneath them the only evidence of the late nights she had pulled to finish the McFarlane audit. Wavy, caramel-coloured hair, flecked with streaks of auburn, pulled up into a butterfly clip. She let her hair out and fluffed it with her hands, massaging her neck for a second.

Thomus made her feel stupidly tense. She wished he didn't get so under her skin. She rubbed her temples in a circular motion, mimicking the stress relief techniques she had seen in an article in the tea room the other day. Was it making her feel better? Hard to tell really. She splashed some more water onto a towel, cooled her neck, and patted herself dry with some more paper towel. Right. Time to get back to work.

Pulling her hair back up into the clip, she studied herself, trying to imagine how others would see her. Her nose was small—a ski jump, her brother had called it. She had laugh lines around her eyes and her cheekbones were high. Medium lips—not too large, not to thin. She smiled at herself, checking her teeth for evidence of lunch. Her features were even, almost symmetrical. She had read once that symmetry was one of the key characteristics of attractive people. Did Reyna think she was pretty? She frowned at herself, waggling her manicured eyebrows. Ridiculous question. Reyna barely knew she existed.

As if summoned by her thoughts, the bathroom door swept open and Zoe yelped, instinctively jumping behind the door, fully expecting to see her boss enter the bathroom. Mel strode through the door and caught sight of Zoe in the mirror. She jumped.

"Woah!" Mel cried, swinging around to face her. "Why are you hiding behind the bathroom door? You gave me a fright. I swear you are not normal!"

Zoe chewed her lip. "I thought you were Reyna," she said, ducking her head in embarrassment.

"So what if I was? Why the hell would you be hiding from Reyna?"

"Shh, Mel! Keep your voice down."

"Reyna's in her office," Mel replied with exaggerated calm. "She's unlikely to hear you from across the office and inside the bathroom. Are we losing the plot a little here do you think? Shall we come out from behind the bathroom door and go about the business of being a sought after and successful, highly paid financial adviser?" Mel smiled, to soften her words. "It is undignified for the Victorian Adviser of the Year to be hiding behind bathroom doors."

Zoe grinned sheepishly. "I was thinking about Reyna and when the door opened I thought it was her. I panicked."

"Fair enough. Well, it's not her, it's me. What are you doing hiding in here anyway?"

"I needed to freshen up. Thomus called me in to his office."

"Oh no. What did Thom-arse want with you? For what reason were you called into the palace de stink?"

She grimaced. "He's cross with me for doing such a good job on the McFarlane audit. They want more information so now we have to have a meeting with them."

"Aha! How dare you be so good at your job as to generate more work for Thom-arse."

"Yeah." She stepped back over to the mirror, adjusting her hair clip. "How annoying am I?"

"Well, sometimes a bit annoying…" Mel smirked at her through the mirror. "Hey, shall we finish off the pamphlet for your seminar program after work tonight? I want to get it done before the next round starts. We could squeeze it in before dinner with the girls?"

Zoe checked her watch. "Damn," she muttered, surprised to see that it was already three o'clock. "I'd better motor if there is going to be an 'after work' today. But yes, that would be good."

At seven o'clock Zoe and Mel were still hunkered down in Zoe's cubicle, making their way through a large plunger of coffee and a comprehensive review of the marketing material for the community financial wellness seminars Zoe had been running. Earlier in the year she had completed an online Diploma in Financial Counselling, qualifying her to provide emotional and practical support to people experiencing financial difficulty. It had been Mel's idea. Hearing that Zoe was no longer entirely content with helping the rich get richer, Mel suggested she learn how to help the poor get richer too.

Zoe had seized on the idea, researching on the Internet until she had found the right course. Combined with her masters in accounting she was perfectly set to design her own seminar series, covering the basics of the emotional and intellectual demands of managing one's finances, including budgeting, getting out of debt, and planning for the future. She was running the sessions on Monday evenings from the office after some manipulation of Thomus.

Naturally, he hadn't been keen to support her idea, but Mel (to the rescue again) had convinced him that with the marketing department on board, they could really drive home a community service message that would look good for the company, and which would simultaneously enhance his own image. He had begrudgingly allowed her to proceed, as long as it didn't encroach on her regular duties, of course. She had approached the local municipal council and struck a deal. They were pleased to be able to offer a free seminar series on such an important issue in conjunction with Azoulay House, agreeing to run advertisements in the local paper and manage enrolments, with Azoulay House supplying the venue and the course. Zoe had been ecstatic when fifteen people had shown up to her first Monday evening seminar. In a show of moral support, Mel had been attending too.

"Do you think management even knows we're doing this?" Zoe wondered, stretching out her shoulders and giving a wide yawn. She gazed at the complex graphic design program Mel was expertly manoeuvring on the computer screen.

"If by management, you mean Reyna, then yes, for sure. I'd say she knows most everything that happens in her own firm." Mel looked straight at Zoe, her normally clear blue eyes suddenly pensive. "God, you really have it bad for her, don't you?"

"I do not," Zoe said primly.

"Whatever." Mel shook her head and changed the subject. "I think we're good. We've got a full suite of marketing collateral to capture the essence of what you're doing. I'll run some of the posters off on the printer downstairs and you can take them to council tomorrow morning on your way to work."

"Yeah and I can see how many have signed up for the new series next week." Zoe stood and stretched, wriggling her hips. "I think my bum's gone to sleep. What time is it?"

Mel checked her watch. "Holy shit, it's after seven. We were supposed to meet the girls half an hour ago."

Zoe shrugged. "So we'll be late. We're always late." She reached over to save their document and then flicked off the screen. "If we leave now we'll make it in time for dessert."

Three cheerful faces, flushed with cheap wine and good spaghetti, greeted them as they walked through the door at La Travoletta.

"You're late," Enid said, pointing at her watch. "If we've told you once, we've told you a thousand times, dinner is at seven."

"We ate without you," Chiara chimed in.

Travis said hi and pulled out a couple of chairs. "Sit," he gestured.

"Let me guess," Enid said, pouring out two generous glasses of red wine and handing them across the table. "Working late?"

"Yep." Zoe took a gulp of the wine and grimaced as the vinegary liquid made her mouth pucker.

They had never really graduated from cheap wine after their university days, everyone agreeing they had more or less developed a taste for it, so why waste money on the expensive stuff. Sometimes, though, she thought they could afford to lift the bar a little higher. Chiara slid a slice of pizza on to each of their plates and Zoe tucked in. She was ravenous. "Mel had a new proposal for the marketing material for my seminars," she mumbled through a mouthful of pizza.

"You what?" Chiara asked, her face confused. "That sounded like you said Mel proposed to you."

"She wishes. I was helping her with the seminar stuff," Mel explained. "Now that she's run a couple of sessions, we wanted to put together some proper collateral so we can advertise it more widely."

Zoe actually felt excited as she and Mel explained exactly what was planned out for the sessions. This program had brought a new element of inspiration into her daily grind. She loved her job, but she had also found herself searching for something more. At the end of the day her work revolved around helping people make money, which was fine, but she was enjoying bringing that skill to regular people as well, not just big business. The corporate world had a tendency to be a bit soulless, so it was refreshing to feel like she was also helping normal, day-to-day people.

She knew her friends found it hard to understand, but Zoe truly loved working as a financial adviser. She loved the puzzle of making the numbers fit together, the excitement of following trails of figures to an answer that was often surprising. Sometimes she felt like a detective, deciphering clues, unearthing missing numbers, and then solving difficult financial problems.

Her friends thought her job was dry and boring. Travis had once described it as "sitting around with a calculator," but for Zoe, it was far more than that. Her solutions had allowed clients to prosper and make the most out of their innovative ideas. What she loved the most was working with clients who were trying to achieve exciting outcomes, like breakthroughs in health care, technological developments, and enhancements in community development. She loved helping businesses manage their finances, so that they could really focus on their creative development.

"Well, I never thought I'd say this," Enid said, tucking a strand of her golden hair behind her ear. "Your program actually sounds interesting! I think even I would like to come along, and I hate talking about money."

"But that's the whole point," Zoe exclaimed, her eyes sparkling. "I want to help people overcome their financial fears and see it as a tool so they can get on with their lives."

"Yeah," Mel said seriously. "It seems like half the battle is won just by taking the fear out of it."

"Count us in," Chiara said, giving Travis a gentle poke in the ribs. "We could use a little help in that department."

Travis sat up straight, knocking his knees under the table. Next to the petite Chiara with her lithe, dancer's body, he looked like a gangly beanpole. "We'll definitely be there. If we're ever going to get a house deposit saved, we could really use some advice."

Zoe beamed at her friends. It had taken forever for Travis and Chiara to admit their feelings for each other, and it still filled her with joy to see them so happy together.

"Careful," Mel warned. "Zoe will give you too much advice if you let her. She'll probably start with, 'if you're trying to save for a house deposit, don't waste all your money on cheap booze and eating out at restaurants with your friends.' At least that's what she told me."

"It's probably true," Travis mused. "Ah well, you can't win 'em all. So, what does the esteemed Thom-arse think about it all?"

"Actually, he hasn't mentioned it since he authorised it. It's entirely possible that he has forgotten about it. The only time I've mentioned it to him was when he approved it, and that was after Friday drinks when he definitely had more than a couple of champagnes in him."

"Speaking of, who wants a top up?" Enid waved the bottle. "We've got another one of these to get through people, so drink up."

"Me, please," Mel said, passing her glass over the table. "And can we order dessert now? I want ice cream."

"We all ready for the Tough Mudder run next weekend?" Enid asked.

Travis groaned. "My hamstring is still playing up."

"We'll carry you through Trav," Mel said. "We can give you a chair lift if your hammy gives out. Or Chiara can throw you over her shoulder, fireman style, and run you through to the finish line."

Zoe grinned, enjoying the mental image of Chiara powering for the finish line with a lanky Travis draped across her. People always underestimated Chiara's strength because she was so slight, but as a professional dancer her muscles were phenomenal and Zoe knew she could outmatch any of them in the strength department.

"Would you do that for me, babe?" Travis asked, and Chiara kissed him on the nose in answer.

"These events are definitely not as easy as they were back when we were at uni," Zoe said.

"Easy for you to say," Mel replied. "You're still running almost every day. The only place I'm running to is flab town." She poked at her nonexistent belly.

"Get out, Mel," Enid said. "You haven't got an ounce of flab on you."

CHAPTER FOUR

Reyna (Friday p.m.)

Reyna watched Thomus jiggling his foot as he tilted back in the chair across from her. Clearly their conversation was making him agitated.

She chose her words carefully. "I've given you a lot of leeway Thomus. But it's important to me that you understand the difference between being supported and taking advantage."

"I should hope you know that I do," he replied peevishly, flicking an imaginary piece of fluff from his pant leg. "I don't know what I've done to receive this kind of attention."

"Perhaps it's more about what you haven't done. I see you leaning heavily on your team."

"It's good for them to step up."

"Yes, but again, there's a difference between stepping up, and being stepped on. As their manager you need to give them credit for their work, guide their hands, contribute your own knowledge." She took a deep breath and went on, "I know that since Dave died you've had your share of struggles, and if there is anything I can do to help you I will, but I won't let you take liberties with your team. That wouldn't be fair on them or you.

We've worked together for a long time and I know you're better than this."

Thomus set his lips in a grim line, swallowing hard as he looked at his hands. "I'm trying," he said finally. "I just can't seem to make myself care about anything."

"Fair enough." Reyna decided to be straight with Thomus. "But what should I do in the meantime? Here I am with a manager who doesn't care and it's affecting his decision-making. You're making yourself, and me, look bad, incompetent in fact."

He shook his head and met her gaze, flinching a little. The bags under his eyes betrayed the sleepless nights and daily struggle he still had, dealing with his partner's death.

"I'm sorry," he said, uncharacteristically quietly. "I don't mean to let you down."

"I know that. The problem is you're letting yourself down. You won't want to stay at Azoulay House forever Thomus, and god knows the financial world is a den of gossip. If you develop a bad reputation amongst the staff here, it will follow you around wherever you go. And then it won't matter how brilliant I know you to be, people won't want to work with you. I'm already hearing murmurs."

He sat up. "What kind of murmurs."

"Speculation. People wondering why I keep you on."

His cheeks flushed hotly. "If you want me to leave—"

She cut him off. "That's not what I'm saying. I'm trying to tell you that I know you, but I'm not the only person who counts. You need to pull it together. I get that nothing can erase the incredible pain you feel about losing Dave. I get that life just feels like a terrible slog that you have to somehow make your way through, believe me, I do. But we need to make a change here or you'll do your career a permanent damage. Are you still seeing the counsellor?" She asked, changing tack.

He shook his head.

"Time to go back?" Reyna suggested, gently.

He blew out a sigh. "Maybe."

"I'm asking you to. As your boss," she added for good measure. She just hoped she was getting through to him.

"Okay, okay."

"Good. We'll catch up again next week. I know it's been a hard few years Thomus," Reyna said, her voice soft with understanding. "But you will get through this."

He cleared his throat and rubbed his chin, ducking his head in a nod. His normal bravado had all but gone and he looked unbearably vulnerable. As frustrated as she was by his behaviour, her heart did go out to him. Understandably, his partner's sudden and unexpected death of a heart attack had left Thomus shattered. But the lack of a will, the mountains of debt and the refusal of Dave's family to recognise their relationship at the funeral had compounded his loss, leaving him angry, bereft, and financially burdened. A few years back he had been a charismatic and intelligent manager, just shy of arrogant as he strode about the office at the top of his game, but nothing Reyna couldn't handle. His decline over the last few years had her wondering how much longer she would be able to keep him on.

"Next week then," Reyna said, closing her notebook. She gave him what she hoped was an encouraging smile. "Call your counsellor."

"Gather round people," Reyna called, tapping a teaspoon against her glass to get the group's attention.

Their monthly Friday afternoon drinks had a tendency to get a little rowdy. As much as Reyna was not a fan of socialising at work, she had instigated this ritual as an opportunity to give back to the staff and build morale. Over the last few years it had become an institution in itself, with staff rating it as a high priority. IT had even set up a video link so that all four national sites were now connected for the monthly catch-up. Reyna made a point to use the opportunity to praise the firm's hard workers and set the bar for those who could afford to push a little harder. She had even begun handing out a monthly "innovation" award. The accompanying dinner-for-two voucher at an upmarket restaurant had become its own motivational factor for the more competitive staff.

She cleared her throat, taking a small sip of champagne as she waited for the room to quiet. "Okay. Welcome everybody.

Another Friday, another excellent month gone by. I'd like to start by congratulating Meryl and Stacey in the Sydney team for their successful handling of the BioCon demerger." A cheer came over the loudspeaker from the Sydney team, who were seen on the video link clinking glasses and patting a pixelated version of Meryl and Stacey on the back.

"Not only did you finish a day early," she continued, "the clients were highly satisfied and both parties have signed a partnership agreement with us for ongoing consultancy, so well done Meryl and Stacey." She paused to look down at her list.

"We've had some big jobs this month; John's team has been working hard with Friedman Industries, and Thomus's team has finalised the McFarlane audit. Thom, I hear there is a potential partnership in the works there too?" Reyna scanned the room looking for Thomus. She wasn't sure he'd show up after their talk earlier, but she was relieved to see him stepping forward.

"That's right, Reyna," he called. "I've been in negotiations with them and I'm hoping to have them signed up within the month. Given their international interests it will be quite a coup for the firm to have them on board."

Reyna resisted rolling her eyes. Of course he would take all the credit for the team's hard work. Disappointing after the chat they'd just had. She knew his team would be smarting at his response.

"Another great team effort," she said, smiling around the room. "Well, I won't take up any more of your time this afternoon. Thank you all for your continued hard work. Azoulay House would not be the same without each and every one of you. So raise your glasses and let's congratulate…Meryl and Stacey—winners of this month's innovation award." The crowd applauded and the room dissolved immediately into loud chatter and a clinking of glasses.

Platters of cheese and crackers had been set out around the room. Staff were encouraged to have something to eat and to drink responsibly. The last thing Reyna wanted was for anyone to have an accident on the way home. Since her sister and brother-in-law had been smashed off the road by a drunk driver, she was acutely aware of the toxic mix of alcohol and driving. Thankfully, she had only had to intervene a few times over the years—a firm hand under the elbow to guide someone away from the drinks table and into her office for a long and boring chat over a cup of coffee while they sobered up. People had caught on quickly and all it took from her these days was a meaningful look and her employees got the message. Friday afternoon drinks were not a privilege to be abused.

Reyna circulated, making small talk with the staff. Nikki, her PA, hovered close by, ready to attend should Reyna indicate she needed anything, adamant that her role was to be by Reyna's side at all times during business hours. Reyna had a sneaking suspicion that if she would allow her, Nikki would be by her side at all hours, regardless of business.

"Excuse me, Reyna," Kylie from IT broke in. "The national offices are signing off the video link now."

Reyna took the cue, stepping over to the webcam to thank the staff for attending. She reminded them to stay safe and drink within their limits, before shutting off the connection.

She enjoyed spending time at the national offices but had limited her travel as much as possible over the last six months since bringing Holden home. He stayed with her parents when she had business that she absolutely had to attend to in person, but she felt strongly that it was important to disrupt his life as little as possible, given the trauma he had experienced. She relied heavily on her management team to run their ships smoothly, which was another reason why she was becoming so frustrated with Thomus. If he didn't lift his game his attitude would start to undermine his team, and she just didn't need that right now.

And on that note, she was more than ready to wrap up her week and get home to Holden. If she left now she'd be in time for ice cream on the couch before bedtime. She also knew that if she let it drag on too long, people would drink more than was appropriate at work.

"Nikki, let's call it a day now, okay?" she said quietly into her assistant's ear.

"Absolutely."

Nikki snapped to attention, gathering up the detritus of the party. Reyna and a few others helped to stack plates and glasses into the dishwasher and clean off the benches while others slipped away, happily chatting with each other. It was important to Reyna to pull up her sleeves and show herself as an active and involved leader. Morale was high and she felt pleased with the way things were rolling out. She had worked with her HR manager to implement a new pay structure at the beginning of the year which had given many of the staff, especially the juniors, a helpful lift in their wages, and she was not immune to the effect it appeared to be having on their commitment. Staff retention was up, managers were coaching their staff toward career progression, and the firm was really growing into a proper, national family.

With the kitchen put back to rights, she ducked into her office to grab her briefcase and a bunch of files she could work on over the weekend when Holden was busy. He liked to watch cartoons on Saturday mornings and she would open up her laptop and sit next to him on the couch, doing her best to concentrate against the background mayhem of Looney Tunes. Growing up, she and her sister had also watched Looney Tunes. It was hard to believe it still existed, but Holden loved it and she was happy to indulge him. She flicked off the light to her office and slipped out the door, closing it firmly behind her. It would be good to get away from the office for the weekend.

"Night, Reyna," a voice called behind her, causing her to momentarily startle.

She swung around and saw Zoe walking up the corridor toward her.

"That was some great work on the McFarlane audit, Zoe," Reyna said, waiting for her to catch up as she locked her door. "I could see your hallmark stamped all over the outcomes there."

"Thank you." A faint blush stole across Zoe's delicate cheekbones. "It was definitely a team effort."

"Anything nice planned for the weekend?"

"I'm doing Tough Mudder on Sunday with some friends. It's an endurance-based, cross-country obstacle course," she added, clearly sensing Reyna's confusion.

"Sounds intense," Reyna said as they walked down the hallway.

"Oh yeah, super intense. It's basically twenty kilometers of insane challenges and mud. Lots of mud."

"And you're doing this why?"

Zoe laughed. "It's actually loads of fun."

"Running for hours through mud?"

"So much mud. We'll all need a hose down afterward, that's for sure. But yeah, we have a lot of laughs. How about you?"

"Me?" Reyna was momentarily confused, wondering if Zoe was asking if she would need some kind of hose down.

"Yeah, any weekend plans?"

"Oh, right." Of course, she thought, feeling strangely stupid. "Nothing too serious. Just a quiet one for me." She was careful with her personal life at work. She felt no need to share her deepest, darkest goings on with one hundred and fifty of her colleagues. She knew she hid behind the distance that her role as CEO created, but she was thankful for it. She was not a fan of mixing her work and personal life.

"Enjoy the run Zoe," Reyna said by way of farewell as she pushed open the door to the car park and stepped out into the darkness. She wrapped her coat around her tightly, warding off the chill of the wintery evening.

"Have a great weekend," Zoe called after her as the door swung closed.

Starting her car, Reyna cranked the heating, and pulled out of the car park, shivering as she waited for the warm air to permeate the car. A strange sense of loneliness crept over her as she drove, focusing on the flickering red taillights of the car in front. As much as she didn't envy her running through all that mud, Zoe's weekend did sound like fun. She realised she was jealous. It had been a hell of a long time since she had been free to muck about with friends all weekend. She guessed Zoe to be early thirties, not so far apart in age from herself. She was obviously a capable operator, a real asset to the firm. Reyna didn't know everyone in the firm, it had grown too large for that kind of personal touch, but with the results Zoe was achieving it was hard not to notice her. She was attractive too. Reyna couldn't deny that. Zoe's athletic build and wide-mouthed smile definitely helped her stand out amongst the crowd. If they had met in a bar, well, Reyna would have been interested, that was for sure. But that was not how they had met, she reminded herself sternly. She was Zoe's boss and there was The Rule.

Reyna had made The Rule for herself very early on in her career: Never Sleep With The Staff. It had stood her in good stead, even when it had occasionally been difficult to uphold. Of course there had been attractions, glances, and serious temptations, but Reyna had been steadfast. She had seen the result of management having casual dalliances with their staff at other firms—broken hearts, lost jobs, acrimony, and loss of reputation. None of that was for her.

The fact was, her love prospects were slim to none right now. And it wasn't like she was getting out and about to meet people. These days she was lucky to squeeze in time with Samira and John. All the rest of her socialising, if you could call it that, was done with her staff, and they were covered by The Rule. These days she felt like her closest relationship was with her laptop. Or Nikki. She shuddered, thinking of her well-meaning but officious assistant. Not only was Nikki far too young for Reyna's tastes, she was painfully self-conscious and took herself very seriously. Nikki had a habit of looking at her like a starving cat planning an attack on an unsuspecting mouse, and the last thing she needed was a lovesick kitten for an assistant. She needed someone who could get the job done. With a sigh, she realised she would need to keep an eye on Nikki and make sure things didn't get out of hand.

Setting a high standard for herself was important to Reyna. She knew others would be happy to cut corners and obfuscate the truth in order to make a deal, but she would not tolerate the merest whiff of that. It had been a strain having to watch Thomus so carefully recently, but thankfully he didn't appear to be doing anything untoward, just not doing too much of anything at all, she thought ruefully. Reyna had climbed the career tree quickly herself. After university, the combination of her natural intelligence and learned business acumen had seen her through some high profile managerial positions, allowing her to rapidly build experience. She had taken a leap setting up Azoulay House seven years ago, but it had paid off in spades. Her love life, however, had not seen such success. And, she admitted to herself, things were unlikely to improve any time soon, given her work and child-rearing commitments.

The reflection of the streetlights shimmered on the wet road, like a mirage. A light, romantic rain had begun to fall and she flicked on her windscreen wipers. Tonight would have been the perfect night to have a lover to come home to. Someone to curl up with and listen to the rain on the roof, feeling safe and secure inside the bedroom together. Unbidden, an image of Zoe came to mind, curled up on Reyna's couch with a book, looking at her with inviting eyes. She quickly chased it away. It wouldn't do to entertain those kinds of thoughts. She knew from experience that even thinking about breaking The Rule was tantamount to disaster. Anyway, regardless of all her rules and (lack of) opportunity, it would be madness to even consider starting a relationship with what she had going on right now. No, her love life was so firmly off the table. It wasn't even in the same building as the table. Or the same street. Or universe.

She had to face facts. She had prioritised her work over her love life, and now she had a child to put in front of everything and everyone, so things were doubly doomed. She pushed her clamouring libido down and turned onto her street, enjoying the arch of the trees that lined the little cul-de-sac. The warm twinkle of the lights in her neighbours' houses reminded her of the comforts of home. She was not alone she told herself as she pulled into her driveway. She had her parents and now there was Holden to love. And love him she did. Already, over the past six months, a fierce desire to love and protect him from the world had arisen within her, surprising her with its intensity. For the first time, she was learning to put somebody else's needs entirely before her own. She stayed in the driveway for a moment, the engine running as she enjoyed the warmth of the car, the chilly winter evening uninviting. It wasn't that she had been selfish before; she knew she was a good friend, she always did whatever she could to help her parents out, and she had loved her sister devotedly, but her sister had moved to England a long time ago and their relationship had sustained itself with annual visits and long chats on the telephone. She just really hadn't had the need to sacrifice herself for anyone else. Until now.

She snagged her briefcase and left the warmth of the car, trotting up the front steps of her house. She heard Holden's laughter from within and paused in the hallway, taking a moment to enjoy the sound. She was actually quite terrified of her new role as quasi-mother. There were no rulebooks here. She had had no training as a parent. She had read a bunch of books when she had first brought Holden home with her, but they had made her even more stressed, talking about the importance of the bond created at birth, the partnership between parents, etc. It had filled her with anxiety—she had none of that. She knew she could never replace his parents and she would never want to. She just wanted to do her best to give him a good life.

"You worry too much," John had told her. "Just let your instincts take over. Your heart knows what to do."

"Yeah," Samira agreed. "And don't forget, you're a CEO. That's like being a parent to hundreds of crazy, messed-up adults, who will probably be far more challenging and difficult than Holden will ever be."

She smiled, hearing her dad give a roar of mock rage as Holden came pounding up the hallway, grinning like a banshee.

"Aunty Rey," he exclaimed breathlessly, grabbing her by the waist and swinging around behind her. "Protect me! I stole Papa's last cherry and now he's going to eat *me* for dessert!"

CHAPTER FIVE

Zoe (Friday p.m.)

Zoe lay in the bath, luxuriating in the deep, permeating heat. Why did she always make such an idiot of herself around Reyna? She absentmindedly swirled her hand through a patch of bubbles. If she was not careful, Reyna might mistake her for a dithering fool. And she wasn't. She was a calm, intelligent, capable woman who was punching far above her weight at work. She knew of course that nothing would ever come of her silly crush on Reyna, but for some reason she just hadn't been able to let it go.

She let her ears slide under the water, momentarily blocking out the sounds of the apartment around her, amplifying the beat of her heart in her ears. Really, how had she developed such intense feelings for a woman she barely knew? She didn't even know if Reyna was gay or straight. Not that it made a difference. Reyna was entirely, firmly, one hundred percent off limits. It was the glimpses, the moments watching Reyna giving presentations, speeches, leading a group, conducting their business like a choirmaster that had caught her eye. She made

Zoe want to sing. Not that Zoe knew anything about music, but she imagined it might be that way.

She resurfaced, wiping the ticklish bubbles away from her ears. Honestly, this just would not do. Her friends were over it, and Mel clearly thought she was losing the plot. This evening after she had bumped into Reyna in the corridor at work, she had been as giggly as a teenager. Mel had rolled her eyes, steering her down the corridor to her little blue cubicle.

Leaning against Mel's desk, careful not to disturb any of the teetering piles, Zoe had allowed Mel's admonishments to wash over her.

"Zoe Cavendish it is time for you to wake up and smell the roses, or whatever the saying is. You're acting like a schoolgirl. You need to snap out of it."

"Snap out of what?" Zoe said, aiming for a nonchalance she didn't feel.

"You cannot stalk Reyna in the halls and moon over her."

She tried to be indignant. "I am not stalking her in the halls. Or mooning over her for that matter. I just happened to bump into her."

"Well, stop *bumping* into her okay? It's not doing you any favours." Mel sighed. "We need to get you out and about and get your mind off her."

"Why don't *you* get out and about? It's not like you're seeing anyone."

Mel blushed, piquing her interest. "Wait. Are you seeing someone?"

"No, I..." Mel shook her head, suddenly interested in a book on her desk. She picked it up and turned it over, studying the blurb. "I'm not."

"You are," she crowed. "Why the secrecy? Who are you dating?"

"I'm not dating anyone," Mel hissed, looking sharply around the cubicle as if worried they would be overheard. "Keep your voice down would you?"

"Why? Why should you care if anyone from work hears us discussing your new girlfriend?"

Mel hushed her furiously. "I do not have a new girlfriend. Drop it, Zoe."

She stared at her friend for a moment, confused by the secrecy. They had always confided in each other. "I don't know what's going on here."

"There's nothing going on," Mel said, tidying up her desk and grabbing her briefcase. "You've got the wrong end of the stick. Just as you do with this ridiculous crush on Reyna. You have to let it go now, okay?"

She had agreed, just for the sake of keeping the peace. And anyway, she knew deep down Mel was probably right.

Zoe skimmed her hand over the surface of the bath, gathering a fresh trail of bubbles. It was weird, but she supposed Mel would tell her what was going on in her own time. There was no point in rushing her. Trying to push Mel in a direction she did not want to go was like trying to stop a freight train with your bare hands. Or a tornado. Or a supernova. Still, she felt a twinge of anxiety. Mel was like family to her, closer than her own family really. They had done so much together and it felt strange to think that she might have a secret.

Zoe blew the bubbles off her fingers, watching them cascade through the air. All would be revealed, she decided, when the time was right. Mel didn't often have secrets but if she was guarding this then she would have a good reason for it.

From the kitchen, Zoe could hear her phone ringing. She sighed, wondering if she should get out of the bath to answer it. She sat up and wiped the bubbles from her hair. It could be Mel, ready to talk. As she climbed out of the tub her ringtone stopped, but she towelled herself off anyway. Her skin was beginning to wrinkle up and it was probably time she got out. She padded through her apartment to the bedroom and wrapped herself in a soft white robe.

The apartment was sweet and she had fallen in love with it at first sight, a small red brick block, nestled in a leafy street in the southern suburbs. She was on the top floor. Penthouse suite, she called it. Annoying, her friends pronounced it, as they dragged her furniture up four flights of stairs on the day she moved in. It wasn't fancy, but then neither was she. Inside, an arched doorway led into a little alcove with a wall of windows, where she had set up a big stuffed chair and a shelf of books. The bedroom was just large enough for her queen-size bed, and a little kitchen with bench seats doubled as entertaining space when her friends came around. But the bathroom was her favourite room. The previous owners had done up the tiny room in a nautical theme with a deep claw-foot bath and a round porthole window set into wooden panels, making her feel like she was at sea.

In search of her phone she rummaged through her bag in the kitchen and then spied it on the bench by the kettle. She was surprised to see it was not Mel, but her brother Danny who had been trying to get her. Flicking on the kettle she called him back, perching up on the bench while she waited for him to answer.

"Dan?" she said when the call clicked on.

"How you going?" he asked, his voice gruff down the line.

"All good here. You?"

"Fine, fine. Listen, you're on speaker, Trina's here too," he said, and Zoe could hear a muffled laughing in the background and then her brother's girlfriend called out, "Hi Zoe."

"Hi," she called back, feeling perplexed. It was unlike her usually reserved and serious brother to sound so…jolly. "What's up you two?"

"We wanted to tell you, well, we really wanted you to be here but—"

"Be where?" Zoe asked, cutting him off. "Tell me what?"

"I'm trying to say," Danny paused, and Trina giggled again in the background. "Trina and I…we, um, got married tonight."

"You what?!"

"We got hitched," Trina sang out. "Right next to the Eiffel Tower."

"Sorry." Zoe knew she should be keeping up but somehow nothing about this conversation was making sense. "What do you mean the Eiffel Tower?"

"I forgot to tell you, we're in France," Danny said.

"You're in France, and you got married?"

"That's the sum of it," he said stoically.

"More information please," Zoe said, shaking her head even though she knew they couldn't see her. "How did all of this happen?"

"We came over for the publishing awards. I was nominated—"

"He won," Trina said loudly into the phone. "Danny's company won best new boutique, international publishing house."

"Wow," Zoe said, her head spinning. "Congratulations, Dan. I didn't even know you were going to France."

"Sorry, yeah, I should have said. It all happened kind of quickly. Anyway, Trina and I decided to come to the awards because we'd never been to Paris, and—"

"Oh my god, you're in Paris?"

"Yeah."

"Mum always wanted to go to Paris, remember?"

"I remember. That's part of the reason we got married here. She would have loved it."

"It was so romantic, Zoe," Trina joined in. "We got married in this divine little garden and we could see the Eiffel Tower in the background. I can't wait to show you the photos."

"Well, congratulations you guys. I'm really happy for you."

"Sorry you couldn't have been here," Danny said.

"That's okay, I totally get it. Strike while the iron is hot and all."

Trina and Danny both laughed and there were some more muffled sounds and a squeal from Trina.

"Better go." Danny's voice came back on the line. "Call you next week when we're back."

"Okay, thanks for calling. Safe travels, you two."

Danny rang off and Zoe shook her head again, more than a little surprised by her brother's spontaneous action. Not that it wasn't lovely news. Danny and Trina had been together for almost five years and they were rock solid. Zoe had supposed they'd get married at some point but they had never mentioned it so she assumed it wasn't really that important to them. Her heart twisted as she thought about how much their mum would have loved a Paris wedding. Zoe could just imagine how she would have oohed and ahhed over it as a wedding destination. Would she have gone? Probably not in the end. Even if she had been well enough to travel, before the cancer struck, she would have made an excuse not to go. In her lifetime, she had been far too poor to afford such a luxury, and in her last few years she had been drinking way too much to manage any kind of travel.

Zoe made herself a cup of herbal tea, her heart a strange mixture of joy for her brother and nagging guilt and sadness about their mother. When her phone rang again she assumed it was her brother calling back to tell her something they had forgotten—perhaps they were having a baby as well?

But it was Mel's voice that greeted her. "Hiya."

"Danny got married," she said by way of reply.

"What?"

"Yeah, they're over in Paris—"

"Paris!"

"My thoughts exactly. Anyway, they had a shotgun wedding."

"They're having a baby too?"

"What? Wait, no. I just mean they got married on the spur of the moment."

Mel laughed, and said "shotgun weddings are for when you're pregnant and you need to get married."

"Oh, really? Didn't know that. There's no baby that I know of."

"Regardless, that's excellent news."

"I know. I can't believe how well he's doing."

"You're both doing extremely well."

"True."

"I mean, who would have thought," Mel went on, "looking back at the two of you as teenagers that you'd turn out so normal."

"Hey!" Zoe protested.

"It's just that with everything you guys went through, it's pretty great that you're both so solid."

"I was worried for a bit there that Danny wasn't going to be okay."

"We all were. He was the wildest of the wild. Actually, given the way you both grew up it's kind of crazy that you were such a nerd while he was such a renegade."

"I was not a nerd!"

"Oh, but you were. You even asked Miss Mallory for extension maths work because you felt like the assignments weren't challenging enough."

Zoe laughed, in spite of herself. "I loved Miss Mallory."

"You and the rest of the school. She was way too hot to be a high school teacher. I was so busy drooling over her I didn't learn a thing in her classes. That's probably why I'm such a maths dunce now."

"You're not a dunce, it's just not one of your strengths," Zoe said, trying to be diplomatic.

"Whatever. I can't believe Danny is married."

"I can't quite wrap my head around it either. It feels like I've been worrying about him for such a long time it's strange not to have to do that. But he's actually had his shit together for a while now. Love has been a real godsend for him."

"Which is why you need to go out and get yourself some."

Zoe sighed, sipping her tea. "Not that simple."

"Actually it is. We arrange the date, you go and sit at the table and be your charming self. Anyone with half a brain will love you."

"All that getting-to-know-you stuff..."

"That's the easy part," Mel cried. "Hi, I'm Zoe, I'm a very successful financial advisor—"

"Boring," Zoe cut in.

"And I'm a runner and I've got great friends and family—"

"My parents are both dead and my brother just ran away to Paris to get married."

Mel paused. "I'm thinking it wasn't quite like that."

Zoe felt a lump threaten in her throat. "It wasn't. I'm just sad to have missed it. We're all the family each other has and now I've missed my own brother's wedding."

"It's just a wedding. What's really important are all the anniversaries and years to come after the wedding. And you'll be there for all of that stuff."

"True."

"And if they do have kids you'll get to be aunty Zoe and spoil them rotten."

"Oh my god, that would be so great." Zoe pictured herself doting on a tiny Danny, scruffy face lit up with a smile as she handed him a lollypop. Or maybe it would be a girl, and they'd go horse riding together. Or maybe twins, and she could take them go-karting. She felt her spirits lift. Mel was right, things weren't so bad. "So, what's up with you then?" Zoe asked, suddenly realising it was odd for Mel to be calling her on a Friday night. "Why aren't you out on a date tonight?"

"Can't a girl choose to have a night in and chat with her best friend?"

"She can, but she rarely does."

"Date canceled," Mel admitted.

"Someone special?"

"Nah, just a casual thing. Remember that girl from the Pink Sofa site? With the gardening business?"

Zoe scanned through her mental data bank trying to picture which girl Mel was referring to. "The one with the really curly hair? Always wears a football cap?"

"That's the one."

"She dumped you?"

"Looks like it. But that's okay, I wasn't really into her anyway."

"You'll find someone," Zoe said comfortingly.

"Ditto, Cavendish."

CHAPTER SIX

Reyna (Saturday, a.m.)

"Holden, be careful with the stick, please. You don't need to actually stab him. Just pretend." Reyna turned to Samira. "Well there's a sentence I never thought I'd hear myself say."

Samira's laugh was muffled by the thick, woollen scarf she wore wrapped high around her face. Only the pinkish tip of her nose was exposed to the frosty morning air. Holden was careering around the middle of a muddy field, swashbuckling fiercely with Samira and John's boys, Jessie and Gideon. Dotted around the field were brightly coloured farmers' market stalls, selling all sorts of winter vegetables, cheeses, and breads.

"Happens all the time," Samira said, pulling down the scarf. "The other day I heard John telling Gideon not to pee on Jessie in the bath. Parenting is a riot."

Reyna nodded ruefully. It was probably different if you had done it from the child's birth, she thought, watching as Holden crashed his stick about, parrying the other boys' attacks valiantly. It would be easier with a child you had cared for since it was born. She and Holden had started as mere acquaintances—she a distant aunty who had visited every few years and waved at him from Skype every now and then, and he a lively little boy with a foreign accent and an enormous undercurrent of sadness. It made her heart happy to see him enjoying himself with some carefree abandon.

"Do you ever know what your boys are thinking?" Reyna asked. "Sometimes I ask Holden and he just shrugs and says he's not really thinking about anything. How can you be thinking nothing?"

"Jessie is exactly like that! Gideon will rabbit on forever if you let him. He'll tell you every tiny detail of his innermost thoughts. But Jessie is far harder to crack. Sometimes he stares out the window when we're driving and I ask him what he's thinking about, and he just smiles at me and keeps staring, almost as if he hasn't even heard me. I'd love to be able to take a peek at what's happening in his brain sometimes."

"Holden is pretty much a closed book," Reyna admitted, rubbing her hands together. She wished she had brought her gloves. "I don't know if it's just because we're still getting to know each other or maybe I'm not doing it right..." She winced as Holden dove to the ground to avoid an attack. He would be filthy by the time they left the market.

"Don't worry." Samira rubbed a gloved hand on Reyna's arm. "You're doing great. This is the world's worst situation and you've taken him into your home and your heart and you're giving him love and everything he could possibly need."

"Except his parents and his friends and his old life."

"How could you give him that?"

Reyna shrugged. "I couldn't."

"Exactly. Look," Samira's blue eyes were bright with compassion, "children are awfully resilient. It's the best and the worst thing about them. It breaks your heart in a way, to watch them stumble through painful experiences, and Holden's had the absolute shittiest deal ever, but he's lucky to have you to love and care for him now, and he will bounce back. It's just going to take time."

Reyna sighed heavily. "I hope you're right."

A pair of long arms reached around them both from behind, a coffee cup in each hand. "Coffee delivery," John sang.

"Oh thank god," Samira said, taking the cup gratefully.

Reyna took a sip of the warm brew, enjoying the way her breath steamed around the cup. "I can't feel my toes." She stamped her feet. "Why are we here again? What is this stuff we're looking for, John?"

"Kohlrabi."

"Oh yeah. And why do we need the 'rabi stuff so badly? Don't they have it at the supermarket?"

"Pff! And even if they did, it would be old and flavourless. It's the secret ingredient for my soup."

"Not so secret really," Samira pointed out. "I think a secret ingredient is something no one knows about. We are all very aware of the Kohlrabi."

"You tease now, but you'll be singing my praises when you eat the soup tonight."

"Speaking of tonight, what time should we come?"

"Whenever you like. John will be making the soup and I'll be sitting on top of the heater trying to stay warm. They boys will be waiting for Holden to arrive from the moment we leave here."

Reyna laughed. "I'm glad the boys have hit it off so easily. It's great that they are so close in age. I couldn't have hoped for better for him, really."

"Mum," Jessie trotted up, breathless and indignant, streaked with mud, "Gideon threw mud in my hair."

"He did?" Samira knit her brow. "That's no good. So how did you handle it?"

"I pushed him over."

"Jessie!"

"Well he was—"

"Save it kid. You know the deal. No pushing. That's not the way we react when we're frustrated. What could you have done instead?"

Jessie poked his toe at the ground, as if searching for the answer in the muddy grass. "I could have asked him to stop."

"Correct. So, now you need to apologise."

"But Mum!"

"No buts. Do you want to keep playing or have you had enough?"

Jessie glared at his mum, his mouth turned down in a picture of sulky frustration. Suddenly his face cleared. "I don't want to play anymore. What are you guys drinking? Can we have a hot chocolate?"

"Perhaps. When you've apologised to your brother."

"Sorry Gid," Jessie called over his shoulder. Gideon, who was in the process of rubbing mud into Holden's arm looked over, pausing long enough for Holden to take advantage of the moment and scoop a handful of mud into Gideon's hair. Gideon howled with displeasure.

"Okay, boys," Reyna called, wondering how she would ever get Holden clean again. "I think that's enough now. Come on over. Shall we get a hot chocolate?" She looked to Samira and John for their approval. Samira nodded and Jessie cheered.

Mud fight immediately forgotten, Gideon and Holden raced over to join them. Reyna slipped an arm around Holden's shoulders, giving him a squeeze as they made their way across the muddy field to the coffee van. Holden was filthy and freezing but smiling all the way to his eyes. He snuggled under her arm as they walked and she held him a little tighter. She could not relate to his desire to roll around on the freezing, hard ground, getting pummelled by his friends, but if it made him this happy, he could be as dirty as he liked.

They pulled up a table at the coffee van, the boys warming their hands on their hot chocolates.

"Hey, I got a marshmallow," Jessie cried, holding up a puffy white ball which he immediately popped in his mouth.

"Ooo, me too," Holden said, dropping his into his hot chocolate. "They're so good when they melt."

"No fair," Gideon pouted. "I didn't get one."

"Yes, you did, Gid." John rescued an escaped pink marshmallow from the table. "It rolled off your saucer. Here."

"Excellent!" Gideon cheered. "The pink ones are the best," he said, sucking it joyfully.

"By the way, Yana will be joining us for dinner tonight," John said casually, tipping back his coffee cup to catch the last drops.

"Who's Yana?" Holden asked.

"A colleague from work."

"Why's she coming, Dad?" Jessie looked confused. "It's Sunday. Why do you want to see work people on a Sunday?"

"Yeah, that's like inviting the principal over for dinner," Gideon added and the three boys giggled.

"She's fun," John promised. "I'm sure you'll all like her."

Reyna thought she caught a meaningful glance pass between Samira and John.

"But why is she coming to dinner, Dad? Just because she's fun? Can't you guys just have fun at work?"

"Well." John fiddled with the lid of his cup, snapping it on and off repeatedly. "She mentioned she would, uh, enjoy the chance to make some new friends, so I invited her over."

"She wants to be friends with us?" Gideon wrinkled his nose like the prospect didn't fill him with joy. "She's old, like you guys, right?"

Samira spluttered. "Hey! Who are you calling old? Your father may be, but Reyna and I aren't even forty yet, whippersnapper. Watch yourself."

"How old are you, Aunty Rey?" Holden turned a curious eye on Reyna.

"Don't you know?" Gideon asked. "I know exactly how old my mum and dad are."

"Yeah but she's not..." Holden trailed off, rubbing his finger against a streak of dirt on the table, his eyes suddenly far away.

"I'm his aunty, remember? Nobody knows exactly how old their aunties are," Reyna said smoothly, ruffling his hair. "For all Holden knows, I'm as old as the hills. Anyway," she said, making her voice sound quivery and frail, "back in my day it was considered rude to ask your elders how old they were."

The boys laughed at her, taking turns to copy her silly voice.

"Hey, race you to the mud pit," Jessie said, taking one last slurp from his cup before throwing back his chair and dashing away from the table. The two other boys shot off in hot pursuit.

"So, who is this Yana really?"

John blushed, avoiding Reyna's steely glare. "She's just a work colleague. Samira and I thought it would be nice to broaden our social circle a little."

"It had better not be a setup."

"Rey!"

"John?"

"Give her a chance, you might like her," he said awkwardly, his eyes wide with guilt.

"I don't have *time* to like anybody."

"It's just a casual dinner, Rey," Samira said. "Not like a real setup. If you like each other you might decide to meet for a coffee sometime. If not, there's no pressure."

"Seriously, why are you guys trying to set me up? Are my hands not full enough here?" She gestured across the field to Holden who was attempting a headstand in the middle of the mud pit. "What with work and trying to keep a child happy, my plate runneth over, or whatever the saying is."

"Well I don't think it's that."

"No, it's cup runneth over, isn't it? It's cup runneth and plate full, I believe."

"Whatever you guys! That is not the point." Reyna eyeballed her friends. They stared back with woeful, puppy dog eyes. "Stop it. Those eyes are not going to cut it here. You're both in big trouble."

"Yikes, now I know how your underlings at work must feel." Samira giggled.

"Yes, watch out!" John elbowed Samira. "Boss is on the warpath."

Reyna smirked and shook her head, a smile twitching at her lips in spite of herself. "You're both being ridiculous. But seriously, I do not have time to think about dating anyone."

"*Seriously*," Samira said, throwing the word back at her, "you need to let go of the reins and give yourself sometime to enjoy life. Doesn't being the boss mean you can handball a bunch of stuff to your minions?"

"It doesn't work like that. I want to know, I *need* to know what is going on so I can make sure we're all on the same page. It's like being the captain of the ship. I give the orders, they follow them and we weather the storms. If I'm suddenly not there they won't know what to do."

"You should give them a bit more credit, maybe they already know what to do without your orders."

"Maybe," Reyna conceded, shrugging her shoulders. "But still, I'm not looking to get involved with anyone right now."

"Don't stress, Rey, it's no biggie. Just a casual dinner. Now," John stood, pushing back his chair, "time to go kohlrabi hunting."

"Dig in," John said as he joined them at the table with the last bowl of steaming soup.

Reyna dipped her spoon in and tasted a mouthful, letting the warm broth roll over her tongue. "Delicious," she pronounced.

"Have you thought of joining the soup club at work, John?" Yana asked.

In what was clearly a setup, she had been seated directly across the table from Reyna and seemed to feel it was her duty to smile toothily at her as often as possible. Her hair was cut short and spiky at the back, with a wispy blond fringe set across her brow. Friendly blue eyes and a petite mouth flashed Reyna a complicit smile. "I don't believe the office is aware of your hidden talents."

"Yes, I am mostly underestimated in life," John sighed.

"Oh, poor baby." Samira patted his hand. As Jessie and Gideon noisily slurped their soup she said, "Anyway, it's clearly a hit tonight. It's not a race, Jessie. Just eat it nicely."

"Which bit is the 'rabi stuff?" Holden asked, studying his bowl suspiciously.

"Yeah, I can't see it," Jessie agreed.

"If you could see the secret ingredient it wouldn't be a secret anymore, now would it? It's in there, boys. You'll just have to trust me." John tapped the side of his nose conspiratorially.

Holden took a dainty sip, his face a picture of misgivings. "Tastes like minestrone," he declared, dipping his spoon in for a much larger mouthful. "It's good."

"You sound surprised," John said, his voice filled with mock hurt.

"More bread?" Gideon mumbled through a mouthful.

"Me too, please. Aunty Rey, can you pass it?"

Reyna handed Holden the breadbasket, taking in the scene before her. A feeling of warmth spread through her that had little to do with the soup. Her heart felt suddenly like it was too big for her chest, an overwhelming rush of emotion coming over her. This was family. This was what it was to share your life with others, to invite people in, to eat food together and tease each other. There was dinner with her parents of course, but it was different, to be sitting here as an adult, with a family of her own (tiny as it was), joking and teasing. She had not realised this was missing from her life until now. How terrible that it had taken the loss of her sister's life to show her how empty her own life had been. She suddenly missed Sarit fiercely, searching Holden's face for a glimpse of her.

"What?" Holden asked, his spoon paused between his bowl and his mouth. "Why are you staring?"

Reyna shook her head. "It's nothing, darling." Tears prickled her eyes and she pushed back her chair. "Just popping to the bathroom," she said with a bright smile, her voice sounding forced to her own ears.

In the bathroom she took deep slow breaths, dabbing her eyes with a damp cloth. She didn't want to go back out to the table looking like a tearful mess. It would be embarrassing in front of a total stranger. Sarit's death stabbed at her like this every now and then. She couldn't even begin to imagine how Holden was managing to keep it together. Whenever she tried to raise the subject, he would deflect, preferring to talk about school or soccer or a video game he was interested in. But Reyna knew. A new school, a new home, a new parent. He had been through so much change, so much loss, and so much grief it was an overwhelming cocktail of difficulty for a child. And yet his resilience was shining through, as he stubbornly refused to buckle under the pain, joining in at school and soccer, making friends and adapting to his new routines. The nightmares provided the biggest insight into his struggle to process things. She would regularly wake up to hear him calling for his mother and father, finding him curled up in a tight little ball in his bed, forehead sweaty and hot tears streaking down his cheeks. She would hold him firmly like he was a puppy, careful not to crush him as she rocked him gently. His arms would steal around her and he would sob, sometimes telling her it wasn't fair, his voice breaking over the words, sometimes without words at all.

It was time to try again with the counselling. She had not wanted to push him too hard when she had first brought him home. She thought it would be best to give him time to settle, let him come to her if he wanted to talk. But now she felt it was time to try again. It wouldn't do for his emotions to get locked up inside. She had tried sending him to a counsellor not long after she had brought him home, but he had dug his heels in, refusing to speak with the stranger who asked him what he felt were prying questions.

"I'm fine," he insisted, avoiding her eyes. "I don't want to go, Aunty Rey. His office smells like old people. Please don't make me."

"I can find someone else, sweet pea. It doesn't have to be this guy. How about I ask around for a recommendation?"

"No." He was quietly adamant. "I don't want to go."

And so she had let him have his way, feeling it would be more scarring to force him to keep going than to hit the pause button on things for a bit. But lately she had been reading books about helping kids through grief and decided that she really needed some professional support. She would try to find a new psychologist. He could not be left to muddle his way through with just her for support.

She dabbed her eyes once more and took a gulp of water from the tap. She should go back or they would wonder what had happened to her.

Samira gave her a searching look as she retook her seat at the table. Reyna returned a quick nod as she tucked back into her soup. It really was delicious.

"My full compliments to the chef," she said, nodding at John. "Doesn't even need salt."

He shook his head and turned to Yana. "Reyna spoils everything with mountains of salt. Sometimes I swear I can hear her arteries groaning across the table."

"Vegetarians can have as much salt as they like," Reyna said.

John rolled his eyes. "Here we go again."

"No, really. Meats are full of salt so I figure by not eating meat I'm free to up the salt content of everything else I eat. And my arteries are doing just fine, thank you."

"Well, I'd rather have my arteries shrivel up and die than stop eating meat," Yana said. "I don't know how you do it. I know I should probably eat less meat but I just can't."

Reyna felt a familiar twinge of irritation. This was one of those annoying things people always said to vegetarians. It wasn't like she was some kind of superhero. She'd just chosen to stop eating meat.

"What are hearteries?" Jessie asked, tipping his bowl up to his mouth to slurp the last drops of his soup.

"My apologies for the caveman manners," Samira said to Yana. "Arteries are the tubes in your heart that send the blood to your body, darling."

"Oh, I'm used to it," Yana replied. "I grew up with six brothers."

"Six!" Reyna exclaimed, appalled at the thought. "How on earth did your parents keep up? Seven children!"

"Eight, actually. I have a sister as well."

"You could almost have your own soccer team," Holden said admiringly.

Yana cocked her head to the side, thoughtfully. "Really? We never thought of that."

"You're allowed to play with only seven," Gideon said encouragingly.

"I must remember to tell them that at Christmas."

"Oh my gosh, Christmas!" Samira exclaimed. "How do you manage all the presents?"

"We do a Kris Kringle. My parents realised early on that it would break the bank for everyone to buy each person a

Christmas present, not to mention now all the children and spouses. These days we have to hire a hall for Christmas lunch just to fit everyone in."

Reyna took a moment to absorb that, trying to imagine her own little family eating lunch in a cavernous hall. When she and Sarit were little, her parents had explained they were agnostic. Their mother, born in Israel, had been raised according to the Jewish traditions, and their father had come from Cairo, son of a strict Coptic Christian family. They had met on a university gap year in England and after falling in love and deciding to marry against their parents' wishes, had settled on raising a nonreligious family, avoiding all religious events entirely. Instead they had created their own calendar of special events, celebrating birthdays, anniversaries, and the turning of the seasons. Instead of Christmas they had a summer party each year, celebrating the beginning of the warm weather and long summer to come. There had been plenty of gift giving at each celebration, so they hadn't felt like they were missing out, and Reyna had enjoyed it. She would have to decide what she and Holden were going to do this year, she realised suddenly, glancing at him. It would be Christmas in a few months and she had no idea if he would be expecting to celebrate it.

"Do we do Christmas, Aunty Rey?" he asked as if reading her mind.

"Er, I'm not sure," she stammered, aware that their conversation would sound strange to Yana's ears. "We can. Why don't we work it out over breakfast tomorrow?"

He nodded, tearing another chunk of bread from the loaf in front of him.

"Can we play Nintendo now?" Gideon asked, pushing his empty bowl over to his mother.

Samira slid his bowl back to him. "If you clear the table properly."

Gideon grinned, catching his bowl.

"Cheeky thing," she muttered with a shake of her head.

"Wait, what about dessert?" Jessie asked, looking expectantly between his parents.

"What about your manners?"

"Sorry Mum. But are we…no, could we…um, please may we have dessert?"

"We'll call you back for dessert in a little while. We're not quite ready yet," she replied.

"Thanks, Mum. You're the best." He snatched up his bowl, giving her a resounding kiss as he left the table.

"So, that's what it takes to get affection around here then, huh?" John said. "Where's mine? I made the soup, you know."

"Yeah, thanks, Dad." Jessie dropped his bowl in the dishwasher and cantered out of the room. "Come on, Holden. Super Mario challenge!"

Gideon raced after Jessie with Holden following behind. "Bags being Yoshi."

"Let's see if we can rescue the Princess."

John sighed. "Parenting. It's a thankless task."

"Oh, to be young again," Yana said, smiling across the table to Reyna. "When all you needed to do was rescue the princess in time for dessert."

"I don't know," Reyna countered. "I think a Princess might be quite hard work once you brought her home."

"You're absolutely right. My last girlfriend was a total princess and it was a nightmare."

"I know what you mean," John agreed. "Ow!" he cried, copping an elbow in the ribs from Samira. "I didn't mean you, sweetheart. I was talking about Crista. Remember her?"

"How could I forget Crista? She practically had you on a leash."

"I was dating Crista when I met Samira," John explained to Yana. "She was, well, a bit restrictive."

Reyna snorted. "That's putting it lightly. It's a wonder she let you break up with her at all."

"Yes, well, she didn't exactly," John said, looking sheepish.

"What?"

"I told her I had been called away with the Peace Corps and wouldn't be back for a long time. So she broke up with me."

"Yes, and we couldn't go out anywhere for a whole year because he was terrified we would bump into her."

"Well, how would I have explained it to her?"

"Sounds like a lucky getaway," Yana said. "Wish I'd been so clever as to think of the Peace Corps. What about you, Reyna? Any lucky escapes?"

"One or two," she shrugged noncommittally. "No major disasters."

"I doubt Karen would agree with that," Samira muttered.

Yana raised an eyebrow. "Do tell."

Reyna shot a frown at Samira. Why was she bringing up Karen? Sure, that breakup had been a bit messy, but Reyna had dealt with things as best she could. The timing had been bad. Azoulay House was still in its infancy and she had little time for anything else. It had taken her a while to notice that Karen was drinking heavily and behaving erratically. They had even been considering living together when she had let herself in to Karen's apartment late one night after a work function to find her firmly in the arms of another. Reyna was shocked, but if she was honest with herself, not entirely heartbroken. Karen had been the angry one at first, claiming Reyna was cold. Reyna never gave her enough attention. Reyna was stuck up. And then she had turned contrite, begging Reyna's forgiveness, telling her they could work it out.

"I love you, baby," she had cried, clinging to Reyna like a child in a storm.

"It's not going to work out, Karen," Reyna said gently, extricating herself from the limpet-like embrace. "You're right. I'm too distracted. I've just got too much going on right now to give you the attention you deserve."

"We could move in together."

"I don't think that's such a great idea."

"Why not? We're so good together, baby."

"Karen." Reyna was firm. "I walked in on you having sex with someone else. That didn't feel like we were so good together."

Karen had been inconsolable for months, turning up at Reyna's house in the middle of the night to beg for another chance, becoming angry and accusatory when Reyna did not relent. She had been worried that Karen would come to Azoulay House, but thankfully she never did. Eventually, after one disastrous night when she found Karen swaying on her doorstep with a bottle of scotch in one hand and a large knife in the other, she seemed to have scared herself, and she hadn't come back.

"I'm sure Karen would agree that we ended things as best we could," Reyna said coolly. "Break-ups are never entirely a walk in the park."

"Yes, but what happened? Why did this poor Karen think it was a disaster?" Yana's gossip-hungry tone grated on Reyna. Karen may have been crazy, but she didn't deserve to have it paraded around like some kind of trashy story.

"It was nothing. Just a misunderstanding."

Samira cut in. "So, Yana, tell us what John's really like at the office. He's always saying how busy and important he is, but what's the truth of the matter?"

"Does he now?" Yana shifted her gaze away from Reyna, with a confident smile. "Well, I suppose he's not entirely wrong. He does some pretty good work."

"You see," John said, beaming. "Told you!"

An excited roar came floating down the hallway from the boys' room.

"That'll be the princess saved then," Samira said.

Reyna glanced at her watch. She didn't like to keep Holden out too late on a Sunday night before school.

"I suppose we'll have to make a move soon."

"Time for dessert first?" Samira suggested. "John's made apple pie to go with the ice cream you brought."

"Oh, John," Reyna sighed. "Martha Stewart eat your heart out."

"That's a yes from me." Yana rubbed a hand across her flat stomach. "Although my waistline won't thank you. Who can pass up homemade apple pie and ice cream?"

Certainly not the boys, who asked for second helpings almost before they had finished scraping their bowls clean of the first serve. Not for the first time, Reyna found herself marvelling at how much food an eight-year-old boy could tuck away. Thankfully money was no issue for her, but her heart went out to those who were on minimum wages, trying to manage the expenses of education, clothing, and food for growing children. Life was expensive, and it was no wonder so many people were struggling out there.

"Well, thank you all for a lovely evening," Reyna said, clearing the last bowl from the table. "We'd better be making tracks now if we don't want to be too sleepy for school tomorrow."

"I don't mind being too sleepy for school, Aunty Rey," Holden said. "We can just stay home if we're too tired."

"Some of us have to go to work, sleepy or not," she replied, grabbing their coats from the hallway.

"Wouldn't do for the boss to slack off now, would it?" John joined in. "Why would anyone else bother to come to work if the boss doesn't?"

"Exactly."

"I don't think I would want to be the boss," Jessie said, looking worried. "That sounds hard."

"I would!" Gideon exclaimed. "I would just tell everyone what to do all day, and they would have to do everything I said because I was the boss. I'd be like, 'get me a packet of chips,' and they would have to get me chips straight away."

"If only it worked that way," Reyna said with a rueful smile.

Reyna and Holden bid everyone good night, Reyna declining a last nightcap as they shrugged on their winter coats in the hallway.

"Want me to give your number to Yana?" Samira murmured, giving Reyna a tight hug.

Reyna shook her head. "You're incorrigible."

"There's a woman at my work, Alli, you might like—"

Reyna swatted her friend's arm. "Enough!"

"Fine, fine. Goodnight, Holdy. Sleep well." Samira gave his shoulder a squeeze.

"All right mister, ready to race to the car?" Reyna asked him, helping him zip his coat.

CHAPTER SEVEN

Zoe (Monday a.m.)

What the hell was that noise? Zoe groaned, realising that it was her phone, mercilessly blaring the hideous new ring tone Travis and Chiara had set last night in the pub. Could it be six thirty a.m. already? She felt like she had only just closed her eyes.

"That should get you out of bed tomorrow," Travis had said, narrowly avoiding sloshing his beer onto her phone as he took a large gulp.

"Yeah, this ringtone works a treat on Travis," Chiara added. "No one can sleep through such an assault."

Chiara's friend Petra had taken that moment to whisper in Zoe's ear suggestively that if they stayed up all night there would be no need for an alarm in the morning. Zoe, caught off guard by such a direct approach, had mumbled something stupid about the importance of rest for muscle repair and excused herself to go to the bathroom. Petra, with her short blond bob, upturned nose, and red painted fingernails, had not let up. She had pressed her leg against Zoe's under the table, brushed her hand over drinks, sent searing, meaningful looks over the table, and had finally pulled her in for a kiss at the end of a game of pool. For one brief moment Zoe had been tempted to let herself give in to the embrace, but when Petra's hands crept under Zoe's shirt right there in the pub, she realised this really wasn't what she wanted. If she was going to be with somebody, she wanted to feel a connection; she wanted some zing, some sparkle and pizzazz, not a lecherous fumble in a pool room smelling of beer and old carpet. She had gently extracted herself from the embrace and declined a repeated invitation to spend the night together, joking that her alarm would have to do the trick for now.

Well, the alarm had certainly woken her up. Travis and Chiara had not been wrong there.

Reaching groggily for her phone, she stabbed at it ineffectually, attempting to turn it off without opening her eyes. It was no use. She cracked an eyelid and immediately shut it again, her retina burned by the bright light coming off her phone in the dark room. Incessant, grainy rock music blared from the tiny speaker, forcing her to open both eyes in order to shut it off.

She groaned again. Her body felt like a sack of potatoes that had been repeatedly rolled over by a pickup truck. Why did they do this to themselves? Perhaps a hot shower would help.

She sat up gingerly, her joints moaning with resistance. She swung her legs over the side of the bed and immediately let out a hiss as pain seared through her calves. Yesterday's Tough Mudder course had been punishing.

She pushed herself off the bed with equally tired arms and creaked down the hallway to the shower. It was a challenge to manoeuvre herself over the edge of the bath, but she managed, turning on the shower and gasping as the water took a moment to heat up. How on earth was she going to make it through today, she wondered, adjusting the taps so that the water was almost too hot to bear.

Zoe washed her hair, still finding bits of dried mud even after last night's shower. She'd literally had mud everywhere at the end of the race—up her nose, in her ears, her pants, her shoes, and her hair. She would probably still be finding little flecks of mud on herself for the next week.

She shut off the shower and stepped out of the bath. The hot water had loosened her up a little, but she would have to take some anti-inflammatories to make it through the day. She leaned in to the mirror to study her face. Great, just great. No amount of makeup would fix this baby. She looked like she had been in a bar fight. Her right eye, normally a standard light brown, was bloodshot and surrounded by purple and black, courtesy of another contestant's stray foot as they had climbed the rope netting. Her top lip was puffy (same foot), and she had a long scratch on her left cheek from sliding under a wire fence. Not to mention the fact that she was walking like she needed a Zimmer frame. Oh well, she would just have to do her best. There was too much on her plate today to miss work for a few sore muscles.

She put on her snappiest suit, a dark grey pinstripe with a light grey shirt underneath, trying to compensate for the state of her face. She struggled into her boots and perched at the kitchen counter with her coffee and toast. By the time she had finished scrolling through her work emails (a bad morning habit that she had yet to shake) and responded to a few urgent enquiries that had come through to her inbox over the weekend, she felt ready to go and face the day.

Her phone chimed, alerting her to a message on the Tough Mudder group chat she shared with her friends. It was Mel. She had simply written, *Ug.* Almost immediately another chime followed and a picture of Travis's face showed up on her screen, a graze across his cheekbone and dark circles under his eyes. *Somebody bring me Panadol…*

I too am dying, Zoe keyed in. *Whose idea was this?*

Yours! Enid joined in. *But wasn't it ace?!* A barrage of photos followed from the day, the group warming up, Travis taking a dive into a mud pile while Chiara looked horrified, a red-faced, mud-splattered group celebrating at the end. She smiled. It was comforting to know that her friends were feeling as beaten up as she was. The beer, she decided, as she slid behind the wheel of her car and backed out of the driveway, had not helped. She wasn't hung over. She'd only had a couple, but in retrospect, water would have been a better choice. It would probably also have helped her ease away from Petra more smoothly, come to think of it. Her exit had not been her finest moment. Telling her friends she was going to the bar, she had slipped out the back door and into an Uber, texting them when she was on her way to let them know she had gone.

Oh well, she thought, easing around a truck that was holding up her lane of traffic. Could have been worse. Petra had been nice enough, but there had certainly not been any spark. No quickening of the pulse, no flush to the skin, no rise of the body temperature when she was near. Not like with Reyna.

Stop it, she chided herself. This stupid crush was distracting her, causing her to act like a teenager playing dress up as a financial adviser. She had to pull herself together. She was good at her job. Not just good, great. She knew she actually had a real talent for helping people and businesses manage their affairs, and she didn't want to throw all that down the gurgler by acting like an idiot with a bad case of puppy love.

She pulled into the car park at work and shut off the engine, taking a deep breath. She let the air out slowly through her mouth as if she were blowing up a balloon. Her swollen lip stung and her eye pulsed with a dull ache. Anti-inflammatories were masking the streaking pain in her muscles, but she was still acutely aware of the tightness in her limbs. After this weekend's Tough Mudder course, she had certainly proven to herself that she could face down adversity. Maybe she wasn't quite ready for blind dates and kissing strangers in the pub, but she was done with this Reyna ridiculousness.

"Run into a door handle?" someone asked, for the hundredth time that day.

"Yeah, you been in some kind of brawl, Cavendish?"

She sat down in the large meeting room, acknowledging the comments with a thin smile. It had been an exceptionally long day, what with all the pain and asides about her roughed-up appearance, and she was tired of pretending everyone was hilarious.

"You should see the other guy," she said, relying on the cliché.

"Right, settle people." Thomus clapped his hands, shuffling his papers together at the head of the table. "Figures time. Reyna has asked us to discuss the impact of a possible Vicon Probis demerger and what we would need to do to prepare for such an event."

Zoe opened her notebook, thoughts scrambling through her head. She had some important points to raise here, if she could just order her thoughts and present herself clearly.

The meeting room door opened and Reyna popped her head into the room. "Mind if I join you all?"

"Of course not," Thomus said, rising in surprise to greet her. "We were just about to start discussing the demerger. Take my seat," he said chivalrously.

Reyna ignored him, taking a seat across the table from Zoe, nodding at the group. "Don't let me interrupt, I'm just keen to hear your perspectives."

There was silence, her colleagues reluctant to speak up with the presence of the CEO suddenly overshadowing their meeting.

James, an alpha male with an overly active sense of importance and hair that an environmental group could mistake for an oil slick disaster, cleared his throat. "We're looking at a fairly run-of-the-mill split here. Both companies look good right now and by divesting themselves of Probis, Vicon probably has a better future." He flipped his pen between his fingers. "I recommend Azoulay House advance the idea with a prospectus for each company and strategies for the demerger."

Reyna jotted in her notebook, nodding at him as he spoke. She had worn her hair out today, and it fell in long, dark waves around her face. Her makeup was subtle, a light lipstick, some mascara enhancing her long lashes. Small diamonds twinkled in her earlobes, and to Zoe she looked like a Bollywood movie star.

What would it be like to run her hands through that hair? Her heart gave a disobedient kick.

"Anyone else?"

More silence.

"I would posit that the demerger represents a threat to shareholders," Zoe suddenly found herself saying, "and each business will suffer a loss to their bottom line that may create unsustainability and instability into the future. I think we have a duty to represent this to the company and its shareholders."

Reyna shifted her gaze to Zoe, her eyebrows slightly raised. "That's a strong and combative stance, Zoe. What evidence do you have to back yourself up?"

"By my calculation, the viability numbers just don't add up," Zoe answered, her aches and pains forgotten for the first time. "Without each other, both businesses lose integral cash flow and neither has the numbers to back themselves as an independent operator."

One of her colleagues shifted in the seat next to her, giving her a soft kick under the table. The message was clear: ease up a bit. Perhaps she was coming on a bit strong, but she believed in her calculations and what she perceived to be a duty of care to the public. It would be wrong to recommend to their clients that they do something that would cause hardship to hundreds of shareholders and potentially the resulting business structure.

"Well," James countered, "that's your opinion. I think you're letting fear cloud your judgment. This could be an amazing growth opportunity, and we need to be blazing a trail here for these guys, not creating a climate of fear amongst their stakeholders."

"It's not just an opinion," she said quietly. "It's the numbers. They don't add up."

Reyna made another jot in her notebook. "I'm not sure I entirely agree with you, Zoe," she said slowly, tapping her pen lightly on her notebook.

Zoe flushed, her armpits prickling with sweat. "May I ask why?"

"In a ViconProbis demerger our role is to assist the company by providing financial instruments for the process. It's not actually our role to advise them on the profitability or future sustainability. It's our role to set them up with two financially independent, operational business structures. We can give them points to consider that will create the least disruption for shareholders, but ultimately we should not be advising them for or against the actual demerger."

"Really?" Zoe frowned. "I would have thought it was our responsibility to alert them if we think there is an integral problem."

"They're looking at the same numbers we are. If they decide to go ahead that is their prerogative."

"But what about all the people who've invested in the business and will now take a huge loss?"

"You don't know that they will."

"It's likely."

"Likely or not, we provide the tools, we advise on the process, not the potential outcomes."

"Is this not possibly a bit shortsighted?" Another kick from her colleague, this time sharp against her ankle. She gulped, rubbing her palms on her knees.

"I believe it's called sticking to the brief." Reyna paused, her eyes resting coolly on Zoe. For a moment they gazed at each other, eyes locked together like horns in a bullfight. Zoe's pulse jumped in her neck, heat rising under her collar. And then Reyna turned away. "Anyone else have thoughts to share?"

Zoe focused on the smooth white Formica of the table in front of her, the flow of continued discussion washing over her. She rubbed at a small pen mark on the desk, smudging the little blue line until it faded. She felt stung by the rebuke in Reyna's eyes, the way she had been ultimately overruled and passed over. Of course, Reyna was entitled to do that. She was the boss, but she was surprised by Reyna's position. Zoe uncapped her water bottle and took a long sip of the cool water, shifting the bottle away from the sensitive bruise on her lip. The dull thump of her swollen eye ached deep in her head. This was not her day. Stupid alarm. She wished she had slept through it.

"Well, thank you all for your thoughts," Reyna was saying as she closed up her notebook. Zoe kept her eyes down, studying the lines of her palm. "I won't disturb your meeting any further. Zoe, do you have a moment to pop in to my office this afternoon?"

She sat up with a start. "Yes." Her pulse thumped like a dog's tail.

Reyna pushed back her chair. "Great, come by in an hour."

"So that went well," Mel said as they sat in her cubicle, Zoe recounting the conversation.

"You think?" Zoe said, her face a picture of worry.

"No, Cavendish, I do not think. You called our boss shortsighted. To her face! What were you thinking?"

"I was thinking," Zoe paused, "that she was wrong."

"Oh right, no big deal then."

Zoe dropped her notebook on the desk and sank into her chair. Mel leaned against the cubicle wall.

"In general it's not great to tell the boss she's wrong."

"Yes. She seemed…"

"Frosty?"

"Possibly. I felt it was my duty to speak up, though."

"I can understand that. I wonder why she wants to see you." Mel looked pensive, chewing on the lid of her pen.

"Slap on the wrist?"

"Nah, she'd get Thomus to do that. Anyway, it's almost four so I suggest you get your skates on and go and find out." Mel flashed her a better-you-than-me smile.

Zoe paused before Reyna's door and straightened her suit jacket, smoothing out her pants. There was no sound behind the door and she knocked gently on the thick wood, almost hoping Reyna had forgotten about their meeting and she could slink away.

"Come in."

Zoe pushed open the door and stepped inside. Reyna stood behind a large, modern desk set against a wide window looking out into the leafy street below. Her phone was tucked between her shoulder and her ear, and she was clearly listening to someone, nodding and murmuring in agreement as she paced before the window. She waved for Zoe to enter, gesturing at the seats in front of her desk.

"Sorry," she mouthed. "Won't be long."

She sat in one of the two plush, grey chairs positioned across the desk from Reyna and waited. She rested her notebook on her knee and tucked a strand of hair behind her ear. Through the big window she could see people holding up umbrellas, blurry shapes hurrying through the skinny drops of rain that streaked across the window. Reyna shifted the phone to her other ear, clearly trying to wind up the call.

"Look, I'll have to revisit this with you next week when I'm up in Brisbane. We can have a face-to-face and nut it all out." Reyna glanced at her without appearing to really see her, listened some more and then smiled. She nodded a few times as if the person on the other end could see her, and hung up with a quick goodbye.

"Phew! Sorry about that," Reyna said, her attention shifting to Zoe. She dropped the phone onto her desk and sat down, making herself comfortable in the black leather swivel chair behind her desk.

Zoe chewed the inside of her lip. There was a moment of silence while Reyna flicked to a fresh page in her notebook.

"I've been speaking with Thomus," Reyna started.

"I apologise if I came across as rude in the meeting," Zoe said at the same time. "Sorry, you go," she said, shifting uncomfortably in her chair.

"You feel you were rude in today's meeting?" Reyna asked, her eyes curious.

"Possibly," Zoe replied with a grim smile. "I didn't mean to be, but in retrospect I may have been impolite when I suggested you were being shortsighted. I wasn't meaning you, I just meant the approach could be considered, well, shortsighted."

Reyna smiled gently, a kindness in her dark eyes. "As it turns out, I do actually understand where you're coming from. In principle I probably agree with you, however, in practice we can't operate like that. If you take an overarching view of our firm, as I am required to do, we are not the right people to march on over to this company and tell them why the decision they're making for their own company is wrong. That's just not our role."

"But if we know they're making a mistake?"

"First, no one actually knows if they're making a mistake, but yes, we can take a fairly good guess that this won't work out in the long run. That said, your team's role, should the demerger go ahead, is to be prepared and to deliver using the financial instruments at our disposal. My role as CEO, however, allows me to have some quiet and well-placed conversations that may shed some light where insight is lacking amongst management at ViconProbis."

Zoe wrinkled her brow. "So you would actually talk to them about it."

Reyna placed a hand on her chest. "*I* would. Yes," she said with emphasis. "And that kind of back-channelling is within my role. You guys need to stick to the brief."

Zoe nodded, rubbing her brow as she realised Reyna was right. It was she who had been shortsighted, stepping outside the bounds of her role without even realising the consequences.

"So that's why you didn't agree with me in the meeting? Because you wanted to know what we thought we should be doing?"

"I suppose so. I always welcome robust conversation. If we don't debate our ideas we might miss creative opportunities, but yes, you were playing in the wrong ballpark. Let's move on now shall we?"

"Sure."

Reyna glanced down at her notebook and jotted the date at the top of the blank page. "So," she went on, changing course. "The reason I asked you to meet with me."

Zoe sat up straighter in her chair.

"You've heard of FinCo?"

"I have."

"Have you ever been?"

Zoe shook her head. "Not yet." She was intrigued. FinCo was the prestigious international Financial Services Conference held in a different semi-exotic location each year. Mostly it attracted CEOs and well established financial heavy hitters, but lately an element of disruptive innovation had begun to creep in, with exciting presentations from start-ups and technology companies featuring on the program. Zoe had yet to attend, but she would usually read through the conference prospectus each year with interest.

"This year it will be held in Alice Springs at the start of September and I will be giving a presentation. I want to bring a small team with me from Azoulay House to present at some of the satellite forums and attend the events. The idea is to feed information and developments in the field back into the firm and to showcase our own innovations to the community."

"Sounds like a cool idea."

"I'm glad you think so, because I'm inviting you to come."

Zoe's mouth gaped. "Me?" She was baffled. "Sorry, just to be clear, you're asking me to give a presentation at FinCo? The most highly sought-after conference invitation in the Southern Hemisphere."

"Yes, exactly. Marketing mentioned your financial literacy seminars in last week's management meeting. I couldn't believe this was the first I was hearing of it. It's an excellent idea, and I would like you to put together a presentation based on the sessions, capture the cohort age groups, give an overview of the session trajectories, the types of questions asked, the main issues people are facing, the relationship you've developed with local council, and of course, any outcomes. First, you can show it to me, and then you can then deliver it at the conference. You might like to ask marketing to help you put the presentation together so it is branded with our logos, etc."

She gazed at Reyna, her light brown eyes shining with excitement. "I can do that."

"Excellent. I think your program represents an outstanding opportunity for an organisation like ours to give back to the community. There's not enough work like this going on. The separation between corporate and community is so entrenched. I don't think organisations like ours have even considered ways we can contribute to society on a broader level. Your program is a trailblazer on this account."

Zoe felt a little thrill run through her. This was the kind of recognition you hoped for, but didn't dare dream of—the boss fully appreciating the strength of your ideas. Thomus hadn't given any indication that he was even aware she had started the work, not that he was one for dishing out praise.

"There will be a small group going from the firm—myself of course, you, as well as Meryl and Stacey from the Sydney team. I don't know if you know them?"

Zoe shook her head. "An all female delegation," she said with a smile. "It's good to see in such a male-dominated industry."

"Well, I didn't plan it that way, but the talent lies where it lies."

"Just one thing," Zoe said carefully, "Thomus has asked me to make sure these seminars are done entirely on my own time. I would be absolutely stoked to come to the conference and present with you, but if I'm going to continue to give the program the attention it deserves, it would be good to earmark a bit of extra time for it."

Reyna pursed her lips. "You've been doing it as an extra-curricular activity, so to speak?"

"Yes."

"I wasn't aware that Thomus had made such a request." She made a note in her book and underlined it firmly. "I'll speak with Thomus about allocating you some work hours for this. We are not in the habit of taking people's time for free here."

"Thank you."

"Right." Reyna turned the small, triangular calendar on her desk around to face Zoe. "First week of September. Do you think you can put together a presentation by then?"

"Definitely," she said, writing the date in her notebook. "I'll have four complete sessions to review."

"Sounds good. Nikki will be in touch to book your travel arrangements this week."

Realising the conversation was over Zoe stood. "Thanks, Reyna. It's a great opportunity."

Reyna stood with her and walked her to the door.

"No problem. Actually, Zoe, there is just one other thing."

"What's that?"

"Can I check that you're okay?" Reyna momentarily pressed her hand briefly on Zoe's arm, her eyes full of friendly concern.

Zoe blinked, not entirely sure how to answer, incredibly aware of the place on her sleeve where Reyna's hand had just been.

"It's just…your eye. And your lip. Has something happened?"

Her hand flew to her face, wincing as her fingers brushed her swollen lip. "Ah, yes this." She smiled ruefully. "Tough Mudder."

"The obstacle course thing?"

"Yeah. It can get pretty rough. I was climbing up a rope ladder and the guy in front of me slipped. His foot landed in my face, hence…" She waved her hand in a circle around her face. "Pretty, I know."

"I see. Well I'm glad to hear it. I mean, I'm not glad you got a foot to the face, but I'm thankful that's all it was. It does look a bit ominous. Pretty painful, I imagine."

"You imagine correctly."

Reyna studied her in a way that made her feel like a strange specimen, as if she was trying to determine why someone would put themselves through such an experience. "Each to their own, I guess."

"Sorry for the way my face looks. I don't have any client appointments for a few days so the black eye should settle down by then. Nothing a bit of concealer won't fix. I know it sounds bizarre but it was actually fun."

"Well, I'm glad you're okay," Reyna repeated.

Zoe hesitated, her hand on the door. That was her cue to leave. She met Reyna's unreadable dark brown eyes with her own and a pulse of electricity ran through her. Her breath caught in her throat. They were standing so close. If she just leaned forward she could brush her lips against Reyna's. She imagined the first touch of their mouths meeting, just the thought creating a flush of shock in her abdomen.

Reyna took a step back moving away from the door. "So, we'll regroup on FinCo in a few weeks."

"Sounds good," Zoe said, trying to sound professional. "And thanks…for checking in. I appreciate your concern."

Letting herself out of the office she took a large gulp of air. Had Reyna felt that? Surely you didn't just feel a spark like that all on your own. Was it possible she had been the only one?

Zoe returned to her cubicle and sat down heavily in her chair, rubbing her aching temples. Her judgment was probably not the best today. She rummaged in her desk drawer and fished out some paracetamol, washing it down with a slug of cold coffee from the mug on her desk.

"What did she want?" Mel asked, popping her head around the entrance to Zoe's cubicle.

"To invite me to present at FinCo."

"What!" Mel exploded. "That's amazing."

Zoe smiled wanly. "And to see why I looked as if I had been beaten up."

"Ah, of course. You do look messy today."

"I feel messy today."

"Well go and have another coffee or something, would you? You need to be on top of your game for tonight's seminar."

"My name is Johanna," a middle aged woman said tentatively, shifting in her chair. "I was recommended to come to the sessions by my financial counsellor."

Zoe nodded encouragingly. The group had been introducing themselves and she had been impressed with the level of honesty people were bringing to the table.

The woman took a deep breath and looked around the group. "I spent some time in jail last year and I've been trying to get my life back on track ever since. My husband cleared out and left me with the kids just after my youngest was born, and it turned out he had racked up a whole bunch of gambling debts. I just couldn't get on top of things."

The group murmured in empathy for her, one participant shaking emphatically. "Rotten," he said.

"It was," Johanna agreed. "I was on my own, my family is over in Western Australia, and I couldn't make enough money to cover rent and food, let alone child care fees while I was working. I was a shop assistant and one day I took some money from the till. My manager didn't seem to notice so I realised that if I took cash and deleted some sales from the computer I could get away with it. I'm ashamed to say I did that for a year before I got caught. One evening I was closing up and I took more than usual, thinking I'd replace it as soon as I got paid, but I didn't know that the manager had installed a camera over the till and he decided to press charges. They had months of footage of me stealing from the business and I was sentenced."

Johanna looked at Zoe, her eyes filled with pain. "The shame was unbelievable. They put my children in care and I went to jail. Thank god they have a recidivism reduction program that focuses on financial counselling, and I've been able to get some help. I didn't know I could get government assistance while I was working. And I've been granted a council flat for the next five years while I get back on my feet, so rent is really reduced. Now I can just focus on earning enough to feed and clothe my babies. They're back with me now and I'll never do anything to jeopardise them again." A tear slid down her cheek and she brushed it away quickly. "I'm here to learn how to manage my finances better so I can get ahead."

Zoe's heart constricted painfully, watching the obvious shame and guilt etched on Johanna's face. Johanna's story reminded her of her own mother's struggle to manage after their father had died, her battle with poverty, despair, and alcoholism and felt a powerful empathy for the woman sitting before her. "And I hope together we can do just that," Zoe said. "Thank you for sharing your story with us, Johanna."

At eight p.m. the last of the group had straggled out of the building and Mel and Zoe switched off the lights in the conference room, using a special fob to set the alarm for the building.

"I think tonight went really well," Mel said as they stood by their cars in the dark of the parking lot. "You have so much knowledge to offer. It's actually quite inspirational watching you deliver this program."

Zoe shivered, turning up the lapels of her jacket. A cold wind whipped through the empty lot. "That was the best one we've done so far," she agreed. "They were a great bunch. I like that it's such a diverse group of people."

"Same. This might sound weird, but I've never actually met anyone who's been to prison before."

"Neither. My first time."

"How amazing that she was brave enough to share her story with us."

"Totally. I'm so glad we're doing this."

"So am I. What a huge day. Me and my black eye need to go home to bed."

Zoe blipped her car open and slid into the driver's seat, starting the car. She buzzed down her window, calling out to Mel who was getting into her own car. "See you in the morning."

Mel waved and Zoe pulled out of the lot, mentally calculating how long it would be before she could get home and put her feet up. Pain was pounding around her eye like waves on a cliff face and her muscles felt tight and stiff. She drove a route she knew well, taking a shortcut through the wintery back streets until she reached her block, pleased to see the warm and inviting orange light she had set up in the bedroom window shining from the street.

She creaked up the stairs and let herself in to her apartment, dropping her key onto the hook by the door.

"Honey, I'm home," she muttered to herself, flicking on lights and the heating as she made her way into the kitchen.

She pulled on the old-fashioned chain hanging from the corner of the kitchen and the lightbulb flickered and blew with a small pop, leaving the room in semi-darkness. Damn. She switched on the torch on her mobile phone and fumbled through the bottom kitchen drawer, searching for a candle. She was sure there was one in here somewhere. In a moment she had three separate candles installed on the bench, their soft yellow light sending warm shadows around the little room.

Not bad, she thought, putting on the kettle and settling on a barstool as she waited for it to boil. She should use candles more often, she decided, enjoying the romantic light. Still, it would be helpful to replace the bulb sooner rather than later. Candles were not quite so practical for her morning rush through the apartment to get breakfast and get out the door.

Sitting at the bench with a hot cup of peppermint tea steaming in her hands Zoe thought about Johanna. She reminded her so much of her own mother, struggling to make ends meet and do the right thing for her children. She took another sip of her tea, scalding her mouth. Sadness charged at her like a wounded bull, followed swiftly by a deep, slow-burning anger, and then guilt. Always the gnawing guilt. She should have done more to help her mother. Should have helped her get off the drink, helped her start afresh. She and her brother had tried to get her to counselling but their mother had refused to go, refused all attempts to help her, and gradually they had just all accepted it as the status quo. But the guilt lingered on.

A card stuck to her whiteboard caught her eye. It was still where she had left it after Enid had slipped it into her hand, some months back when they had been out for dinner, held in place with a little magnet from their cycling trip the previous year to Tasmania. She eased off the bench and fetched the card, running her finger over the embossed edge. *Dr Singh, Psychologist.* Would it be too weird to see a psychologist? Where would she even start? She couldn't really imagine having to tell a complete stranger her feelings, but Enid had assured her it would be helpful. Enid's brother had seen this particular psychologist when he and his wife had divorced, and he had sung her praises to Enid.

Zoe had been apathetic at the time. Now, sitting at her kitchen bench, she flipped the card over, noting the long string of qualifying letters beside the psychologist's name. There was a quotation printed on the back of the card that she hadn't noticed before.

"*Sometimes asking for help is the most meaningful form of independence. – Unknown.*"

Perhaps she would call in the morning.

CHAPTER EIGHT

Reyna (Saturday, two p.m.)

Reyna checked her watch again. If they didn't pick up the pace now they would be late.

"Let's move a little faster, Holdy," she urged, placing a guiding hand behind his shoulder blades.

"I am moving," he mumbled, refusing to be hurried. He was quick when he wanted to be, that was for sure. She had seen him tear down the field after a soccer ball as fast as his growing legs would carry him, but now, not entirely happy about the appointment, he was dragging his feet.

"Let's run," Reyna suggested, breaking into a little jog beside him.

Forgetting himself, he smirked.

"What?"

"You're running."

"Yes, and you're not. Come on please, Holden. It's rude to be late."

He allowed himself to be jogged along, now openly laughing.

"You run funny," he said.

"Do not." She stuck out her tongue at him.

"Race you," he cried, taking off at full speed down the street.

"Damn," she muttered, chasing after him. It had been a long time since she had run. Why run when you could walk, was her motto. She enjoyed dancing and swimming and the occasional game of tennis, but she avoided running like the plague. She felt so ungainly when she did it. Perhaps he was right, maybe she did run funny.

"Stop, Holdy. It's the grey building," she called as he ran past their intended destination.

He stopped and plopped himself on a set of small concrete steps, whistling as if he had been waiting for her for hours.

"I win," he crowed when she caught up with him.

Reyna checked her watch again, catching her breath. One minute to spare. She hated to be late. It reeked of disregard and selfishness. God help those who arrived late to her meetings at work. She had perfected her disapproving "you're late" stare, and she knew the sight of it was enough to raise the heartrate of her employees. Composing herself, she straightened her shirt before they went through the double doors at the top of the steps.

Inside the building a large silver sign hung on the wall, announcing the presence of treating physicians Snider, Lohs and Singh. A receptionist with dark grey hair pulled into a neat bun sat behind a large marble counter underneath the sign.

"We have a two p.m. appointment with Dr. Snider," Reyna said, handing an appointment card over the counter to the receptionist.

The receptionist pushed her glasses up her nose and fiddled with her mouse, tapping some keys on her keyboard. "Holden and Reyna Azuolay?"

"Yes, that's us," Reyna said, thankful once again that her sister had kept her maiden name and passed it on to Holden. It made these kinds of moments so much easier.

"I'll just need your Medicare card and other details filled out on this form. Take a seat through those doors," she said, handing Reyna a clipboard and gesturing to a set of frosted glass doors behind them.

Through the doors was a waiting room, decorated in a tasteful olive green. Rows of chairs lined both sides of the room, and a section in the corner was designed especially for children. A generic print of a rural landscape hung on the opposite wall, and a magazine rack showcased a bunch of well-thumbed cooking and gardening magazines that she had no desire to read. She settled herself in one of the chairs next to the play area.

"Cool, they have Hot Wheels," Holden announced, dropping down on the floor to play with a brightly painted car and accompanying ramp.

Reyna watched him pushing the car up and down the ramp, vigorously smashing it into the sides and making his own sound effects. It amazed her how easily he could become absorbed in a game, especially if it was imaginary.

"You're sure you're happy to go in without me?"

"Yes, Aunty Rey," he said, distracted by his car which had just spun 360 degrees and flipped entirely off the ramp.

"It's just that if you've changed your mind, I can come in with you, I'd be happy to."

He looked up for a second, contemplating her with a serious look in his eye. "I'm okay to go in by myself. Will you wait for me out here? Just in case I want to leave?"

"Of course." She reached down and swept a curl from his forehead. "I'll be right here."

"Good." He returned to his game, conversation over.

He knocked his car recklessly over the little course, then she looked away, hearing muted voices outside the frosted doors they had just come through. She prepared herself for the psychologist to enter. They had chosen Dr. Snider based on a recommendation from a lady Samira worked with. Further research had shown him to be a friendly-faced specialist in children's issues with a trail of commendations and reviews from satisfied parents on the clinic's website. Holden had taken some convincing, but in the end Reyna had bribed him with the promise of a new fandangled robotics set if he would give it a month, and he had readily agreed. She felt a little guilty about bribing him but decided the possible gain would far outweigh the parenting faux pas.

"You can wait through those doors," Reyna heard the receptionist say as the door to the waiting room pushed open. Reyna looked up, ready to see another patient enter the room. Instead she found herself face-to-face with Zoe Cavendish, who had stopped stock still in the doorway, her eyes wide with confusion. The swelling on Zoe's lip had gone down but there was still the gash on her cheek and a telltale smudge of purple around her eye where the bruising had been.

"I—" Zoe stopped, her face visibly paling as she took in Reyna and Holden.

"Hello," Reyna said simply, slightly taken off guard herself. It was always a bit awkward bumping into people from work, but this setting had an extra level of discomfort. She couldn't ask Zoe what she was doing there, nor did she particularly want to go into her own reasons for being found in the waiting room of a psychology practice with a small child in tow.

"I—" Zoe said again, and took a step into the room, letting the glass doors swing shut behind her with a quiet thud.

Holden turned around to study the newcomer.

"You're not Dr. Snider," he said.

"No," Zoe agreed, hovering beside a chair as if she couldn't decide if it would be worse to sit or stand.

"Actually Holden, this is Zoe. We work together."

"Hi." Holden studied her for a moment with his serious brown eyes, and then clearly decided his game offered a better level of entertainment, turning away to resume the car demolition.

"Hi," Zoe said to his back, sitting down with a rush in one of the olive chairs.

The doors to the waiting room pushed open for a second time, and this time the friendly face Reyna had seen on the clinic's website entered the room. He was shorter than Reyna had expected, his collared shirt and black jeans more casual than the head shot with the shirt and tie had depicted.

"Holden?" the man said in a deep, warm voice, smiling at the boy with a smile that reached right up to his bright blue eyes as Holden turned from his game.

"Yes." Holden stood up, continuing to clutch the car.

"I'm Dr. Snider. Nice to meet you." He held out his hand and Holden took it with his own small paw. Holden's curls bobbed as he gave the hand a vigorous, single shake.

"Well, you do have quite the grip," Dr. Snider exclaimed. He turned, glancing between Reyna and Zoe, as if trying to decide who belonged with Holden. "Reyna?" he asked, his twinkling blue eyes making the right choice.

"Yes, that's me." Reyna stood.

"How about we all catch up at the end of the session," Dr. Snider suggested. "If you come back in say, forty-five minutes, Holden and I should be done talking and you could join us for a quick cuppa?"

"That would be good. Is it okay if I just wait here? I promised Holden I'd stick around."

"Absolutely. Would you like a coffee while you wait? I can have Doreen bring you something." He gestured behind him, obviously referring to the receptionist they had met earlier.

"I'm fine, thank you."

"Okay, then. Well, how about we go get started Holden? Are you ready to check out my office? You can bring the car if you like. I actually have some pretty cool toys in my office as well."

Holden nodded, gripping the little car tightly.

"Right. This way then." He held open the glass doors. "See you in a bit, Reyna. Doreen will show you in."

Reyna smiled encouragingly at Holden. His face was a mask of apprehension as he followed the doctor through the glass doors.

"Did you know they let me have a robotic Lego set in my office?" she heard Dr. Snider say as the doors swung closed. "And a much bigger Hot Wheels set."

Reyna sat back in her chair and rummaged through her bag for her bottle of water, aware of Zoe's eyes on her. She found the bottle, opened it, and took a long sip, before meeting the gaze.

"I didn't know you had a son."

"My nephew."

"Ah."

for the staff, and judging by the bills she received, they were using it. She did what she could to support them, conscious that they were exchanging their hard-earned intellectual knowledge for the advancement of her firm. Sure, they were paid well, but running a successful business was about more than just paying people well. People needed to see that they were valued; they needed recognition and evidence that management cared, that they were not just another, expendable cog in the wheel. That was why she had started up the innovation awards.

It was, however, becoming much more difficult for her to maintain that degree of personal touch with the growth of the firm. Being spread out nationally meant she didn't always have eyes on what was being said and done. Thankfully her management team worked hard, and the company's enviable results continued to speak for themselves, but it was strange to find she didn't always know all the details of what was happening in her firm. She had to work hard to keep the lines of communication firmly open so that things didn't slip under her radar. Occasionally she had come across bad behaviour that had been shielded from her view, due to the sheer size of the firm. She also relied heavily on her regional managers to maintain the ethos of the firm, but every now and then a bad egg slipped through the net. Was Thomus becoming one of these? This business of making Mel and Zoe run the workshops on their own time was poor form indeed. She would keep a close eye on him for now.

Her mind flashed back to Zoe, unusually pale but pretty in her casual attire. Reyna felt a strange jolt inside her. There was a vulnerability to Zoe that she had a sudden urge to soothe. She was clearly uncomfortable to have been found in the waiting room of a psychologist's office, but well, they had both been caught off guard. Reyna was certainly not interested in the personal details of her life being broadcast around the office. She was sure Zoe would feel the same way. She would try to catch up with Zoe during the week to reassure her of her privacy. Hopefully Zoe would afford her the same respect. Her thoughts snagged again, catching on the soft woollen jumper

Zoe had been wearing, pausing over the exposed skin at her neckline. What would it be like to feel that up close, to slide her hands underneath the soft wool and feel the warmth of skin against her palms?

Reyna shifted in her seat abruptly, shaking her head as if to dislodge the inappropriate thought. Her pulse quickened and she stood, pacing in the little waiting room. Where had that come from? She took a deep breath, letting it out slowly and rubbed her palms on her jacket, as if she could brush away the thought. It had been a long time since she had been intimate with someone, she realised, mentally counting backward to her last relationship, if you could call it that. More like a fling really. It had been almost eighteen months.

She picked up a gardening magazine from the rack and sat back down, flipping the pages without seeing them. She missed the closeness, the intimacy of discovering another body in the darkness, surrendering herself to the moment, hands held over coffee, the thrill of a woman's lips on her own. But there was no room in her life for any of that anymore, she thought, staring down at a DIY hanging flower garden with an ache in her abdomen. She knew her friends would continue to try to find women like Yana and Alli to set her up, but she couldn't even begin to imagine having the time or energy to devote to a relationship. And anyway, she thought, as she glanced around the psychologist's waiting room, her needs, her wants, those kinds of desires just had to take a backseat. She had a growing boy to raise and a demanding firm to run. Surely there was no space for anything more.

CHAPTER NINE

Zoe (Sunday, p.m.)

"You what?"

Four pairs of eyes around the table stared with horror at her.

"I bumped into Reyna in the psychologist's waiting room," she repeated with a baleful look at her friends. She gave the remainder of the red wine in her glass a swirl and drained it. "It was kind of a nightmare. I mean, she was totally professional and everything but I was so embarrassed. I've got no idea what I even said."

"I wonder why she was there," Chiara mused. "Did she say anything?"

"She was there with her nephew. I didn't ask her about it."

"Her nephew," Mel repeated. "That's kind of strange. How old is he?"

Zoe shrugged. "I don't know. He looked young, maybe ten or something. The more important question is, will she now think I'm some kind of deranged lunatic who has to see a psychologist? Definitely not the impression I was hoping to give at work."

"Don't worry about it," Enid said confidently. "Pretty much everyone has a psychologist these days. She'll just think it's normal."

"None of you have one."

"True, but none of us have been through what you've been through, sweetie." Chiara reached across the table and gave Zoe's hand a squeeze, her eyes full of empathy.

"So, you all think I'm messed up."

"No," Enid strung out the word. "You just need a little help to sort through your emotions that's all. What did the psychologist say?"

Zoe took a deep breath, tracing a finger across a water droplet on the table. "Dr. Singh said that my internalised belief that I should have done more to help my mother has led me to believe I'm not worthy of a proper relationship now. So I have developed feelings for someone entirely unattainable because I know I will never be called upon to act on it."

The eyes stared again.

"I'm sorry," Mel said, her brow wrinkled in confusion. "She said what?"

"She said that my internalised belief—"

"Wait, don't just say it all again. What does it mean?"

"I think she's saying," Enid interrupted gently, "that because Zoe feels guilty about her mum, she doesn't think she deserves to have a happy relationship. So, her crush on Reyna is easy because it's never going to happen. It makes sense."

"Thanks," Zoe said. "I think."

"Did you tell her you had just bumped into Reyna in her waiting room?" Travis thumped the table with his fist. "I mean, what are the odds of that?"

"I didn't."

"Why not? I would've thought that's just the kind of thing a psychologist would want to know. Maybe she would have said, 'Oh wait, you bumped into each other here? That must be fate. Forget everything else I've said.'"

"Yeah, right. Maybe I should have. I didn't want to tell her everything all at once, you know?"

Mel narrowed her eyes. "Isn't that kind of the point?"

"I don't know. Got to save something for the next session, right?" Zoe glanced through the crowd at the bar, where an attractive redhead with an array of tattoos and piercings was wiping the counter. "I think I'm ready for another drink. Anyone else? My shout."

"I'll come with you." Mel slid off her barstool and tucked her arm through Zoe's. "Help you carry."

They made their way through the Sunday night crowd of hipsters and university students who frequented this particular bar. A group of boys sporting chequered shirts and oversized beards ribbed each other at the pool table, squabbling over the appropriate cue to use for a difficult corner shot. Zoe and her friends had enjoyed coming here in their own uni days and revisited it every now and then for a trip down memory lane. Tonight felt more like a trip through a dark alley, Zoe thought, her mind clouded with heavy thoughts. Dr. Singh's words had struck home. It felt like a key unlocking an important door, but she was scared to open it in case some other demon lurked behind it. Wouldn't it just be better to keep that door closed and move on?

At the bar the redhead nodded at them, her sculpted biceps flexing as she hefted a tray of cleaning glasses onto the bench.

"What can I get you?"

Mel gave their order, engaging in some friendly banter. "Come here often?" she asked, showing off her dimples to full advantage as the redhead pulled the cork from a fresh bottle of Shiraz, deftly pouring out five glasses.

"Four nights a week," she said, wiping a drip from the top of the bottle with a flourish and popping the cork back in. She fluttered her eyelashes at Mel. "Clearly you don't come here often enough."

"Clearly I don't," Mel agreed. "Perhaps we can rectify that. Will you be here tomorrow night?"

The redhead fluttered some more and Zoe inwardly rolled her eyes. Mel was an outrageous flirt, but no one could deny she got the job done. "I'm not working tomorrow night. Night off."

"Oh." Mel fished her credit card out of her wallet and handed it over. "Shall I take you out somewhere instead then?"

The redhead smirked. "Maybe." She waved the credit card over her machine and handed it back, holding onto the card for a moment too long as Mel reached for it. "Come see me before you go." She let go of the card.

"It's a date."

Mel took the tray of glasses, deftly balancing them on one hand.

"I thought you were seeing someone," Zoe muttered as they stepped away from the bar. She placed a hand on Mel's shoulder, steering her toward their table as Mel attempted to continue dimpling at the redhead over her shoulder.

"What? Who me?" she said casually, depositing the tray in front of their friends.

"I definitely got the impression the other day that you were seeing someone."

"Oh that," Mel breezed, handing out the glasses. "It wasn't a thing, too complicated."

"Right. Did you guys know about this complication?" Zoe asked. Her friends looked as baffled as she felt.

"Not me," Enid replied. "Do tell all, Melanie."

"Really, there's nothing to tell. It turned out to be a nonstarter. Now, I'll just return this tray." With a flick of her hair she tucked the tray under her arm and trotted back to the bar.

"Something weird is going on with her," Zoe said, perching on her stool. She rubbed her temples, trying to massage out the stress of her weekend. "Maybe she should see my psychologist."

"Speaking of," Chiara continued, picking up the thread. "Did she give you any advice? Tell you what to do next?"

"She did. She said I could go on some dates. Replace thoughts of Reyna with positive thoughts about other things I'm looking forward to. I can't remember everything she said. I took notes, though."

"Sounds like good advice. So, shall we get moving on setting you up?"

"Who's setting who up?" Mel asked, shimmying back to the table. She waved a slip of paper in front of her with a look of glee. "Guess who's got a hot date tomorrow night?"

Zoe shook her head. "You're incorrigible."

"I'm proactive."

"Zoe's psychologist says she needs to start dating," Enid advised. "Maybe you can bring her with you."

"Thanks a lot, Enid. Anyway, she said I *could* start dating. Big difference."

"Oooh, yes," Mel crowed. "Where shall we start? Who do we know who would be perfect for Zoe? Wait! Who have we already tried?"

Zoe tuned out, letting her friends discuss her as if she wasn't there. She wasn't ready to start dating. If the psychologist was right, and she had stopped dating because of the guilt she felt about her mother, she was pretty sure it would take a bit more than just one session to get over it.

CHAPTER TEN

Zoe (Monday, a.m.)

Zoe sat on the floor in her kitchen lacing her runners and eating a banana. First light was beginning to creep into the sky and everything seemed very still around her. She loved the quiet of the morning. If she got up early enough, there was no traffic on the roads, no people crossing in front of her, only the occasional light on in a passing house. It felt special, like she was getting some extra secret time in the universe that everyone else was missing.

She stood and did a little jog on the spot to test the tightness of her shoes followed by slow lunges to warm up her muscles. It would be cold outside, the heating in her apartment giving her a false sense of the temperature. She tucked a key into the little pocket in her running shorts, tossed her banana peel into the compost bin, and headed out the door. The stairwell was brightly lit, causing her to squint against the harsh fluorescent light as she skipped quickly down the stairs.

A gust of wind greeted her at the bottom of the stairs and she shivered, striding out onto the pavement to get warm as quickly as possible. Finding her rhythm, she took a familiar path through the quiet suburban streets leaving her mind free to roam. She had been so overwhelmed by her visit to Dr. Singh she hadn't even begun to process it. But she did her best thinking in moments like these, when her body was occupied, legs pounding to the tempo of her heartbeat. Was Dr. Singh right? Was she really trying to avoid finding love because of the guilt she felt about her mum's death?

She crossed the street, checking for cars over her shoulder. She liked listening to music while she ran, but it wasn't safe in the mornings, especially in the winter when it was still so dark. She liked to be able to hear what was going on around her.

Thinking about her mum brought up the familiar stab in her abdomen, and she stumbled, breaking her stride momentarily. It had been a year and a half since her mum had died. Surely that was time enough to process the emotions. Although, she admitted to herself, if she were honest, she hadn't really done anything proactive about it. She had just waited for the emotions to run their course, expecting it would all settle in time. She hadn't cried much in the beginning. She had felt an empty tickling loss, like there was always something missing but she couldn't quite put her finger on it. She had been caught a few times going to ring her mum after work, sitting with her mobile phone in her lap and a hollow ache in her breast. But a few months later the tears had come, taking her by surprise while she was watching a very average film late one night. In the film, the little girl's mother had died and Zoe found herself sobbing uncontrollably on her couch, curled up in a tight little ball of anger and disbelief, the movie playing on in front of her.

She had fought waves of grief, almost nauseating in their intensity, for a month or so after that, but they had gradually eased. She had been left with the overarching feeling that something had changed deep within her, but she had no idea exactly what it was or if it was okay that it had. Sometimes she felt adrift without her mum to care for, to plan for, to check in on. And sometimes she felt so relieved not to have to do any of those things any more that she burned with shame at the feeling. Had she done enough? She told herself she had done all she could, but shouldn't she have tried harder? Why hadn't she pushed her to go to a rehab center, even an AA meeting, something to help her clean up and fight the cancer? But even as the familiar question plagued her she knew it would have been impossible. Her mother would never have gone.

Stopping to grab a quick drink at the fountain in the park, she stretched out a twinging calf muscle while she caught her breath. How this all tied in with her feelings for Reyna she didn't understand. Surely she hadn't just invented a crush to stop herself from finding a proper relationship. Had she?

She checked her watch. It was time to head back or she would be late to work. She picked up the pace, pushing herself harder, enjoying the burn in her muscles and the elevation of her heartbeat, blood pulsing swiftly around her body. She supposed she didn't have much to lose by trying Dr. Singh's idea. She had thought about it last night, trying to pinpoint something she was excited about that she could focus on instead of thinking about Reyna. She realised she had plenty to choose from. She was excited to put together her presentation for FinCo, not to mention the upcoming trip to Alice Springs. She had never been there before, but pictures of the place looked amazing and she was seriously looking forward to exploring it. As an added bonus, she had looked up the expected weather and it would be warm and sunny, the perfect antidote to the chill of Melbourne's winter.

Yes, she had plenty to look forward to and focus on instead of Reyna, she decided, making a final tired push up the hill to her building. Her legs trembled as she reached the stairwell, and she wobbled up the four flights into her apartment. She kicked off her shoes and wrapped a towel around her shoulders, setting the coffee percolator on the stove. It was a new day, a new chance to make better choices. Leaning against the bench, she sipped a glass of water as she waited for the coffee to brew.

The award she had received for Victorian Adviser of the Year caught her eye, acting as a book stop on the end of the shelf. She had worked incredibly hard last year. Every year really. But after her mother's death she had really just lost herself in her work, treating herself to time out with her friends, occasionally seeing Danny, but for the most part, setting the bar high for excellence in her field. It was gratifying to know that work had not gone unnoticed, but she realised with a sting that an award was a poor substitute for the warmth and enjoyment of another human being.

She added a dollop of cream to her coffee and settled on the floor, doing some light stretches before her shower. Was she ready to start dating? She had convinced herself for so long that this crush on Reyna was genuine. It was hard to imagine looking at anyone else. But of course, Dr. Singh was right. Zoe knew nothing about Reyna so how real could this crush actually be? It had been a shock seeing her in the waiting room with her nephew, a boy who had looked so similar to Reyna that Zoe had assumed at first sight that he was her son. And wasn't that exactly the point? Reyna could have a son. She could have a whole family Zoe knew nothing about. She could like Mongolian throat singers and scary movies and Hawaiian pizza for all Zoe knew. She eased up from the floor, peeled off her running gear and stepped into the shower.

She had just over three weeks to prepare for FinCo and she wanted her presentation to be brilliant. What better event to focus on?

CHAPTER ELEVEN

Reyna (Thursday, p.m.)

Being five thirty p.m. on a Thursday, the tea room was deserted when Reyna went in to make a fresh pot of tea. An unavoidably late meeting with an executive group she belonged to meant her parents were with Holden for the evening. As she stood by the sink cleaning out her teapot, she hummed gently to herself, a tune she had heard on the radio with Holden that morning on the way to school. Suddenly she became aware that someone else had entered the room, and she looked quickly over her shoulder, embarrassed to have been caught singing to herself.

"Only me," Zoe said. She raised her empty cup by way of greeting. "One last refill."

"You're working late," Reyna said, making room for her at the sink.

"I'm working on a very important presentation for a very important financial conference I'm attending in a few weeks," Zoe said with a grin. "Coffee is my best friend."

Reyna acknowledged her humour with a smile of her own. "I can't drink caffeine this late in the day. I'd be up all night."

"Sometimes being up all night can be fun," Zoe said, and then seemed to catch the double entendre in her words, her gaze flicking away from Reyna's. "I just meant back in the day, you know? Trying to finish off an assignment for uni, my friends and I would brew up a never-ending pot of coffee and settle in for the night to get it done. I guess it sounds weird but it was fun."

"I think we definitely have different ideas of fun," Reyna said, thinking of the obstacle course Zoe had described as "fun" the week before.

They prepared their drinks in silence, Reyna slowly dipping her tea bag into her favourite ceramic mug as she waited for it to steep.

"Tea has a fair bit of caffeine too," Zoe said, peering into Reyna's cup. Reyna caught the scent of her perfume, a subtle hint of orange blossom, suddenly aware that Zoe was standing quite close to her. Her hair was back up in its clip today, showing off the line of her neck and the delicate shape of her ears. Reyna could see the fine silver necklace she had spotted in the waiting room, nestled in the curve of her throat. She had an overwhelming desire to rub her thumb over that curve. From under her lashes, her eyes met Zoe's, a sudden heat streaking through her body.

"It's herbal," Reyna said, swallowing hard, resisting the urge to take a step back. She held up the little cardboard tag on her tea bag. "Actually, I'm glad to catch up with you, Zoe." Reyna removed the tea bag from her cup and tossed it in the bin, attempting to sound casual. "I wanted to tell you, well, to ask you really... The other day when we bumped into each other at the clinic, I was there on private business for my nephew and I would prefer it if you didn't mention it to anyone here."

"Sure, of course. Same for me, I guess. I mean, not the nephew part, but I wouldn't particularly want it bandied about the office that I'm seeing a psychologist."

"It's a deal."

"Did it go well for him?"

"Excuse me?"

"For your nephew. Was it a success?" Zoe's look of concern was disarming.

Reyna frowned, studying her cup. For the first time she noticed little lines in the porcelain, a sign of its age. "I suppose," she said, torn between the desire to share and keeping her professional boundaries intact. "I think it will be a bit of a journey."

"Exactly. My friends seem to think I should be all sorted after one session, but I feel like it could take a bit more than that."

"Well, best of luck with it all. I'm glad to see you've sought help," Reyna said, thinking of the bruises. "If there's anything we can do within the organisation to support you, please don't hesitate to sing out. Just speak with your manager."

Zoe snorted and then seemed to catch herself, as if suddenly aware that she was speaking with the boss. "Oh yes, it's all fine thank you. Some old emotional scars from the death of my mother. No need to speak with Thomus, thanks."

"Oh. Your mother." The surprise in her voice escaped before she could help herself.

"Yes," Zoe frowned. "Why did you think I was there?"

"Well," she took a small sip of her tea, "I thought, the bruises," she trailed off, feeling lame.

"From Tough Mudder?"

Reyna nodded, dialling up a half smile like a peace offering.

"Oh." Zoe looked taken a back. Then suddenly she laughed, her face clearing in that way the sky does when the sun slides out from behind a cloud. "Actually I was worried you had thought that. Really, it's a hectic course. Everyone ends up with cuts and bruises everywhere. I wasn't just making it up."

"I'm relieved to hear it. When I saw you in the psychologist's office so soon after coming to work with a face full of bruises, I assumed the worst."

"Well, it does happen and I guess you can't be too careful."

Zoe was taking her misassumption very well. Reyna wasn't so sure she would have been quite so understanding.

"Seeing as you're here," Reyna found herself saying, "and you're working on your presentation, would you like to show it to me? I have an hour before my conference call starts."

"Sure, that'd be great." Zoe looked genuinely pleased. "Your desk or mine?"

Reyna smiled. It had been a while since anyone had invited her to their desk. Usually she issued the invitations and it made sense to sit in her office where the space was bigger.

"Why don't we sit at yours?"

Zoe's cubicle was neat and functional with a touch of the personal. A photograph of a striking man with a bushy ginger beard and Zoe's eyes was taped to the wall on her left. Although you couldn't see his mouth for the beard, his eyes indicated he was smiling.

"Danny, my brother," Zoe said, following Reyna's gaze. "He won an award recently for a book he published."

"Nice," she said. "He looks just like you." They were seated side by side in front of Zoe's computer, Reyna on a swivel chair Zoe had borrowed from her neighbour's cubicle. The cubicles were really only built for one, and their elbows bumped as Zoe manoeuvred her mouse to bring up the presentation. Reyna relaxed into her chair, allowing Zoe to lead her through her work. It was quiet on the floor, most other desks abandoned at the late hour.

She was impressed. The presentation Zoe had put together was carefully thought out, showcasing a program clearly designed to help those without the skills to successfully manage their own money.

"I think we should look at expanding your program, Zoe," Reyna said. She allowed herself to lean closer as she pointed at a graph on the screen. "This section here where you measure knowledge before versus afterward, how did you do this?"

"I got everyone to fill out a questionnaire." Zoe flicked her mouse to the next screen. "It's a basic financial health check people do at the start of the course and then again at the end. You can see people have reported a better understanding of how to design a budget, how to manage yearly expenditure on a fortnightly income, et cetera. It's all here. In terms of expansion, I was actually thinking I could put this together as a package that could be run by anyone from any of our centres. We could even develop an online course for people in regional areas who can't make it in to one of our centres." Zoe's eyes shone with enthusiasm as she spoke.

"It's really fantastic work." She looked admiringly at Zoe. Here was a young woman who was hitting bull's-eyes in her corporate work, who still wanted to do more. It was a rare quality. "I like your ideas and I think after FinCo we should discuss this further. I'd be happy to support you to spearhead this program for the firm nationally."

"That would be ace." Zoe beamed, directing the full wattage of her smile at Reyna who felt she could almost bask in the warmth of it. She liked how down-to-earth Zoe was. She wasn't stuck-up, trying to guard her work or self-aggrandise. She knew many of Zoe's colleagues wouldn't have missed a chance to self-promote to their boss, but Zoe was refreshingly different. She actually seemed to want to make a difference in the world.

She checked her watch. "I'd better get moving. My conference call is in five and I need to prepare a couple of documents."

"Of course."

"I won't be here in the Melbourne office for the next few weeks, so I won't have a chance to catch up with you again before FinCo. I'm happy for you to email me through the final presentation for a look over, but otherwise you're clearly on the right track and I'll see you there."

"No problem. Going somewhere nice, I hope?"

"I'm just working from home before the trip. My nephew…" She paused, unsure how much detail she wanted to discuss. It would be easy to share with Zoe, with her open smile and clear brown eyes, but she should be careful of her boundaries. Then again, Zoe had already seen her with Holden at the psychologist's office so she had already had a window in. "My nephew has been through some rough times. I just want to be around more for him before I go away for the week."

Zoe nodded encouragingly. "Sounds like you're a very caring Aunty."

Reyna shrugged. "I do my best."

CHAPTER TWELVE

Reyna (Monday, two weeks later, Alice Springs)

The plane touched down on shimmering black tarmac with a bump that made the passengers collectively gasp. A few further skips, like the plane was some kind of giant rabbit, and they pulled up sharply at a freshly painted red railing, next to a sign that read Welcome to Alice Springs Airport. Some passengers clapped, and there was a general buzz of chatter and excitement throughout the plane.

"'Scuze me honey, do you mind?" The grey-haired American tourist sitting next to Reyna waved her camera. "Just wanna take some photos."

Reyna leaned back, allowing the woman access to the little oval window. She held her breath as the woman oohed and ahhed, smelling heavily of the plane's burnt coffee. Terminal staff on the ground wore broad-brimmed hats and dark glasses to ward off the harsh glare of the midday sun, set in an overwhelmingly bright blue sky. The windows of the terminal building behind the railing were also set with a dark glass, but the white bricks caught the light and threw it back, causing Reyna to rub her tired eyes. She had pulled late nights to stay on top of her workload over the past two weeks, fitting in as much time with Holden as possible around school hours, and she felt edgy. That happens if you burn the candle at both ends, she thought ruefully.

"It looks hot outside, don't it?" the lady asked, shifting back into her own seat. Reyna took the opportunity to retrieve her handbag from under the seat in front of her and fished out her sunglasses.

"It certainly does."

"I read on the innernet that they're having a heat wave. Unseasonably hot for the beginning of September. I can't wait to get some sun on my skin."

Reyna was also looking forward to the warmth. Melbourne had served up an icy cold snap over the last few weeks, complete with frosty mornings and single-digit temperatures. Holden had been jealous when they had looked up the expected temperatures for the week ahead, begging her to take him with her.

"I wish I could, darling, but you've got school."

"I can take my schoolwork with me, Aunty Rey. I'll be so good. You'd hardly even notice I was there. I heard we could go for a camel ride in the desert there."

It had been hard to say no to him, but she had promised him they would go back together for a holiday in the future.

He would have loved the hotel. Little sets of units dotted amongst sandy vegetation, ringing a sparkling blue swimming pool with a diving board at one end and a kid's splash pool at the other, complete with a waterslide in the shape of a giant frog. A small group of children took turns sliding down its shining pink tongue with shouts of glee.

In the middle of the pool was a swim-up bar where a man in a crisp white shirt and hotel regulation blue shorts perched on a shaded platform serving fresh coconuts and cocktails. Room key in hand, Reyna settled her sunglasses on her nose and followed the young concierge to her room, allowing him to wheel her suitcase over the cobblestone path. She could already feel the heat radiating up from the path through her thin flats and was glad of the shade provided by a row of trees. It must take a lot of water to keep all this going, she thought.

"These individual units here closest to the pool are our executive suits. We call this the Banksia section," the concierge told her as they stopped at her door, with a wave of his hand at the surrounds. "The hotel goes in concentric circles. Behind these are the Wattle units, and behind those are the Yellow Gum units. The double-story complex at the back is the Desert Spring Circle where most of the regular rooms are."

Reyna nodded to show she was following along.

"You would have seen the main building when you came in. That's where the conference centre is and also the bar and restaurant. If you need anything during your stay, Ms. Azoulay, please just press nine from the telephone in your room."

He took her swipe key and brought her bag into the room for her, pulling back the heavy drapes to reveal a small back veranda with a tasteful cane table and chair set. The branch of a large, smoky-blue gum tree hung over the setting, providing some much-needed shade. The air conditioner already purred, and the temperature of the room was a welcome relief from the dry heat outside that seemed to suck the very moisture straight from her skin.

"Here is your minibar," he said, opening a cupboard to reveal the prerequisite fridge stocked with champagne and chocolates that she would not consume. "And here's your tea and coffee. It's complimentary of course."

She thanked him and pressed a small tip into his hand saying, "I can take it from here." He flashed her a toothy grin and repeated his instructions to just press nine if she needed anything at all and closed the door with a click behind him.

She kicked off her shoes and lay back on the bed. Thankfully it was nice and firm. There was nothing worse than a soft hotel bed. God, she was tired. She longed for a quick nap, but there really wasn't time. The conference program would begin in an hour and she needed to freshen up before she got started. She wondered briefly if Zoe had arrived yet. She had almost expected to see her on the plane, but there had been no sign of her in the boarding lounge, and Reyna had not spotted her when she had taken a walk down the plane's aisle to stretch her legs. She yawned and stretched, rubbing her neck to ease the tension. Perhaps a cool shower to freshen up, and then she would head over to the main building to sign in for the conference and claim her name tag and conference bag.

The shower pressure was strong and she relaxed under the steady spray until she noticed the sign discreetly fixed to the wall, which said that Alice Springs relied on a finite supply of ground water and it would be appreciated if guests would keep their showers brief. Guiltily, she immediately shut off the shower and wrapped herself in a soft, white towel. Padding around the room in her bare feet she hung her shirts and trousers in the cupboard and put her toiletries in the bathroom. She actually enjoyed staying in hotel rooms, fitting her life into the new dimensions of one small room. It was like an enforced downsizing and she enjoyed the minimalistic experience of it. And although she already missed Holden with his goofy smile and his earnest eyes, it was nice to have a small break from stepping on Lego pieces and trying to create a semblance of order in the house.

She slipped into a wine-coloured cotton shirt, which had somehow managed not to crumple in her suitcase, matching it with a pair of white linen trousers. She knew the colour scheme made the most of her black hair and olive skin. She had chosen her outfits carefully for the conference, maybe even more so than usual, refusing to ask herself exactly why. Pushing thoughts of a wide smile and acorn-coloured eyes from her head, she had told herself it was always important to look her best at industry events.

Tucking her room key into her pocket, she grabbed her laptop bag, slid her feet back into her flats and left the cool of her room. The heat permeated the shaded path, causing her shirt to cling uncomfortably to her skin. Thankfully it was only a short walk to the main conference area. She looked longingly at the cobalt blue of the swimming pool, imagining the cool of the water breaking over her head as she dove in. She would definitely have to get up early tomorrow to swim before the conference program started. If she were lucky, there would be time for a quick dip tonight.

The conference check-in area was humming with activity as people located their name badges and conference bags, greeting each other with exclamations of recognition. Reyna gave her name to a delegate who crossed her off the list and handed her a special presenter's pack. She would be giving her talk tomorrow, which was good timing. She could settle in and get the lay of the land, but she didn't have to wait so long that nerves would take hold, or worse, people would be burnt out. She felt sorry for those people who had to give their presentations on the last day. Most of the audience had done their dash by then and were barely making a show of listening to be polite.

"Reyna," a familiar, gruff voice called above the chatter. She turned to find Meryl, a short, stocky woman with the build of a garden gnome but the brains of a Nobel Laureate smiling placidly at her. In contrast, her partner, Stacey, was positively willowy, standing an entire foot taller and whippet thin. Together they produced some high-calibre outcomes for the firm, and Reyna thought of them as "the dream team."

"Hello ladies," she said warmly. "When did you arrive?"

"We came in yesterday," Meryl said in her low growl. "Wanted to get a head start on looking around. Neither of us have been to Alice Springs before. Have you?"

"I have, but it never ceases to thrill me. Did you do anything special yesterday then?"

"We had dinner in the botanical gardens," Stacey said, her eyes dreamy. "It's called Olive Pink, and the sun set right over the park as we ate. It was seriously magnificent."

"Well, from the magnificent to the slightly more mundane." Reyna waved at the table. "Have you picked up your packs yet?"

"Yes, we got ours yesterday," Meryl replied. "Did you see who's giving the plenary address?"

"It's Jessica Myers." Stacey jumped in before Reyna could answer. "Her work with the Government around the GFC was absolutely pivotal to Australia avoiding a recession."

Reyna raised her eyebrows appreciatively. The conference always waited to release the details of the plenary speaker until the first day, and Jessica Myers was a real coup. It would be interesting to hear what she had to say on such an important period in Australia's recent history. And it would be good to catch up with her. They had gone to university together and Reyna had not seen her in many years, not since Jessica had moved to Canberra to work as a high-level political advisor.

"Perhaps it's a good idea to go and find some seats," Reyna suggested.

"Save me one, would you?" Meryl checked her watch. "I'm going to duck to the loo before it starts."

Reyna and Stacey entered the main presentation room, finding a group of seats for the three of them at a large table fairly close to the stage. The table was dressed with a stiff white cloth, and there were glasses of ice water and bowls of mints at each setting. Reyna smiled politely at the other delegates at their table, most of whom were chatting in small groups. Preparations were clearly underway for the conference to begin imminently, as a technician tested the microphone and the lights dimmed. Reyna caught a range of different accents amongst the predominantly Australian chatter, signifying the international status of the conference. She particularly looked forward to catching some of the Asian speakers, as she hoped one day to extend the reach of her firm into Asian partnerships. She found herself craning her neck to scan the crowd, wondering if Zoe had arrived yet. Surely she would be here by now. She wouldn't want to miss the plenary address, but with a few hundred delegates gathered in the room it was difficult to tell.

Meryl slid into her seat just as a balding man dressed in a sharp grey suit took to the podium and tapped on the microphone.

"Phew, just made it," she whispered. "The line for the loos was ridiculous."

"Ladies and gentlemen," the man began and a hush fell over the room. "Welcome to FinCo." He smiled expansively at the crowd, like he was taking an opportunity to show off his full set of bright, white teeth. "Before I invite our plenary speaker to the stage, I would like to review a little bit of housekeeping."

She tuned out, having heard this type of speech many times before. He would tell them where the bathrooms were, the timetable for meals, and all the usual bumph that she could find out with a quick glance at the program. A flash of brown hair with telltale streaks of auburn caught her eye a few tables in front. *Zoe*. Her hair was up in its usual clip, exposing the nape of her slender neck. She appeared to be listening intently to the speaker, her head tilted slightly on an angle, and then, as if sensing Reyna's gaze on her she turned around, locking eyes with Reyna. Reyna felt her breath momentarily catch in her throat as she nodded by way of greeting. Zoe returned the nod with a shy smile that made Reyna swallow nervously.

"And so, without further ado, I would like to introduce Ms. Jessica Myers."

Zoe turned back to face the podium.

Reyna stared in front of her, clapping along with the rest of the crowd, barely seeing what was before her, trying to get a handle on her jumping pulse. What on earth had just happened? Her mind raced as she reached for her water glass and took a shaky sip. She had been on her own for a while now, it was true, but it would not do to fixate on one of her employees. She almost blushed at the thought.

It was the thrill of the conference, she decided, pushing away the knowledge that she'd been to a hundred of these things and never felt quite as she did right now. And she'd definitely had way too many late nights recently. It wasn't healthy to be so sleep deprived. She probably just needed to relax and enjoy herself a little. It would be good to have some adult company for the week. She enjoyed spending time with Meryl and Stacey whenever she visited the Sydney office, and the week to come promised to be full of intellectual stimulation and enjoyable adult conversation. She would get some sun, swim in that divine-looking pool, and catch up with her peers. That should be enough to get her back on track. And perhaps when she was back in Melbourne, she might let Samira and John talk her into one of their setups. Just not with Yana, she thought with a shudder.

Her eyes swam back into focus as a woman in a tight red dress mounted the stage and walked with a swing in her hips to the podium. She adjusted the microphone and flicked her lustrous black hair over her shoulder. The crowd, already mesmerised, waited in hushed anticipation. Jessica had always been a showstopper.

"Good afternoon everyone," she said in a husky voice. "What a pleasure it is for me to stand before you today here in the heart of Australia, Alice Springs. I would like to acknowledge that this meeting is being held on the traditional lands of the Arrernte people and pay my respects to elders both past and present. I would like to acknowledge that sovereignty was never ceded. I know some of you have come to us this week from overseas, and many from interstate. I hope you will join me in enjoying all that this town has to offer while we are here together over the next five days, exploring new ideas, learning from the past, and imagining what could be for the future."

Her voice was compelling. She had always been able to command a room, even back in their university days when she would take the floor during a tutorial to give her considered and highly intellectual point of view on a contentious topic. Reyna admired her charisma. It was hard not to. Jessica was an attractive woman, and in the past Reyna had wondered if there was a spark between them. There had been the odd flirtation back in their university days, but they had always both been so busy, aiming high, working hard, it had never amounted to anything. Would it now, she wondered? Perhaps over a late night drink.

"She's just so great, isn't she?" Stacey whispered beside her, cutting into her thoughts.

Reyna nodded, feeling like a naughty schoolgirl who had been caught daydreaming in class. She really needed to focus. People would want to discuss Jessica's talk, and it would not do for her to have no idea what had been said. She could hardly say, *Oh I'm sorry, I missed most of what she said. I was too busy thinking about my love life!* Or lack of it.

For the next forty-five minutes Jessica spoke without notes, in an engaging and confident manner, about Australia, its global position as a leader in finance, the strategies and fiscal instruments that had been used to leverage it through the Global Financial Crisis, and the creative vision required for the country to continue to thrive. She placed a call for action from the leaders in the industry to strive for excellence and pleaded with each and every member of the audience to raise the bar on ethical practice. It was an impassioned speech and the audience lapped it up, showing their appreciation with a roar of applause when she finally stepped away from the microphone. It had been an impressive performance and Reyna was not immune to its effects. It reminded her of how proud she was of her own firm, and all that they were achieving, not to mention the high ethical standards they maintained. Once again she was pleased to have been able to bring Meryl, Stacey, and Zoe to this conference to represent the firm. She knew they too would be well received.

There was a crowd forming around the conference foyer where a group of long tables had been set up with afternoon tea. People were selecting mini cupcakes, fruit, little Danishes and platters of biscuits from towers of food, but Reyna bypassed these in favour of a strong cup of tea. If she ate anything sweet now she would just feel sleepy during the rest of the afternoon's presentations.

Zoe appeared at her elbow, balancing a small plate of fruit and Danish in one hand, conference brochure and coffee cup in the other.

"Would you mind tipping a bit of milk into my coffee, please?" Zoe said. "I seem to have run out of hands."

Reyna obliged, pouring as she said, "Say when."

"Perfect, thanks."

"When did you get in?"

"I arrived yesterday at lunchtime. What an amazing place."

"Isn't it just. Did you get to look around at all last night?"

"Yep. I borrowed one of the hotel bicycles and went for a ride along the Todd River into town. I don't suppose it's likely to rain is it? I'd love to see that river flowing. "

"It's highly unlikely with this heatwave."

The Todd River was a wide, sandy riverbed that rarely saw much water. It was dry most of the time, dotted with towering red river gums and spiky native grasses. Locals considered themselves lucky to see it flow year in and year out.

Zoe's mouth turned down. "Damn. I bet that's a sight to see."

"It is. Locals say that when you see the Todd flow three times you'll stay in Alice Springs for life. I've only seen it once myself."

"Oh, you've seen it. Was it magical?"

"It was pretty impressive. The banks flooded overnight and we woke up to impassable roads and a cascade of water streaming down the river. The water was a deep, brown red like the colour of clay. I took a lot of photographs."

"We?" Zoe asked, her wide brown eyes innocent.

"My family and I. It was a long time ago when we were kids." Thinking about her sister and their family trip to Alice Springs all those years ago gave Reyna a sudden deep pain in her heart. "I'd better go," she said, placing her teacup back on the table. "I'll catch up with you later."

She saw the confusion in Zoe's eyes as she turned abruptly and walked away. She was conscious that she may have sounded curt, but she was unable to do anything about it, driven by an urgent need to get away from the chattering crowd. Her eyes stung and she blinked furiously, taking deep breaths in through her nose as she left the conference centre and stepped outside into the baking hot air. She walked quickly down the path toward her room and stopped at the door, leaning against it for a moment, protected from view by a tropical-looking shrub with large, flat leaves. She could see the pool from where she stood, trying to get control of her thoughts as she watched a pair of children splash raucously in the shallow end.

She and Sarit had done just that when they had visited as a family back in the 80s. Not that they had stayed anywhere this fancy. It had been a little motel with an oblong-shaped pool. They had played Marco Polo for hours. She had not thought about that trip in a long time. That was the problem with memories; they could strike like a brown snake and paralyse you in seconds if you accidentally stumbled across them.

Feeling calmer, she checked her watch and realised the next session was due to start. She would have to forgo spending time in her room. As she stepped onto the path, she nearly collided with Jessica, who was heading away from the conference centre.

"Reyna! How fantastic to see you." She swooped down and kissed Reyna lightly on both cheeks, reminding Reyna of how tall she was. "I saw your name on the program and was looking forward to catching up with you."

"You're looking well, Jessica. That was a wonderful talk you gave. I know I'll be chewing over the issues you raised for some time to come."

"I'm glad you liked it." Her eyes gave Reyna the once-over. "How do you manage to look this fantastic in such heat? Life is obviously treating you well."

Reyna smiled noncommittally and said, "Always. Are you heading back to the conference centre? I'm interested to hear the next talk. John McDonald is presenting on the implications of rising interest rates for equity with limited liquidity."

"Actually, I was going back to my room to freshen up. Do you have plans after dinner tonight? We should get together for a drink later."

It was tradition on the first night of the conference for everyone to share a meal at the conference centre, and it was always a very spirited event. Reyna enjoyed the opportunity to catch up socially with her peers, a chance she didn't get very often.

"I'd like that." There went her early night, but it would be fun to catch up. "Shall we meet in the bar?"

"How about poolside, eight o'clock?"

"Sounds perfect."

Jessica put her hand on Reyna's arm, giving it a firm squeeze and said with a flutter of her lashes, "We are long overdue, Rey. See you then."

And with that she tapped off down the cobbled pathway in what Reyna noticed were a pair of serious stilettos, her hips swinging.

CHAPTER THIRTEEN

Zoe (Monday, p.m.)

Zoe stood in one of the large lines for dinner, holding her empty plate against her chest as she shuffled forward with the rest of the conference goers toward the buffet. People sprinkled themselves around the room, settling in small groups at large round tables with their overflowing plates of food. Zoe wasn't sure why a buffet always seemed to lead people to stuff themselves. There was clearly plenty of food to go around and no one would starve, but there would surely be a lot of food wasted.

Meryl joined her in the line. "Don't mind if I step in here with my friend, do you?" she said to the lady standing behind Zoe, who if she did mind, simply shrugged. "Stacey's nabbing us some seats. I spotted you in the line and said we'd bring her back a plate of food."

"She doesn't want to choose for herself?"

"Nah, been to one conference buffet, been to 'em all. Anyway, she's not picky."

Zoe wondered for a moment if Meryl and Stacey were a couple. They seemed to know each other very well, and there was a certain easy intimacy between them that implied there was more to their relationship than met the eye.

"You two work together in Sydney? Have you known each other long?" she asked, attempting to sound casual as they inched forward toward the buffet.

"About twenty years. We actually met at a conference not unlike this one in the States. She was over there on a sabbatical and I was working for an Aussie firm that had international offices."

"And you stayed in touch all those years?"

Meryl gave her a searching look, like Zoe was missing a screw and it was up to Meryl to work out where to put it. "You know we're together, right?"

"Oh, uh, no. I'm sorry, I didn't mean to pry."

"It's fine. I thought everyone knew."

"Even Reyna?"

"Of course, Reyna. We told her when we came on board that we're a package deal. You don't get one without the other."

"Wow. That's amazing. Is it ever difficult? Working together and living together and stuff? What happens if you fight?"

"We don't really fight. Sometimes I get huffy and Stacey tells me not to sulk. Sometimes she gets sad and I realised I've stuffed up. I just apologise and wait for her to tell me what I've done wrong. It usually blows over pretty quickly."

Zoe smiled, appreciating the candid insight into their lives. How incredible it would be to have such ease with another person. Would she ever find something like that? Well, first, she admitted to herself, she would need to actually go out on a date with someone. Perhaps it would be worth opening the door a crack and letting her friends set her up with someone. It was starting to feel a little lonely on Zoe island.

At the table she picked at her food, listening to two young, clean-cut men in expensive suits discuss the likelihood of an imminent stock market crash. She wasn't actually that hungry.

Her head was swimming with information from the talks she had attended so far, and the din in the room was rising as people finished their meals and began to talk in earnest.

"When interest rates go up, you can bet your bottom dollar the market will tank. Get out while you can, man," one of the men said.

"And if it does, I *will* be betting my bottom dollar because I'll be buying up all the cut-price stock you bailed out of on the cheap, *man*," the other replied, banging his fist on the table.

Zoe tuned them out, letting the conversation wash over her. It had been a long day. She had been up before sunrise to climb Anzac Hill, or Untyeyetwelye as the local Aboriginal people called it according to her guidebook, and had not been disappointed. She had ridden out to the hill on one of the hotel bicycles, climbing carefully in the grey light of dawn. From her vantage point she had watched as a deep red and orange sun had slowly spread across the sky, inching up to paint the MacDonnell Ranges in front of her in soft purples and blues. She had stayed up there, sitting crossed-legged on a stony patch of ground, as the town had awoken, cars beginning to take to the roads, people weaving past on bicycles, until eventually it was morning. The sky faded to blue and the landscape settled into a dusty green and brown. It was only a short hike down the hill, and a ten-minute ride back to the hotel. She would definitely like to do it again before the week was out, if she could fit it in before the day's activities began.

Dessert was brought in to the dining room and people began to queue up again to fill their plates with what looked to be chocolate mousse and strawberries.

"I'll go line up," Meryl declared, pushing back her chair. "Zoe, you want?"

"Not for me thanks," Zoe said. The last thing she felt like was dessert. Perhaps it was the heat, but her appetite had all but disappeared. She refilled her water glass from the ice-cold pitcher on the table and took a long sip. She hadn't realised how thirsty she was. She would have to remember to drink more in this weather.

She wondered where Reyna was. She hadn't seen her since Reyna had walked off in the middle of their conversation at the tea table. Zoe had no idea what she'd done to offend her, but the look on Reyna's face had been clear. Zoe had breached some kind of no-go zone and Reyna was displeased. She wondered if she should say something or would that make it worse? She had only been making polite conversation, and if she had somehow put her foot in it she was equally likely to stumble into the same minefield a second time around. She sighed, trying to concentrate on the conversation around her, but she felt unsettled. She checked her watch and realised with a shock that it was already almost nine p.m.

"I think I'm going to pop out for a bit of air," she said quietly to Stacey.

"Everything okay?" Stacey asked, her brow crinkled with concern.

"Oh yeah, absolutely. I just feel like some time out."

"I get that. Meryl could stay here chatting with everyone for hours, but I get kind of tired after a while. The whole introvert thing."

Zoe nodded. She wasn't exactly an introvert, but she had taken a test once at uni that said she definitely wasn't an extrovert either. Somewhere in between she supposed. You couldn't always fit people neatly into boxes.

"Think I'll head to bed soon. Catch you guys in the morning?"

"Definitely. We'll have an early breakfast if you want to join us. Meryl wakes up hungry and likes to hit the breakfast buffet by seven a.m."

"Sounds good, I might squeeze in a bike ride before breakfast, but I'll probably be back by then."

It felt good to get out of the stuffy dining room and into the cooler night air. She actually shivered a little, remembering that the temperature at night in the desert was always much cooler. It felt good to be cold after the furnace of the day.

In the darkness, she could see the shapes of people dotted around the pool, quiet murmurings and the occasional bark of laughter drifting across the water. It would be nice to sit by the water for a moment before bed and feel the stillness of the desert evening. The pool, which had looked so inviting during the day, was now lit up with an array of discreet yellow lights, creating a warm and romantic environment. She hadn't had a chance to swim yet and she realised there were actually people in the water now, their heads bobbing in the darkness like seals. She let herself through the gate in the pool fence and scanned for an empty lounge chair, spotting one over by the children's splash pool.

She plonked herself onto the chair and leaned back, letting the tension flow out of her body. It was going to be a big week and she needed to pace herself.

"Zoe?"

She sat up with a start as she realised Reyna was saying her name from the table next to her. She was seated with a woman whose silhouette Zoe couldn't identify in the dark. There was a candle flickering at their table in a glass jar and an ice bucket with a bottle of something sticking out of it. "Oh, hi. I didn't see you there." She eased herself up off the lounge with a little groan.

"Are you hurt?"

"No, just tired."

She stood and stepped into the light of their table.

"Zoe, this is Jessica." Reyna gestured to the woman sitting at the table, who on closer inspection she instantly recognised as Jessica Myers, the conference's plenary speaker. "Jessica this is a colleague of mine, Zoe Cavendish. Zoe is one of our star employees at Azoulay House."

"Great to meet you, Jessica." Zoe extended her hand. "Your talk today was excellent." Jessica took Zoe's hand in both of her own and pressed it lightly, her skin smooth and cool to the touch.

"A pleasure to meet you, Zoe Cavendish," she purred, holding Zoe's hand for a moment longer while she smiled slowly in the candlelight. "Will you join us for a glass of champagne? We have a whole bottle to get through and neither of us seem able to make much of a dent in it."

"Well, I…" She trailed off, unable to think of a reason not to stay. Would it be awkward with Reyna? She glanced at her as if to ask for permission and immediately felt irritated with herself, as if Reyna cared what she did. "I'd love to," she finished, pulling out a chair and sitting decisively.

"Wonderful. We don't have another champagne glass but if you don't mind using a water glass, I'll pour you a drink."

"I'm not fussy." She glanced again at Reyna, aware of the dark eyes on her. It was impossible to read her expression but her face had a serious, contemplative look.

"How have you enjoyed the first day, Zoe?" Reyna asked.

"It's been a blast already." Zoe took the glass Jessica had poured and raised it to her lips, enjoying the feel of the bubbles on her tongue as she took a sip. "Everyone has so much knowledge to share, there are so many great people to talk to, and we're in Alice Springs. What more could I ask for?"

Reyna smiled at her and Zoe felt a warmth spread through her. Probably just the champagne.

"Cheers to being in Alice Springs." Jessica held up her glass and the three of them clinked glasses.

Their conversation in the candlelight was easy, touching on Reyna and Jessica's history, things they were looking forward to about the conference, and the sights of Alice Springs. They finished off the bottle in the ice bucket as the conversation flowed.

"I climbed Untyeyetwelye this morning," Zoe said, pronouncing the syllables carefully. "It was amazing and I'm going to do it again tomorrow. Would either of you like to join me?" Was she crazy? The voice of her friends in her head said she most definitely was, inviting the plenary speaker of the conference and the CEO of her firm to join her on a pre-dawn bike ride.

"What time will you go?" Reyna asked. "Is it far?"

"Well, you have to get up at six to make it in time for the sunrise, but it's only a ten- minute ride from here. We can use the hotel bicycles if you'd like to come. They have plenty of them available."

"I think I would like that," Reyna said slowly. "I haven't seen a good sunrise in a long time."

"Oh, you won't regret it! The colours are to die for."

"Well, I'd just about die if I had to get up at six in the morning and get on a bike," Jessica snorted. "Take some pics, though. I'd love to see them when I'm done sleeping."

"You're all bluff, Jessica," Reyna told her friend. "I know you. You're the first one up in the morning and definitely the last to bed."

"True. But when you work for the government you have no choice. Politicians never seem to sleep. They're always too worried about news cycles to sleep. But really, that's the only kind of cycle I'm interested in at that time in the morning. I don't think I've been on a bicycle since I was twelve years old."

"If I'm getting up at six in the morning I'd better get to bed now."

"Actually," Zoe corrected, "we need to leave at six, so you'd better get up a bit earlier than that."

"Right. Where do I meet you?"

"I can pick you up from your room if you like? The bikes are stored in the rec shed and I've got the passcode." Zoe drained the remnants of her glass and stood, noticing the buzz of the champagne in her limbs. "I think I'll hit the sack too."

"Great. Why don't you walk back with me and I'll show you where my room is? That way you'll know where to come in the morning."

"Sure. Goodnight, Jessica. It was lovely to meet you."

"Goodnight to you both. I might stay up a little longer and see out the evening. I'd love to see those photos if you're around tomorrow night, Zoe? Over a drink perhaps?"

Zoe blinked. A drink with Jessica Myers? "It's a date," she said.

"Perfect," Jessica replied. "Let's all go to town. Reyna, you'll join us? There's a great little rooftop bar I'd like to check out. We can meet in front of the hotel at nine."

Zoe felt her cheeks flush, glad the darkness hid her embarrassment. For a second she had thought Jessica was actually inviting her out, but clearly she had misread the situation. Thank god neither woman had seemed to notice her words.

Zoe followed Reyna out of the pool area and onto the cobblestone path that led to the first circle of units.

"I'm just down here," Reyna gestured. "Number seven."

"I'm in the Desert Spring building. I have a nice view of the hotel from my balcony."

"A view is good."

"Bit of a hike to breakfast, though."

"And here I was thinking you liked exercise. So, this is me." Reyna stopped on the pathway. Her unit was set back amongst a screen of foliage, the door hidden from view of the main path.

"All right. I'll come back before six then. Sleep well, Reyna." Zoe touched her lightly on the arm, realising it was out of character for her to do so. Oh well, she could blame the champagne.

"Goodnight, Zoe," Reyna said, her eyes shying away from Zoe's as she headed for her door.

Zoe courted sleep with a hot shower and a cup of chamomile tea, grateful for the soporific effect of the alcohol in her system. When it did come, she dreamt over and over that she had slept through her alarm and missed the sunrise altogether, waking anxiously to check the time on her phone repeatedly through the night in case she really had overslept and missed the morning with Reyna. When her alarm finally sounded she woke with a start and quickly switched it off, the sound grating against the silence of the desert morning.

She cleaned her teeth and dressed in layers by the light of her bedside lamp. It was cold and dark now, but she knew from yesterday morning that by the time the sun came up it would be warm enough to shed her jacket on the ride back to the hotel. Switching off the lamp, she let herself quietly out of her room, careful not to let the door slam and wake her sleeping neighbours. She jogged down the stairwell rather than waiting for the lift and made her way to Reyna's unit, enjoying the absolute stillness around her. The birds were not awake yet, and there was nothing moving at the hotel.

At Reyna's door she tapped quietly and took a step back, wondering if Reyna had managed to wake up on time. Would she be ready? Would she have changed her mind?

She leaned against the doorframe while she waited. Should she tap again? Would that seem rude? If Reyna was still asleep, there wouldn't be any point in waking her now. Perhaps she had forgotten. Zoe could just creep away and do the ride on her own, as she had originally planned. It had been ridiculous to think that Reyna, the CEO of her firm, would want to join her on a dawn bike ride! Perhaps she would tap just once more, and if she still didn't answer she would leave. She raised her hand to knock and the door swung open, leaving Zoe standing at the doorway with her fist in the air. She quickly put it down, trying not to stare as Reyna stepped out onto the pathway. She was wearing a pair of soft, grey track pants, baby blue flats and a puffer jacket, zipped up to her chin. Her hair was damp, as if she had just showered, a loose strand stuck to her cheek. Zoe had to shove her hands in her pockets to resist the urge to reach out and tuck it behind her ear. Reyna looked younger without her makeup, almost vulnerable in the shadows of the pre-dawn.

"Sorry, I was just looking for my jacket."

"No worries. Ready to go?"

"As I'll ever be." Reyna shot her a hesitant smile, as if she had been debating the merits of this experience with herself and lost. "You might have to go slow for me. I'm not a big professional athlete like you."

"You'll be fine. Come on, let's get the bikes."

The helmets were stored on a shelf at the back of the rec shed and Zoe grabbed two, tossing one to Reyna.

"Pretty sure they're just one size fits all so try that on."

She wheeled her bike out into the open and adjusted the straps on her helmet. Reyna appeared to be struggling with hers.

"You all right?"

"I can't seem to shorten the straps."

"Here, let me help you."

Zoe rested her bike on the ground and took the straps from Reyna's hands, sliding the toggle up the strap in order to shorten it. "Try that?"

Reyna fumbled with the straps, trying to meet the two ends together under her chin.

"I've got it." Zoe took the two ends and gently clipped them together, careful to avoid touching Reyna's skin. It would be so easy to run her thumb along Reyna's cheek, to graze her lips with her own. Her abdomen constricted, her heart thudding. Heat spread through her. She took a step back and said quickly, "That should do it."

The ride out to Untyeyetwelye was an easy, flat route. She remembered the route well enough from the previous day that she didn't have to stop and check the directions. They rode silently, side by side through the darkness. A few cars passed them, their headlights illuminating the road and the surrounding gum trees for a brief moment, and then they were picking their way through the darkness by the light of the torch on Zoe's mobile phone.

"I did ask the hotel if they had any bike lights, but unfortunately they don't," Zoe apologised as they pedalled down a long straight road. "I didn't think to bring mine with me, but we're actually nearly there."

"I don't mind. It's kind of nice riding in the dark. Makes it feel like an adventure. Anyway, my eyes are pretty much adjusted now."

Adventuring with Reyna, Zoe thought. Who would have imagined that? She felt a little thrill run through her as she pushed on the pedals and stood, letting the bike coast for a moment. She felt good. She felt free.

"Now you're just showing off."

"What? No, it's fun that's all. You should try it."

"I'd fall off."

"Nah, it's harder to fall off a bike than you think, once you get moving. You've just got to look straight ahead to keep your balance."

Reyna followed her instructions, looking straight ahead as she pedalled some more and then suddenly she too stood on her pedals. "Woo," she called, shaking her head in the breeze. "Doing it!" Her bike gave a small wobble and she sank back down onto her seat, laughing. "I haven't done that for an age."

Zoe's heart soared like a bird on an updraft. If I could sing, she thought, I would want to do that right now. Sadly her voice was about as birdlike as a crow. Regardless, she felt weightless, like she had been airlifted out of her normal life and dropped into a moment that had been reserved especially for them.

"It's pretty good, isn't it?" she called, pedalling hard to feel the rush of air against her face. The sign for Anzac Hill loomed in the darkness and she pulled up, waiting for Reyna to catch up.

"Hey, you said you'd go easy on me, Lance Armstrong!"

"Sorry." Zoe grinned. "We can leave the bikes and walk up from here."

They dismounted, linking their bikes together with a chain Zoe had procured from the hotel, and headed up a small gravel track. As the track got steeper their pace slowed and Reyna slipped, her foot sliding out from under her on a loose stone. Zoe reached out her hand and grabbed her by the elbow, holding her up. Reyna gave a shaky laugh.

"Got you," Zoe said.

"I don't think my shoes are really cut out for this. I didn't actually bring any runners with me."

"That's okay. We're nearly there. Just hang on to me until we reach the top."

Zoe linked her arm through Reyna's, holding her close to support her as they finished the last few meters of steep ascent. As fit as she was, she felt breathless, as if she was finishing Everest, conscious of Reyna's body pressed against her own.

At the top, they stood for a moment, arms still linked, watching as the morning lights began to flicker on in the township. There were others dotted around the top of the hill, getting out cameras and tripods, obviously gathering to watch the sunrise.

"We made it then," Reyna said quietly, her body warm against Zoe's.

"Want to sit down?" Zoe suggested as they looked around the hill.

"Sure."

"We should sit on the side where the sun comes up. There's an empty bench."

Reluctantly, she let Reyna's arm slip from her own and they made their way over to the bench and sat down. She checked her watch. The sky was beginning to glisten with the first hint of red dawn light. "It won't be long now."

"There's The Gap." Reyna pointed toward a craggy break in the ranges where the road ran into the township.

"Oh yeah, I came in through there on my way from the airport. God, I love this view. The landscape here is just phenomenal."

The edge of the sky above the ranges was beginning to glow a deep orange, the bowl above their heads lightening to a pale blue. Reds streaked the across the sky as if smudged on to a canvas by a carefree artist.

"It feels ancient. That's what I like about this landscape. It's like you can actually see the history of the land out here. Melbourne is so covered in buildings and asphalt you can't really see or feel anything."

"I did a walking tour back home recently with an Aboriginal elder, where we visited sites that were sacred to the Aboriginal people of Melbourne, and she told us about their meaning and significance. It was really special, but I know what you mean. I was standing at this riverbank at a giant weir, on a man-made platform with bicycle paths and bench seats all over the place, trying to imagine what it had been like a few hundred years ago. You don't have to try so hard out here, that's for sure."

"I wish Holden could have seen this."

"Holden?"

"My nephew. He really wanted to come with me but he had school. He would have loved this."

"Young boys do seem to love an adventure."

"True. Holden is no exception, and he hasn't seen outback Australia yet."

"Yet?"

"He's from England." Reyna gazed out over the landscape, her face serious. "I brought him back to Australia to live with me when his parents died."

"Oh wow," Zoe said, searching for the right words. "That's huge. For both of you."

"It has been. Hence the psychologist's office. He's actually doing pretty well all things considered, but I felt like he could use a bit of extra help with the emotional side of things. I guess there's only so much you want to tell your aunty."

"So he lives with you? Like, all the time?"

"Yep."

"You're his parent now."

"Sort of. An aunty type of parent. He's staying with my folks while I'm in Alice, but that's why I've been working from home so much recently. I've been trying to be around more for him. It's been a big adjustment for both of us, I guess."

"I didn't know," Zoe said lamely. Why would she have known? It wasn't like she and Reyna had ever really had a personal conversation. "And that means you lost…"

"My sister and brother-in-law."

"God, that's awful."

Reyna bit her lip, her eyes far away. "It was pretty bloody awful."

They sat quietly together, contemplating the landscape before them.

"So now you're, raising Holden on your own?" Zoe asked tentatively, hoping she didn't sound like she was prying.

"Yes. Just me. No parenting experience, no partner, no real idea what I'm doing."

"I bet you're doing great. Losing your parents is insanely hard, but he's lucky to have you to support him."

Reyna glanced at Zoe. "You lost your mum a little while back, didn't you?"

"About a year and a half ago," Zoe replied, surprised Reyna remembered.

"It must have been tough."

"It was a bit. Things hadn't exactly been smooth sailing for her. She had a hard life. My dad died when I was six and she had to provide for us all. It was a struggle."

"I can't imagine how difficult that would have been."

"My brother and I didn't really know why everything was so hard at the time. You don't as a kid, you're too busy thinking about yourself."

"I think that's pretty natural," Reyna said, shifting slightly so their shoulders touched.

Zoe was instantly aware of the pressure. "I wish we had realised what was going on. We might have been able to help her."

"You were just a kid? What could you have done?"

"I don't know. Got a paper round, something. She needed help and she didn't have it. It plays on my mind a lot," Zoe admitted.

"I can understand that. So you've lost your mum and your dad."

"Yeah. I guess I'm also an orphan. Just a really old one." She cracked a lopsided smile at Reyna.

"Well there you go. I didn't know that."

"As they say, you learn something new every day," Zoe said. "Oh, look, here it comes."

The first crest of the sun's blood-red orb showed itself above a length of rocky cliff, turning the sky into a tequila sunrise. Beside Zoe, Reyna fished her mobile phone out of her pocket and stood, turning three hundred and sixty degrees as she took photos to get the full effect. Zoe merely let her eyes record the event, having done the same thing herself the previous morning. Photographs didn't do it justice, though.

She gazed at Reyna, her edges blurred against the sunrise. Reyna's hair, now fully dried, curled softly around her ears, tucked into her puffer jacket which was still zipped up to her chin against the chill of the morning. Zoe rubbed her arm, sure the skin still tingled from where they had touched earlier. She wished she could reach out and pull Reyna gently back onto the seat, wrap an arm around her, and kiss her. As if sensing the gaze, Reyna turned, her face an unforgettable picture of serenity against the riot of the sky.

"What is it? Is something wrong?"

"Everything is perfect," Zoe murmured. "I'm just admiring the sunrise."

Reyna considered her for a moment, her dark eyes opaque. Then, she slowly turned back to the sunrise.

Zoe hadn't realised she was holding her breath, letting it out now with a quiet sigh. Her resolution to focus on anything but Reyna appeared to have taken a dive.

Reyna settled back on the bench seat and they watched the colours fade almost as quickly as they had appeared. Within ten minutes the oranges and reds had been replaced with a warm yellow light.

"We should probably head back," Reyna said, rubbing her neck and stretching. "I'm presenting this afternoon, and I should go over my presentation before the day gets started."

"For sure." Zoe kicked out her feet and jumped up. "Hang on to my arm. It will be slippery on the way down the hill."

"Thanks." Reyna took the proffered arm and they headed down, Zoe choosing their path carefully in deference to Reyna's unsuitable shoes.

At the bottom they retrieved their helmets and slipped them on.

"Argh," Reyna exclaimed in frustration. "What's wrong with this thing? Why can't I make the clips work?"

"Here, let me help. It's hard when you can't see what you're doing."

Once again, Zoe took the ends and clipped them together. Her hands hovered under Reyna's chin. There was a thin, pale scar on the edge of her jaw that Zoe had never noticed before. She ran her thumb lightly across it. The air around them seemed to stand still.

"What's this scar from?" she said, her voice sounding husky to her own ears.

"Would you believe I fell off my tricycle when I was four?"

"I kinda would, yeah."

Zoe studied Reyna from under her lashes, her thumb still tracing the tiny scar. "You're so very beautiful." Her heart was hammering in her chest. Slowly, holding Reyna's eyes with her own, she leant forward and brushed her lips over Reyna's. She was almost shocked by the soft velvet. An arc of electricity jumped between them, heat immediately coursing through Zoe's body.

And then Reyna broke away, taking a step backward, her fingers nervously skating over the strap of her helmet as if to check that it was fastened.

"Zoe, I—"

"Of course, no, I know," Zoe jumped in, cutting her off before she could say whatever dreadful words she had ready. Zoe turned away, busying herself with unlocking their bikes. "We best get going if we want to make it back in time for breakfast."

They pedalled the short ride back in silence, Zoe's inner voice more than making up for their lack of conversation. What the hell had she just done? Probably cost herself her job, that's what. Why on earth hadn't she thought of that before? You couldn't just go around kissing the boss and not expect there to be ramifications!

At the bike shed they parted quickly, Reyna thanking her briefly for the ride, Zoe nodding, doing her best to avoid Reyna's gaze.

With the bikes securely returned to the shed, Zoe hightailed it to her room, sinking onto her bed and curling up with a pillow. She didn't even bother to turn the lights on, the darkness of the room suiting her mood. She had made a giant error of judgment and she cringed, imagining what her friends would be saying if they were here.

She cried hot tears into the pillow, furious with herself. Reyna could accuse her of sexual harassment. It was a disaster. She was a disaster. Peeling off her clothes she made for the shower, running the water hot and hard as her tumultuous thoughts finally settled. Undoubtedly, not her finest professional moment. She should have been focusing on her presentation and thinking about how to make the most of what the conference had to offer, but instead, here she was larking about like she was some kind of kid on a school excursion with a crush on the teacher. Even if she discounted the stupidity of her actions, it was embarrassing. She had set herself up for instant rejection, and her rebellious heart smarted, thinking about the look in Reyna's eyes as she stepped away from the kiss. What had it been? Compassion? Pity? She was hard to read.

Towelling herself off she gave herself a stern look in the mirror. Should she call her friends? Ask them for advice? That would just add to the embarrassment, she decided. What she needed to do was apologise to Reyna, quickly, before things got out of hand. Maybe if she wrote her a note and slipped it under her door, she wouldn't have to actually see Reyna and speak to her. That way she couldn't be accused of harassing her any further.

She wrapped the towel around her resolutely and grabbed her notebook from the bed, scribbling quickly before she changed her mind. *Sunrise must have addled my brain. I'm really sorry. I acted inappropriately. Can we please pretend that didn't happen?*

She used one of the hotel envelopes on the desk to seal the letter and wrote Reyna's name on it. She could deliver it now while Reyna was at breakfast and then try to stay out of her way for the rest of the conference. She hoped fervently that Reyna would be understanding. It was all she could really hope for.

Zoe dressed quickly in a sleeveless, collared shirt matched with a pair of light trousers, and slipped on her sandals. It was set to be another warm day and the heat greeted her as she stepped out of the building and made her way back down the path to Reyna's room.

At the door, she paused. Should she knock? Should she just slip the note under the door? She was just trying to decide what to do when the door flung open and Reyna stepped out, right into Zoe's arms. Zoe jumped back, letting her go as if Reyna were a burning ember. Reyna looked confused as she regained her footing.

"I didn't hear you knock."

"I hadn't yet. I was just coming to give you this," Zoe handed Reyna the envelope.

Reyna took it and nodded, a muscle in her jaw flickering with tension.

"It's an apology. I hope you can forgive my behaviour. I don't know what came over me but please be assured it won't happen again."

"Okay, yes thanks." Her tone was clipped. Zoe's heart sank. Reyna was obviously really angry.

"Really, Reyna, I'm so sorry, I—"

Reyna cut her off, "Actually, you couldn't have come at a better time."

Zoe paused, confusion warring with contrition in her mind. "Sorry, what?"

"I can't seem to log on to the Azoulay House network and the file I was working on for my presentation is on the network drive. I should have saved it onto a USB but I didn't. I just assumed I'd be able to get it from the network drive, but now I can't access it. Do you know your remote login details?"

"Oh no, that's awful. I can log in for you, but that will only help if you've saved it in one of public drives."

Reyna's face fell. "It's in my personal folder. And I can't get through to IT to work out what's wrong."

"Do you want me to take a look? It could be that your network folder has unlinked itself from your profile. That's happened to me a few times and I think I can remember how to get it back."

"Please. I was just on my way to the conference IT crew to see if they could help, but if you think you might be able to take a look?"

Reyna stepped back from the doorway, holding the door open for Zoe to come inside.

"Sure, of course."

She followed Reyna into the room, trying not to look too curiously around her. The room was set up differently from her own. Where hers was simple and functional, Reyna's had a touch of opulence that was missing from Zoe's. The tasteful, dark grey carpet was thicker, and the bed was a king size with what appeared to be an inordinate number of pillows. The sheets were still rumpled and Zoe averted her eyes, trying not to imagine Reyna lying between those sheets, possibly in her pyjamas, possibly not. There was a large mirror, edged in a wooden frame set behind the desk, upon which sat the offending computer. Zoe drew up the plush leather desk chair in front of it and took the mouse.

"It lets me log in to the main terminal, but from there I've got nothing, no network drives, no personal drives, just a blank screen."

Zoe skated the mouse over the screen, hoping like hell she could remember the complicated set of instructions she had received from IT when this had happened to her. Thankfully she loathed calling IT so much she had taken notes the first time it had happened, following them successfully when it had occurred again. She hovered over the start menu, scrolling through options until she found the control panel, trying to visualise her notes now.

"I'm pretty sure you have to disconnect all the preference settings and re-map the drives. I think I can remember how you do it."

Reyna didn't answer. She stood behind Zoe, looking over her shoulder. Her eyes met Zoe's in the mirror in front of them, her mouth set in a tight line, her brow pinched with worry.

"Do you want to grab a cup of tea or something while I do this? It could take a while."

"No, I'm fine."

"Right."

Zoe navigated her way through the control panel, trying to ignore Reyna's scrutiny.

"Oops," she said as she realised she was in the wrong menu. "Not this one."

She tried a few other options, her eyes once again meeting Reyna's in the mirror.

"Do you think you can remember?"

Zoe nodded. "Yeah, just give me a sec. I need to find the thingo."

"The thingo?"

"It's some kind of menu," she replied with a grimace. "I forget what it's called but I'll know it when I see... Wait, this is the one."

Relieved to be looking at a list of options she recognised, she carefully checked the boxes she remembered and went through the advanced suite of options, muttering the steps under her breath as she proceeded.

"There," she said. "I'm pretty sure that will have fixed it. If we restart the computer now it should all come up."

They both watched as the screen flashed blue, waiting in silence for the login box to reappear. When it did, Reyna leaned over her shoulder, tapping in her username and password. She held her breath, conscious of Reyna's cheek so close to her own, Reyna's hair brushing against her ear, her breath on her neck. She didn't move as the company logo appeared and the home screen loaded, Reyna continuing to lean over her as she took the mouse and navigated to the files menu. She could feel the curve of Reyna's breast pressed against her shoulder as she clicked through the file stems, accessing her private folder, until she reached the presentation file itself, double clicking on it to open it.

"Oh my god. Thank god, it's here," she breathed as the screen filled with the first slide of her presentation. Zoe took a shaky breath as Reyna walked away from the desk and sank into an armchair across the room, another feature that was noticeably missing from Zoe's own room. "I appreciate your help, Zoe," Reyna said, her tone once again formal, in control.

"It's no problem." She stood, hovering near the desk. "I'll leave you to it then."

Reyna looked up at her wearily, her face drawn and pale. "Before you go, we should probably talk. Can I make you a cup of tea?"

"Oh, no, I'm fine really. It's fine, I can just—"

"Please. Sit."

She slid back into the desk chair, tucking her hands under her thighs so she wouldn't fidget.

"What happened this morning was…" Reyna paused, turning her head to gaze out the window as if something outside could help her find the right words. "…outside the scope of our operational relationship." She turned back to Zoe with a searching look. "Do you understand what I mean?"

"I think so. You mean we work together so we shouldn't, uh…"

"Yes."

"Right. Understood." Her chest felt heavy, empty, as if someone had scooped out her lungs and her heart and left her with a raggedy hole.

"I want us to be clear. I am not in the market for a relationship, and even if I was, it would never be with someone from the firm. I hope I hadn't given you the wrong impression. I apologise if I had."

The hollow feeling in her chest expanded, and she nodded, not trusting herself to speak in that moment. Reyna apologising to her. She had not envisaged this. "You hadn't," she managed.

"Good. Well I'm glad we're clear. I value your input at the firm. You're an intelligent and skilful operator and I hope this morning's…strangeness hasn't jeopardised that."

"No, of course not. If you don't mind me asking, why aren't you in the market for a relationship?" She bit her lip, wishing she could have stopped the question before it had popped out. Way to make things worse, Zoe, she chastised herself. Couldn't she just quit while she was ahead?

Reyna studied her, a wariness in her eyes, and then she nodded and said, "My nephew, the firm, my family. I can't… Well, let's just say there's too much at stake. Those are my priorities and there just isn't room for any other…distractions."

"Fair enough."

"No hard feelings?"

Zoe dialled up a weak smile. "None."

"Right, well…" Reyna stood and Zoe followed suit. "I think we can agree to put that behind us and move on. Thank you again for your help, Zoe. Have a great day."

Have a great day, Zoe thought as she left the room, cognizant of the sound of Reyna's door softly clicking shut behind her. She had slept like hell, missed breakfast, and badly messed up with her boss and it wasn't even eight o'clock yet. Not exactly the makings of a great day. Oh well, at least she hadn't been fired.

CHAPTER FOURTEEN

Reyna (Tuesday, p.m.)

Reyna slipped into her bathers and donned a pair of sandals, wrapping a sarong around her waist. She grabbed her room key and her book, put on her sunglasses and headed for the pool. She had opted to skip the last presentation for the day, which promised to be both dry and ponderous, never her favourite combination, in favour of a quiet moment by the pool. Her head felt thick and heavy, and as she opened the pool gate, she was grateful to see there weren't many with the same idea.

She neatly folded her sarong and dropped it on a banana lounge in the shade with her book and kicked off her shoes. If there had been a beach or a river nearby, she would have gone there, but given she was in the desert and the nearest watering hole was at least fifty kilometres away, she settled for the pool. It actually looked quite inviting, its peacock blue, shiny tiles sparkling in the afternoon light. There were a few people sitting at the bar in the middle of the pool, sipping colourful cocktails and laughing. She didn't feel too much like laughing, she realised. With a sigh, she eased herself into the water and ducked her head under. The cold shocked her and she rose above the surface, pushing her hair out of her face and gulping air.

What a day. She leant back against the side of the pool and tipped her head back, squinting toward the sun, which was still high in the sky. Hard to believe that was the same sun she had watched come up this morning. That felt like a lifetime ago.

A thrill ran through her as she reviewed the events of the morning, remembering Zoe's lips, light as a feather, touching her own. A sudden, sweet ache arched through her abdomen and she ducked her head under the water again, trying to short circuit the memory. Oh body, don't betray me, she begged. Now was not the time to forget herself over a pair of acorn-coloured eyes and a head of auburn-streaked hair. Not to mention a set of the softest lips that had ever touched her own. Her lungs burned and she came up for air, propelling herself along the length of the pool with a lazy breaststroke.

Her presentation had been well received, and she was glad to be done with that. There was always a tension that hung over her before she gave a talk. Now she could try to relax and enjoy the rest of the week. *Without thinking about Zoe.* Clearly that was not going to be as easy as she'd hoped.

Her day had been peppered with flashbacks of the surprise kiss at inappropriate moments: introducing herself to the audience, chatting with an old colleague over lunch, listening to a lecture on government lending for private business. She had finally surrendered and left the conference for the day, realising that the thoughts were not going to leave her alone until she sorted through them. She swam harder, pushing herself through the water until she arrived at the other end of the pool. Clearly she was attracted to Zoe. It wasn't an entirely surprising revelation, but she hadn't exactly been prepared for this either. Alarm bells had tolled when she had agreed to the early morning bike ride, but she had chosen to ignore them. Just some sightseeing, she convinced herself. She knew Zoe had been the one to kiss her, but somehow she felt guilty, as if she had willed Zoe to do it and then slapped her for it. Not cool.

So now she would just have to avoid Zoe. It couldn't be too hard given the number of people at the conference, but it wasn't ideal. And if they did bump into each other, she could always hide behind her role as CEO and be strictly business. Thankfully, Zoe had taken it well when she had broached the subject this morning, but Reyna was pretty sure Zoe would be giving her a wide berth from now on anyway. She had invited Zoe in to her room on impulse, but she wondered now if that had been a wise move. She had sincerely needed the help at that moment, and what else could she have done? The woman was literally standing on her doorstep in her hour of need. It had been hard though, not to pull her in for another kiss, for a taste of her soft, wide mouth.

Her groin pulsed, heat generating between her legs despite the cold pool water. Oh god, she thought, climbing out of the pool and heading for her sarong. Wrapping her sarong around her, she set her mouth in a firm line, summoning her inner strength. She sat down on the banana lounge, opening her book to the folded page. This morning had been an aberration. Time to move on.

From behind her closed eyes Reyna felt a presence move in front of her, changing the light behind her eyelids.

"Catching up on some sleep?" came Jessica's drawl.

Reyna's eyes flew open. "It's called relaxing. You should try it sometime."

"Actually, I do it all the time. I'm just surprised to see *you* doing it."

She shrugged. "I needed some time out."

"Right, well don't forget we're going to that rooftop bar tonight. I'll meet you out the front at nine, okay?"

She had forgotten Jessica's plan from the night before. She couldn't possibly go out for drinks with Jessica and Zoe now. That would send entirely the wrong message. "Oh, no Jessica, I think I'll stay close to the hotel tonight. I've had a big day and I'm not in the mood to go out."

"What! Not you too."

"What do you mean?"

"Zoe also begged off. Said she's got a headache or something. Seriously, you Melbourne girls are no fun."

Oh well, she supposed if Zoe definitely wasn't going to be there, there was no harm in her going. "Fine, fine, I'll come."

"Good." Jessica smiled archly. "You won't regret it." She waltzed away from the pool area leaving Reyna to wonder if Jessica was flirting with her. Jessica, she realised, flirted with everyone. It was her modus operandi.

She sighed and reopened her book, trying to find the place where she had put it down and closed her eyes earlier. Clearly she had romance on the brain today.

At ten past nine she made her way past the front desk and out to the hotel's entrance. She had opted for a simple, sleeveless black dress which gently hugged her curves, leaving her hair to fall across her shoulders. She saw Jessica on the steps with a small group and headed toward her.

"Reyna," Jessica called. "Fashionably late as always. I've picked up a few others to join us. You remember Walter and Caroline from Silo Corp? And Jacquie from Waterhouse Group?"

Reyna nodded, saying hello and smiling at the group. She had met Walter and Caroline at various functions over the years. She had actually worked in the same company as Jacquie not long after university for a few months.

"Here's our taxi," Jessica said as a van pulled up in front of them. The driver got out, opening up the side door and gestured for them to enter.

"I ordered a maxi to fit us all in. We're just waiting for…Ah, here she is."

With a jolt, Reyna looked over to see Zoe trotting down the steps to join them.

"Sorry I'm late."

She looked a picture in a sea-green shirt that exposed her midriff, and a pair of flared black linen pants, cuffed around her waist with an oversized belt. Flashes of the tanned skin around her flat belly were visible, sending off warning signals to Reyna who froze with her hand on the taxi door. What was Zoe doing here? She was supposed to be feeling unwell.

"Just in time," Jessica said, ushering Reyna into the taxi and squeezing in behind her. They all settled into the cab and the driver pulled away from the hotel. Reyna sighed inwardly in frustration. This wasn't meant to happen. She was trying to avoid Zoe, not head out on the town with her.

"I'm glad you're feeling better, Zoe," Jessica said.

"Thanks, turns out the headache passed. I'm keen to get a look at the nightlife in town."

Reyna gazed out the window, watching a blur of gum trees flash by in the fading light as they sped into town. It was a short trip and she found she hadn't had to say much before the taxi driver announced they had arrived.

"I don't see it," Walter said, squinting out the window. They were stopped in a car park at the back of town.

"It's just down that alley. You'll see a red door. Can't miss it, mate."

They thanked the driver, paid him and left the cab, Reyna following behind as the group entered the alleyway. They heard it before they spotted the red door with a chalkboard hung on it. The words "follow the music" were scrawled on it in white chalk. Sounds of thumping bass spilled out from above, filling the alleyway, and they opened the door to a set of thin wooden stairs, just wide enough for them to climb in single file. The music intensified as they reached the fourth floor and Jessica pulled open another red door to reveal a large open terrace with a DJ at one end, a dance floor in the middle, and a crowd of well-dressed partygoers making the most of both. Music flooded across the terrace, a light show pulsing in time with the beat. Reyna stood still, letting her senses adjust to the onslaught. It had been ages since she'd been in a club. A soft desert breeze floated across the rooftop. She had never been in a club where you could see the stars.

"Come on," Jessica called. "Drinks."

Reyna followed the group to the bar, allowing Jessica to place a glass of pinot gris in her hand. They spotted a table at the edge of the room by one of the glass panels that acted as walls. It was too loud to talk, but everyone attempted it anyway, shouting into each other's ears to try to be heard. Zoe, seated across from her, was laughing at something Jessica said, her head tipped back and her wide smile lighting up her face. Jessica's arm was casually draped across the back of Zoe's chair. Reyna looked away, her chest strangely tight. Was there something between them?

"Do you want to dance?" Walter shouted, his face so close to hers she could feel his warm spittle on her cheek. She left it there, feeling it would be rude to wipe it away.

"Not yet," she called back. "I'll just find the bathrooms."

She slipped from her chair and weaved through the crowd, spotting what looked to be a bathroom door at the end of the terrace. She was not disappointed, and inside she closed herself in a cubicle and sat down on the lid of the toilet seat. She felt like she was floating above her own body tonight. She was suddenly desperately not in the mood to be at this bar. Why had she come? She missed Holden and her home, their home. This…being in a club in the middle of nowhere with a buzz in her head from the alcohol, watching a woman she could not be with flirt with someone else… This was a strange form of torture and she wished she wasn't here. She would grab her handbag and slip out she decided, flushing the toilet for show and leaving the cubicle. She washed her hands and pulled open the bathroom door and for the second time that day, walked straight into Zoe's arms.

"We have to stop meeting like this," Zoe said with a shy smile, catching Reyna around the waist as she stumbled forward.

"Yes." Caught off guard, Reyna was aware her tone sounded cold.

"Sorry, it was just a joke," Zoe said, her eyes wounded as she dropped her hands and stepped aside.

Reyna nodded as she slipped past, unsure what to say. God, she was really making a mess of this. She made her way back to the table and drained her drink, reaching for her handbag to make a quick getaway.

"Your shout next then, Reyna," Jessica called across the table. "I'll have the same again."

Hiding her frustration, she smiled politely at the group. She could hardly leave without paying her round. She took orders and threaded her way through the throng of dancers to the bar, Walter's hand in the small of her back as he accompanied her to help "carry the drinks." Another one she would have to let down gently, she thought.

She was actually grateful for his help as they squeezed through the crowd to the table, balancing the assorted drinks between them. Walter had convinced her to get one more for herself, which she had, finding herself unable to explain she was leaving. Zoe had returned from the bathroom and studiously avoided Reyna's eyes as she distributed the drinks.

The music seemed louder, as if the DJ were in competition with herself, and the dance floor was beginning to fill up.

"I'm ready to dance," Jessica announced to the table. "Who's coming?"

Reyna shook her head, as did Walter, opting to stay at the table with her, but Jacquie and Caroline were keen.

"Come on, Zoe," Jessica cried, grabbing Zoe's hand and pulling her gently from the table. "I insist you dance." Jessica towed her away, laughing as they made their way to the dance floor.

"Pull up okay for the end of financial year?" Walter said into Reyna's ear.

Oh hell, Reyna thought. She smiled politely and kept her distance, raising her voice to be heard over the music. "Yes, no problems. You?"

Walter leaned in and gave her a detailed rundown of their end-of-financial-year woes and the problems with their new accounting software. It was hard work but at least she was not required to say anything in response.

Instead, she let her eyes drift around the room, settling on Zoe who was playfully waving her arms in the air on the dance floor, laughing as she exposed her midriff. Jessica grabbed Zoe around the waist, pulling her in close and they danced together, Zoe's arms around Jessica's neck. Jessica was saying something in Zoe's ear. She was grinning. And then they were swept from her view as others danced in front of them. *Damn.* Reyna flashed with irritation. She did not need to see that.

Walter droned on. Reyna finished her glass of wine, aware that she was drinking too quickly. Jessica and Zoe danced back into view, Jessica's hands on Zoe's hips, Jessica spinning her around, Zoe losing her balance and Jessica scooping her into her arms and nuzzling her face into Zoe's neck. And then, laughing together, they disappeared back into the crowd.

"Walter," she said, cutting him off mid-sentence. "I've actually got to head back to the hotel. I forgot I have an important phone call to make."

"No problem," he cried, jumping up to follow her. "I'll see you back to the hotel."

"No." She held up her hand with a gentle smile. "I'm fine, thanks. Really. Please stay here and enjoy yourself."

And with that, she flung open the little red door on the side of the terrace and ran down the stairs, holding onto the rail tightly to keep her balance. She called a taxi as she reached the bottom and stood in the alley, trying to convince herself everything was just fine.

She woke at six, after a night spent tossing and turning in the hotel's comfortable bed. She had been unable to get the image of Zoe dancing with Jessica out of her mind. She had also been unable to stop imagining what it would have been like if *she* were dancing with Zoe, where *she* would have put her hands. Done with the pretence of sleep, she threw back the covers and tossed on her sweatpants. Perhaps she would grab an early breakfast and a cup of tea to take back to her room.

As she let herself out of her room she was surprised to see someone walking down the pathway in the semi darkness. As the person got closer she realised it was Zoe, still in her sea-green crop top and flared pants from the night before.

"Good morning," Reyna said, her clipped tone clearly giving Zoe a start as she stepped onto the pathway.

"Oh, hi," Zoe said, pulling up short, her hand on her heart. "You gave me a fright. I didn't see you there."

"Big night?"

"Yeah, I guess. It was fun. You left early?"

Reyna felt a flash of anger. "Zoe, I brought you to this conference to learn and to participate, to represent Azoulay House, not to stay out all night partying and getting drunk."

Zoe's eyes widened. "I am not drunk, thank you. And I haven't stayed out all night partying. My room—"

"Save it, Zoe. I'm not your mother and as your boss, I don't need to hear your excuses. Just make sure you are on top of your game today. I expect you'll be attending the full suite of today's program."

"Of course I will." Her cheeks were flushed, her tone indignant. "I'm trying to tell you—"

"Good, well, have a good morning then." Reyna stalked down the pathway toward the main hotel complex, aware that she had been bitchy and cold, but too mad to care. Clearly Zoe had not returned to her room last night. Had she spent the night with Jessica? Who else? From the way she was behaving, it must have been Jessica's intention from the onset of the evening. So that was what Zoe was after. A roll in the hay, a conference dalliance. Well thank god Reyna had not allowed the kiss to get out of hand. She burned with embarrassment as she thought about the grandiose speech she had given Zoe the morning before. *I'm not in the market for a relationship*, she had said. She cringed at the memory. Obviously Zoe wasn't either.

The restaurant was almost empty when she entered and she found herself a table and sat down, her appetite suddenly gone. She regretted showing Zoe her anger. She should have kept it together. What Zoe did after hours wasn't her business, as long as she wasn't besmirching Azoulay House's good name. God knows people got up to a lot worse than a late night shag at a conference. She had heard stories of all-night drunken parties, where it was all in as far as sex was concerned. Reyna had always steered clear of that kind of thing, opting for the sensible, controlled behaviour that befit her position as a leader in the industry.

She had a momentary flicker of jealousy and then she shooed it away in irritation. Jealous of wild, drunken parties? She would not be where she was today if she had indulged in that kind of behaviour. And Holden would not have the kind of aunty who could have stepped in and provided for him at a moment's notice. No, she had made good choices. But why was that suddenly leaving her feeling dry and boring?

"Can I get you anything, ma'am?" a waiter asked, approaching the table.

"Just a black tea, please," she answered, smiling at him grimly. It was Wednesday. She would be leaving on Friday afternoon. She had really been looking forward to this conference, but now, as far as she was concerned, Friday could not come quick enough.

"Hi Holdy," Reyna waved at the computer as she sat cross-legged on her hotel bed, her laptop propped up on a pillow in front of her. "Hi Mum, hi Dad. I'm glad I caught you before you left for school."

"Hi Aunty Reeeeeey." Holden's face pixelated on her screen, froze and then caught up with itself in a blur. Reyna cursed the hotel's Internet connection. "Have you seen a crocodile yet?"

"No darling, but I did see a couple of wedge-tailed eagles yesterday afternoon. They were circling above the hotel."

"Cool! Probably looking for mice."

"Eww."

"Well that's what they eat, Aunty Rey."

Her mum leaned forward, peering at the screen like Reyna was somehow inside the computer. "How's the conference, darling?" Her parents were not exactly luddites but they weren't super comfortable with the technology. "Have you done your presentation yet?"

"Yes, it was great, thanks, but I miss you guys. I can't wait to give you a proper squeeze, Holdy. Shall we have takeaway for dinner when I come home on Friday night? Pizza?"

"Nah, we had pizza for dinner last night. And sushi for dinner the night before. Pops reckons we should try as many different country's takeaways as possible before you get home."

"Does he now!" Reyna raised her eyebrows. "Right, well, it will be boiled veggies for you when I get home."

"No way! And guess what I had for breakfast!" He didn't wait for her to guess. "Coco Pops."

She grimaced. "Mum, please don't give him Coco Pops before school. He needs something really low GI and filling to see him through the day."

"I know, darling. It's not my first rodeo. I just let him have a small bowl before we had porridge with banana. Will that do?"

"Yeah." She smiled sheepishly. "Thanks."

"We'd better go, Aunty Rey. Pops and I are riding our bikes to school and I want to go past the skate park on the way. Pops said I can go down the bowl a couple of times before school."

"Okay, sweetheart, go easy. Look after those knees. Have a great day everyone."

"You too, darling."

"See you, love," her dad said, overenunciating into the computer screen.

She smiled as they disconnected, her face feeling strangely out of sync with the ache in her heart. She was lonely. No, she was feeling alone. She didn't know exactly what the difference was, but she knew it wasn't great.

By dinner Reyna felt guilty. She shouldn't have taken her anger out on Zoe. She had spotted her throughout the day, diligently attending the day's offerings, but their paths had not crossed and there had been no excuse to make them do so. Sitting now at a large table with Meryl and Stacey, she scanned the room, but Zoe was nowhere to be seen.

As if reading her mind, Meryl said, "Zoe will be preparing for her talk tomorrow morning. Reckon she's a bit nervous about it."

"She shouldn't be," Stacey chimed in. "From what she told us about it over lunch, it sounds like it will be brilliant. Has she run it past you Reyna?"

"I saw the preliminary draft but I haven't had a chance to check in with her since," she replied, her guilt intensifying. She really should have made the effort to do that. As far as she knew, it was the first time Zoe had presented at a conference, and as her boss, it really was her role to provide her with some guidance and mentorship. "Maybe I should touch base with her after dinner and see how it's going. Do you know which room she's in?"

"Three-eleven," Stacey said. "It's the Desert Spring building at the back. She's right next door to us. Your assistant must have booked the rooms at the same time. Strange you're not with us."

"No, I ah, well, I think Nikki must have booked mine separately. I'm in one of the suites. Anyway, perhaps I'll take her a plate of something. She'll have missed dinner at this rate."

"Great, I was going to do that, but if you do, it'll save me the hike back to the rooms," Meryl said. "We can go for a dip in the pool instead, Stace."

Reyna read the hallway signs and followed the gold-plated numbers down toward room 311. At Zoe's door she hesitated, balancing a plate of assorted items from the buffet in one hand before she knocked on the door. Was this a bad idea? She didn't want Zoe to get the wrong message, but she did feel she owed her this as an employee. She would want to go over any of her employee's presentations with them before a big conference. She had been lax not pursuing it with Zoe. She had seemed so confident back in the office. Reyna had let her run with it. Resolutely, she knocked. There was a shuffling sound inside and then the padding of footsteps to the door. It swung open, Zoe's face registering surprise, and then a mask of wariness.

"You have your presentation in the morning," Reyna said, suddenly unsure of herself.

"Yes."

"I didn't see you at dinner so I thought you might need sustenance."

"I ordered up."

"Oh." Reyna ploughed on in the face of Zoe's standoffish demeanour. "I realised we never went over the final draft of your presentation. You were going to email it to me, but I didn't hear from you. Do you want me to look it over now?"

Zoe leaned on the doorframe, her arms crossed over an oversized V-necked football shirt, a pair of denim cutoffs that barely covered her thighs, her feet bare. Her normally open face was closed off, as if a light had been turned out, her expression unyielding in the harsh fluorescent light of the hallway.

"Thank you, but I think I have it covered. No need to burden yourself."

"Okay, but I'd do this for any employee. It's my role to support you at your first conference."

"It's not my first conference."

"Oh. Right. I thought you said you hadn't been here before."

"That's right. I've never been to FinCo, but I've been to plenty of other smaller conferences, Reyna. I've even given the odd presentation or two."

"Okay, well if you've got it covered." Reyna turned to go, feeling stupid with the plate of food in her hand.

"You can come in if you want."

Reyna hesitated, turning back to look in Zoe's eyes. She raised her chin, willing herself to sound calm, confident, in control. She was the CEO of her firm for god's sake. "It's up to you, Zoe. Like I said, I would usually go over things with any of my employees before a big conference presentation. I just thought you might like that opportunity."

Zoe studied her for moment and then stepped back from the doorframe, holding open the door. Her tone was more conciliatory as she said, "Actually, I'd appreciate that."

She stepped into the room, edging past Zoe. Her laptop was open on the bed, which was rumpled where she had clearly been sitting when Reyna knocked. Reyna looked around and perched on the edge of the desk, setting the plate of food next to her.

"Do you want me to look at your slides or would you like to practice your delivery?"

"Maybe we could do both?"

"Sure. Turn your laptop to face me and start from the beginning."

For the next thirty minutes Reyna allowed Zoe to deliver her presentation, uninterrupted. Zoe was a natural speaker, friendly, clear and concise in her delivery, and Reyna found herself entirely engaged. The content was flawless, and Reyna quickly abandoned any idea of constructive criticism, allowing herself to be swept up in the one-on- one experience of Zoe's full attention.

"And so, any questions?" Zoe asked, concluding her mock presentation.

"Wow," Reyna said, smiling at her appreciatively. "Well done." She clasped her hands together. "You obviously didn't need any input from me. You've got it in the bag."

"Thanks." Zoe dipped her head in acknowledgment, her face serious. "Like I said, not my first time."

"I didn't realise you were so experienced."

"I'm not massively, but I have done it before, and in this case, I designed the program I'm speaking about, so I know my material well. It was fun to put this together."

"It shows. You're definitely not in danger of putting anyone to sleep."

Finally, Zoe smiled and Reyna felt like someone had turned the lights up in the room. "I'm glad of that."

They sat opposite each other for a moment, neither of them speaking. Reyna knew she should probably make the move to leave but she couldn't bring herself to. Not just yet.

"Any highlights of the conference so far?" she asked.

"Apart from your talk?" A smile tugged at the side of Zoe's mouth, in spite of her restraint.

"Nice of you to say, but yes, apart from mine."

"Well, Jessica's was pretty inspiring. I took away a lot from her talk. I'd love to see the industry doing more to raise the bar."

"You're doing that with your seminar program."

"In a way, I guess. But I'd like to see more. You know, shake out the people like Thomus, who are just there to make an easy buck and don't care what they have to do to get it." Her hand flew to her mouth as if realising too late who she was speaking to. "I shouldn't have said that..."

"It's okay. I think I know what you're saying and let's just say I have that situation in hand." Of course she couldn't reveal anything of Thomus's circumstances to Zoe, but it was worrying to note that his team clearly had a low regard for him.

Zoe stretched out on the bed, tucking a pillow behind her head.

"You look tired," Reyna said, easing herself off the desk to leave.

Zoe sat up quickly. "No, I'm fine. Would you like a drink? I have an assortment of interesting looking things in the minibar and I'd love to hear your thoughts on the conference so far."

Reyna laughed. "You know those aren't for free, right?"

"I know. But have you seen what's there? They have Irish coffee cream liqueur."

"Yeah I saw that. I'm guessing it's been in the cabinet forever. I don't think anyone actually drinks that."

"Are you kidding? It's delicious. My mum used to let me have sips of hers when I was little. Let's open it." Zoe rolled off the bed and made a beeline for the minibar cabinet, securing two glasses and the mini bottle of liqueur. "There's even ice in my ice tray. I don't mean to make you jealous or anything," she continued as she retrieved the ice and snapped it out of the tray into the glasses. "Your room might not be quite so fancy as mine."

"Hmm, yes you're right. I might need to have a word with Nikki about this. She really should have requested me a room with an ice tray."

"Heads will roll." Zoe twisted the lid off the mini bottle and poured it evenly between the two glasses. "Here you are."

"A toast?"

"To excellent working relationships?"

Reyna smiled. "To excellent working relationships."

They touched glasses and Reyna took a sip of her drink, surprised to find she enjoyed the thick, creamy liqueur. "You know it's actually not that bad."

"Not that bad?" Zoe sounded outraged as she settled back on the bed. "This is the fancy stuff. Mum would only break this out at Christmastime."

"Wow, Christmas must have been really fancy at your place."

Zoe studied her glass. "Actually," she admitted, "my mum had quite a troublesome relationship with alcohol." She looked up at Reyna from under her lashes, as if seeking reassurance to continue.

"It happens."

"It happened to my mum. In a big way."

"I'm sorry to hear that."

"I couldn't get through to her. Neither of us could, my brother or I."

"It's hard. Once you tip over the edge, I understand it's pretty difficult to clamber back up."

"She tried, I think. I was young. I didn't know what was really going on. She hid it all pretty well. Until the end."

"How did she die?"

"Liver cancer. The doctor said it was from the alcohol. It was quick, thank god."

"Quick can be painful in its way too."

"Right, of course. Your sister."

"Gosh, we've gotten morbid," Reyna said, swirling the ice cubes in her drink and taking another sip. The alcohol burned on its way down, warming her from the inside. "Have you swum in that magical pool yet?"

"I haven't but I'd like to. My boss was insistent that I be present at all the talks today so I haven't had a chance yet." Zoe's eyes were wide, a hint of a smile hovering around her lips.

"Oh, ouch. Well, what are you waiting for. Get your bathers on. No point hiding away in your room. The pool awaits."

"What, now?" Zoe made a show of checking her watch. "It's eight o'clock."

"Perfect time for a swim if you ask me. Go on, you've earned it."

"Only if you come too."

Reyna hesitated. She was supposed to be staying away from Zoe, not flitting off to have a midnight dip. "Sure," she found herself saying, ignoring the little voice clamouring to be heard inside her.

"All right then, I'll just get changed."

Zoe put down her drink and went over to her suitcase, rummaging through for her bathers. A knock at the door interrupted her and she looked up in surprise. "Maybe Stacey and Meryl," she said. "Their room is next door."

From her position on the desk Reyna could see straight down the short hallway as Zoe opened the door to reveal Jessica, ice bucket tucked under one arm, brandishing a bottle of champagne. Reyna's heart sank. "I brought supplies," Jessica said in a husky tone, sliding past Zoe into the room. She pulled up short seeing Reyna leaning on the desk.

"Well, hello there." Jessica raised a perfectly manicured eyebrow. She set the champagne and ice bucket on the bedside table and perched on the edge of the bed. "And where did you disappear to last night?"

"Oh, I just went back to the hotel," Reyna said, trying to sound casual. "I had some work to catch up on."

"Work, work, work, Reyna." Jessica grimaced at Zoe who was still hovering in the doorway. "How dull. Luckily you're not quite there yet."

"Thanks, I think," Reyna replied, irritated by the smug look on Jessica's face.

"So, you started the party without me?" Jessica pouted.

"There's no party," Zoe jumped in. "Reyna stopped by to check on my presentation. Actually, we were just about to go for a swim."

"A swim! Well I can get with that program. Not exactly what I had planned," Jessica winked at Zoe, "but we can swing past my cabin on the way down to the pool and grab my bathers."

They had plans to spend the evening together, Reyna realised, feeling awkward. She didn't need to spend another night watching these two flirting with each other, that was for sure.

"Actually, at the risk of sounding dull again, I really should get back to my room to send some emails. I've asked the Canberra office to prepare a report for me and they can't go any further until I send through some more data. Well done on your presentation, Zoe." She knew her tone was stiff but she couldn't help herself. She was mad with herself for even being in Zoe's room. If she was honest, she couldn't hand-on-heart say she had come here for purely professional reasons. And how ridiculous to suggest a late-night swim. At this rate, Zoe would have every right to question her professionalism. On top of that, clearly there was something going on between Jessica and Zoe, and she was not in the mood to stick around and watch it unfold. "I'm sure you'll be great tomorrow."

"You're not coming swimming now?" Zoe's brow wrinkled with confusion.

"No, I really shouldn't. Enjoy your evening, ladies. See you in the morning." She nodded at Zoe and left the room.

CHAPTER FIFTEEN

Zoe (Wednesday, p.m.)

Confused, Zoe watched Reyna leave her room. The woman was impossible to understand. Just when Zoe thought she had a handle on her, she whisked around and blew in a completely different direction. Hot and cold didn't even begin to cover it. She had been sure Reyna would chew her out after the kiss, but she had been almost pleasant in her response. Definitely friendly. She had been distant and cold Reyna at the bar, and then, the next thing she knew she was being blasted by irate Reyna on the hotel pathway before breakfast. Zoe had been convinced she would be facing some kind of disciplinary action until friendly Reyna had reappeared at her door to help her with her presentation. Who the hell was this woman?

"So shall we stop by my room to get my bathers," Jessica asked, fluttering her eyelashes suggestively.

Zoe sighed. She should have been over the moon with the attention Jessica was giving her. She was drop-dead gorgeous and an internationally recognised intellectual powerhouse, but for some reason, Zoe was not feeling the spark. Still pining after the ever-complicated Reyna, she thought with irritation. Her friends were right. She was beginning to look like a hopeless case. Even amongst all the confusion, her heart still refused to get with the program. *Damn her heart.* There was no reason her body couldn't enjoy the attention. Last night had definitely been fun, even if there wasn't exactly a spark.

She forced herself to smile.

"How about I meet you down at the pool in fifteen minutes? I need to get changed too."

"How about I stay here and help you get changed?"

Jessica eased off the bed and pulled Zoe toward her, covering her lips with her own. The kiss was soft and warm and Jessica's hands ranged over her body. Zoe moved in closer, willing her body to come alive, to ignite under the touch of Jessica's hands.

"Mmm, yes baby," Jessica murmured against her mouth. "Let's ditch the pool. Who needs swimming. I can think of lots of other ways to get wet."

Zoe broke the embrace, laughing at Jessica's outrageous lewdness. "I can't be up late, Jessica. I want to be fresh for my presentation. I actually really wanted a swim."

"Oh, you're not fun." Jessica reached for her but Zoe sidestepped neatly, ducking out of the way.

"Meet you at the pool in fifteen," Zoe said firmly, turning Jessica around and ushering her toward the door.

"Don't leave me waiting," Jessica said as Zoe gently pushed her out into the corridor. "I don't like to wait."

"I won't," she promised, closing the door.

Stripping off her clothes, she retrieved her bathers from her suitcase and suited up. There must be something wrong with me, she worried, adjusting the strap of her bikini. Last night with Jessica had been fun. The combination of the music, the dancing and the alcohol had made Zoe feel loose and easy, enjoying some playful flirtation with Jessica. If it hadn't been for the problem with her key, she probably would have left it there—flattered to have the attention, but no real interest in anything further. But Jessica had insisted on walking her to her room, and when Zoe's room key failed to work, she had been adamant that Zoe should sleep in her room.

"Honestly, Zoe, what else are you going to do? Sleep in the hallway?"

"I'll just go down to reception and get another key."

"It's three a.m. Reception is closed."

"I'm sure they've got a night person."

Jessica had tucked Zoe's arm through her own and led her over to the elevator. "I promise I won't bite. Come and get some sleep."

"We've only just met. I—"

"I have two beds in my room."

"Oh. Okay."

Zoe had allowed Jessica to lead her back to her room, where thankfully, she really did have two beds.

"You are welcome to climb in with me if you get scared in the night," Jessica had said softly, reaching out to tuck a strand of hair behind Zoe's ear. They had kissed then, Zoe surrendering to the moment, wishing she felt more. It had been nice. Soft, sexy in a way, but there was no spark, no elevation of her heartbeat, just, well, nice. She knew Jessica would be madly insulted to have her kiss described as "nice."

When Jessica had suggested they retire to her bed Zoe had declined gently.

"I really need to get some sleep, Jessica. Sorry to be boring but I really want to get the most out of this conference and I need to be on top of my game."

"You're turning me down for a conference?"

She laughed nervously. "I'm not turning you down, I'm just… suggesting we reschedule?"

"Fine. One more nightcap then."

"Honestly, not for me. I've had enough tonight. If you don't mind I'm ready to crash."

She suspected Jessica was unused to being turned down. She had pouted and made a show of pouring herself a large tumbler of scotch, keeping the lights on until well after Zoe had crawled into the bed and pretended to fall asleep. *Just get into her bed*, her brain kept repeating. But she had resisted and eventually Jessica had switched off the light and gotten into bed herself. Zoe had listened to her breathing gradually slow until a soft snore indicated Jessica was asleep. Then she had tried to relax herself, taking deep slow breaths, trying to imagine her limbs sinking into the pillowy mattress. But sleep had eluded her. Her mind kept flashing back to the moment she had kissed Reyna. It had been over so quickly she could almost believe it hadn't happened.

But it had. And now, with Reyna acting like a spin-off of Jekyll and Hyde, Zoe was struggling to know how to act. She had tried humble and apologetic, but Reyna hadn't seemed to want that; she had tried friendly and professional, acting like nothing had happened, but Reyna had met that with anger. When Reyna had arrived at her door this evening, Zoe had still been furious from their encounter that morning. How dare Reyna make assumptions about her professionalism based on a chance meeting.

It had looked bad, she admitted to herself, as she grabbed a towel and headed for the stairs. And Jessica turning up in her room just now would only have added fuel to the fire. Was there a fire? Was she having a thing with Jessica? Did it matter what Reyna thought? Her mind buzzed with questions. Reyna had made it clear she wasn't interested, so she supposed it didn't really matter what Reyna thought. Except that it did.

Because for a moment, back there in her room, she had thought Reyna might have changed her mind. "Wishful thinking, Zoe," she heard her friends say as she unhooked the pool gate and threw her towel on a banana lounge. There were a few small groups of people dotted around the tables, but Jessica wasn't there. Zoe stood at the edge of the pool and dipped in a toe, relieved to find the temperature was bearable. She wasn't really one for arctic swimming.

Zoe dove in to the water and resurfaced in the middle of the pool. She flipped onto her back and floated, gazing up at the moon. Venus, in all its mystical glory, was glowing brightly just underneath it.

Star light, star bright, first star I see tonight…

Her brother had always told her there was no point wishing for something you knew you'd never get. That was just a waste of a wish. But even as a kid she had been unable to heed his advice. As a child she had wished hard for her dad to come back. He hadn't. As she had gotten older she had wished at every birthday for her mum to get happier. She hadn't. And as a teenager she had wished fervently for a computer, desperate to keep up with her schoolwork and her peers, struggling to manage the workload at the library, until she had realised all the wishing in the world wouldn't help her, but an afterschool job would. She had gotten a job at the local newsagency, stacking the shelves after school, and then she had graduated to a before school paper round, and eventually she had saved enough money to purchase a bottom of the range computer, but her very own computer nonetheless. But when it had come time to purchase it, she hadn't been able to bring herself to do it, knowing their mum was struggling just to get food on the table. Instead she had handed over her envelope full of cash and watched as her mother had cried with relief.

I wish I may, I wish I might...

It hadn't cured her of wishing, though. Perhaps if she just wished hard enough tonight, Reyna would walk through the pool gates and dive into the pool next to her. They would hold hands in the water, heads close, looking up at the moon. Reyna would cup her chin in her hands and kiss her, her tongue gently probing Zoe's mouth.

Have this wish I wish tonight.

"Yoo hoo, Zoe."

Zoe righted herself looking over at the pool gate. Jessica waved at her.

"What's the water like?"

"It's fine," Zoe replied. Danny was right. There was no point wishing for something that wouldn't come true. Better to make the most of what was right there in front of you. "Just fine. Come on in."

Before she went to bed that evening she rang Mel.

"Jessica Myers wants to sleep with you and you're calling *me*?" Mel's voice was a shriek down the phone. Zoe held the receiver away from her ear, wincing dramatically, even though she knew Mel couldn't see her.

"Yes, that's about the sum of it."

"Let me get this straight. It's what, ten thirty there?"

"Yeah."

"And you've come back to your room, after what basically constitutes a midnight swim with one of Australia's hottest women, to telephone me?"

"Um, yes."

"Why, exactly?"

"I don't know what to do."

"As in sex-wise? What are you telling me, Zoe?"

"No!" Zoe exclaimed, almost blushing down the phone. "It's not that. It's just that I don't think I really like her that way. You know, *like* like her."

"I'm sorry, did we just fall backward through time into high school and I didn't notice? What do you mean you don't know if you *like* like her? We are talking about the same Jessica Myers, right? Even I know who Jessica Myers is and we've both agreed she's a picture of absolute loveliness crowned with the intellect of a Rhodes scholar. What's going on here, Cavendish?"

Zoe sighed, tucking the receiver under her ear as she crawled into bed and pulled the sheet up under her chin.

"I don't know. She is pretty amazing and it seems like she's into me, but I'm not really feeling it."

"Are you okay? You sound a bit out of sorts."

"I kissed Reyna."

"You what?!"

"I kissed Reyna, and now everything's all screwed up."

"Okay. Tell me everything. Start from the beginning and leave nothing out."

Zoe filled her in. She told her about the bike ride, the slippery shoes, the sunrise, the kiss. She told her about the awkward conversations afterward, the attention from Jessica. Ten minutes later she sighed and said, "so that's everything."

There was silence down the phone.

"Mel? You there?"

"Yep. Look, I think you might be overthinking things."

"Why? What do you mean?"

"I know that it feels huge to you that you kissed Reyna, but that's just it. *You* kissed Reyna. It doesn't really mean anything, and it sounds like it really hasn't changed anything. You were lucky she didn't fire you, but apart from that, it sounds like she's just trying to move forward, business as usual."

"I guess."

"And now someone's come along who sounds like she totally fancies you and she's just what the doctor ordered. She's smart, she's fun, she's good-looking and she's into you. What would your psychologist say?"

Zoe blew out another sigh, feeling like an old balloon. She had already considered Dr. Singh's opinion. She had heard her quiet, considered voice clearly in her head whenever she stopped to think. "She'd say I'm avoiding Jessica and investing in Reyna because I know it's impossible and I won't have to actually get involved."

"And do you think that's what's happening?"

"Maybe. I don't know. My mind tells me I really like Reyna."

"Can your mind be trusted at the moment?"

"Well I bloody hope so, I've got my presentation in the morning and a job to hold down."

"Exactly. So why chase after the unobtainable and fill your life with heartache when there's someone jumping up and down in front of you saying, 'pick me, pick me.'"

"I don't think Jessica is exactly the jumping type."

"You know what I mean."

"She's more the gliding type. And the sexy dancing type."

"Right. So, she's sexy dancing in front of you and you're, like, looking around her going, 'um, hello, is anybody out there?'"

She knew Mel was right. She was being obstinate and stupid. She had promised herself she would move on from Reyna and she had completely failed at that.

"You know what?" Mel said. "You have your presentation in the morning. Why don't you go to sleep now and try to forget all this for a day? Focus on yourself for a change. You've got great things going on with your career and this conference is a big win for you. Maybe just let the other stuff resolve itself around you."

Zoe snuggled down under her covers. "I knew there was a reason I chose you for my best friend. You're so good at the Pep Talk."

"And I'm *incredibly* good looking."

"Right. But that didn't really figure in my best friend choosing."

"Whatever. Go to sleep now. Wow them tomorrow. Take yourself off on some kind of cool adventure. Just enjoy it all and come home refreshed. Forget these crazy ladies for a bit."

"Thanks Mel, I will."

"Good night, Zoe."

"Night."

Zoe put her phone on silent and switched off the reading light next to the bed. She was too tired to read tonight. She slept fitfully, dreaming repeatedly that she had forgotten her PowerPoint file, that she couldn't find the room she was supposed to be in, and that she kept turning up to give her talk in her pyjamas. When the alarm finally woke her at six thirty a.m., she reached for it groggily, glad to be awake.

In fact, the presentation was a huge success. The room had been full, no mean feat in itself when there were competing program items, and people had asked insightful questions, using up her entire allotted timeslot with still more hands raised.

"I'm sorry I haven't gotten a chance to address all your queries," she said when the MC, who was sitting side of stage, tapped her watch, giving her the wind-it-up signal. "But I will be around for the rest of the week, so if anyone wants to chat further about the program I'd be happy to."

She left the stage and joined the crowd in the room who were taking a chance to stand up and stretch and chat before the next presentation began.

A shoulder gently bumped her own. "Nice work, Zoe."

She turned to see Stacey standing next to her, with Meryl and Reyna behind her. Zoe had spotted the three of them during her presentation, seated together about halfway down the room, and acknowledged them with a smile and nod.

"Yes, well done," Reyna agreed. She smiled politely at Zoe, her eyes giving nothing away. "You handled yourself extremely well."

"It was excellent," Meryl enthused. "They were eating out of the palm of your hand! I hope ours goes that well, Stace."

"Thanks, guys," Zoe replied. "You'll be great. You're old hats at this."

"Looks like there's still a couple of people who want to speak with you," Stacey murmured, gesturing behind Zoe.

Zoe turned to see a man and a woman hovering behind her. Both were wearing lanyards indicating they were from Financial Literacy Australia.

"Do you have a sec?" the man asked. "We'd love to catch up with you about how you integrated your program with your local council. We're thinking this kind of thing would work really well with some of the programs we're looking at."

"Would you like to grab a cuppa with us?" the woman asked. "It's not quite morning tea time but we could get a jump on the crowds. Unless you're heading to another presentation?"

Zoe found herself turning to Reyna, a question in her eyes. Would Reyna think she was somehow shirking her responsibilities if she didn't attend the next presentation?

"Of course, go." Reyna gave her a nod. "You're entitled to an hour off after what you've just done."

"Thanks." She knew she had done well and she was pleased with herself, but she wished she could see it reflected back at her through Reyna's dark eyes. Reyna seemed even more untouchable than usual, her gaze now focused on her conference booklet as if she were already moved onto the next thing. Her dark hair fell over her cheek and Zoe felt a sharp pull in her heart, wishing she could reach out and smooth it away. She gave herself a mental shake, firmly pushing the thought away.

"Lead the way," she said to the pair.

They talked the whole way through morning tea and right up to lunchtime, the pair asking her question after question about how she had gotten her program off the ground, discussing the issues particularly of relevance to them, grilling Zoe about the demographics and the roll out.

"We're all about promoting financial literacy across the board," the woman who had introduced herself as Evie said. "We're focusing on programs for women, for children, for prison offenders, for people with intellectual disabilities. Basically, if they're a vulnerable cohort, we're interested in providing programs. The difficulty is getting access to these cohorts. The bridge you built with council interests us. We really need more of this kind of thing in the community."

"I'm surprised you're at a conference like this," Zoe said. "I would have thought it's too..." She searched for the right word. "Corporate?"

"I know what you mean," the man, Graeme, said, rubbing a hand across his stubbly chin. "When we looked at the agenda we were also a bit worried about that, but there's actually been quite a bit of activism. Your presentation, for example, was one of the reasons we were interested in coming."

"Wow, I'm so glad. Tell me more about what you guys are doing."

They talked on and as the crowd rolled out of the conference rooms to gather in the dining room for lunch, Evie looked suddenly guilty.

"Oh my gosh, we've kept you for ages. Thanks so much for your time, Zoe."

"No worries at all. I've really enjoyed speaking with you both."

"I know you have a fancy finance job and everything," Graeme said with a grin, "but you could really make a difference to the world with this kind of stuff. Here's my card. If you ever want to get a bit more involved in the community side of things, give us a call."

Zoe took the card and tucked it into her laptop bag. "The firm I work for is great. I mean they're supporting me to do this, for instance, but these programs are definitely something I want to do more of. I'm actually thinking of putting together a training package so our other national offices can easily implement it themselves. Who knows, maybe other organisations will come on board in the future."

"Another great idea," Evie acknowledged. "Send it over to us when you're done okay? We'd love to look over it."

"Deal."

Graeme stuck out his hand. "It's been great meeting you. I think we'd better let you get on with your day now."

Zoe shook hands with both of them and left the dining room, deciding she had earned a little break in her room. She wanted to change her clothes and take a moment to chill after the intensity of her morning. Besides, she was too jazzed to be hungry.

She had just stepped out of the conference centre when a husky voice said in her ear, "Going somewhere?"

Jessica, looking radiant in a bright yellow skirt with a crisp white shirt, wrapped an arm around her waist.

"Your presentation was a smash."

"Thanks! I didn't see you there."

"I snuck in up the back after you had started. Didn't want to be stuck in the front row in case you bombed. I needn't have worried. You totally nailed it."

"Er, thanks," she said, unsure if Jessica was joking.

"Hey, I'm just teasing. Where are you going anyway?"

"Back to my room. I need to freshen up."

"Now, that sounds like something I could get on board with."

"Jessica, I—"

"Hush, I'll walk with you."

They made their way down the cobblestone path together.

"I'm actually flying back to Canberra this afternoon," Jessica said.

"You're leaving early?"

"Something's come up at work and I need to head back. It was always going to be a long shot getting a whole week away from the politicians. The country's governance is a twenty-four-hour machine. But what can I do? My team needs me."

"That's a shame."

"Is it?" Jessica stopped walking, giving Zoe a searching look. "I get the feeling you won't be reaching for the Kleenex when I leave town."

"Oh, no, I really like you, it's just…" Zoe trailed off, unsure what to say next. Did she like Jessica? Would she be sad when she left? Considering Jessica lived in Canberra, wasn't this all a bit of a moot point anyway?

"Is there someone else?"

"No." Zoe looked up at the sky, trying to work out how to phrase her next sentence. "I'm just not sure what I'm ready for, in life, if you know what I mean."

"I can't say I entirely do, no." Jessica started to walk again. "But if you're talking relationships, that sounds pretty serious. I'm certainly not thinking serious thoughts if that makes you feel any easier."

They made their way back down the path in silence until Jessica said, "I actually get down to Melbourne quite often. Politics is a national game, you know. In fact, I'll be down next month with the Prime Minister's team, assisting with a business briefing." Jessica reached over and took Zoe's hand, capturing Zoe's eyes with her own bright blue irises. "Would you like to meet up for dinner?"

Zoe blinked. Mel would say yes. Enid would say yes, she told herself. Chiara and Travis would be jumping up and down saying yes.

"It's just dinner, Zoe. We're friends. It would be fun to catch up again."

"Okay," Zoe said.

"Well, that's great." Jessica leaned forward and pressed her lips against Zoe's. "A kiss to seal the deal," she whispered. "I won't see you before I leave, but I'll email you."

"I haven't given you my email."

"It's in the program."

"Wow. You're really on top of everything, aren't you?"

"Not quite everything," she said with a suggestive grin. "Yet. Bye, Zoe." She waved a set of perfectly manicured fingers. "See you in a couple of weeks."

"See you then." Zoe watched her walk away, wondering if she had made the right choice. She glanced back down the path and could have sworn she saw Reyna disappearing off the path into her unit.

She walked back to her room feeling uneasy. Had Reyna seen the kiss? Not that it really mattered. She wasn't breaking any rules. She was a free agent and she could date whoever she liked. Hell, it was almost her duty to date someone like Jessica. Her friends would be pleased, she thought, as she climbed the stairs toward her room. But was she?

The afternoon shot past in a blur and Zoe joined an evening tour group to Desert Park. It was an amazing chance to see a whole bunch of native animals at twilight and she was blown away by the experience. As a city girl, she rarely got up close with nature. She had never, for instance, seen a real thorny devil. She couldn't believe her eyes as she watched the strange little creature, covered in thorns and spikes, scooping up ants on the dark red, desert sand. The rest of the group were headed out to a restaurant in town and then presumably a big night of partying, but Zoe opted for a quiet night in her room. Tomorrow would be the last day of the conference and the word was to expect a fairly raucous party that night. She had also signed up for a tour out to a nearby waterhole at the conclusion of the conference, so tomorrow would be a big day. It was best to get some rest now while she could.

CHAPTER SIXTEEN

Reyna (Friday, p.m.)

The bus out to Ellery Big Hole bumped and skittered over a rutted track, shaking the teeth in Reyna's head. Most of the drive had been smooth, down a long, thin, barely tarred road that weaved between mountains glowing red, purple, and brown in the afternoon light. It was dry and the clumps of grasses by the roadside looked spiky and yellow.

"Nearly there folks," the bus driver announced over the loudspeaker. "You might want to hang on to the seat in front for this last bump."

Reyna reached out, grabbing the seat in front of her just as the bus skirted around a large boulder and rolled over a hefty rut, causing Reyna's bum to lift out of its seat and thwack back down. She laughed as the people around her all groaned in unison.

"Jeeze," Meryl complained from her seat across the aisle. "We're gonna be black and blue by the time we get there."

"I wouldn't worry," Stacey said, placing her hand on Meryl's knee. "I think you've got plenty of coverage."

"Oi." Meryl playfully swatted Stacey and they laughed together.

I want something like that, Reyna thought, staring past the empty seat next to her out of the window. But it was futile to think that way. Ridiculous to torture herself so. She had had plenty of chances to make a lasting relationship but she had chosen work instead. And now life had chosen Holden for her and that was that. No room left at the inn. The bus pulled into a car park and the doors swung open with a hiss.

"Right-oh," the bus driver announced. "Take your hats and your sunnies and your towels. We're here for two hours. Plenty of time for a swim and a sunbathe. Just a word: please don't use sunscreen because it comes off in the water and is bad for the wildlife."

Reyna raised her eyebrows. She had never thought of that. She was glad she had opted to put her sunscreen on when she got down here, and not before they left. She could easily cover up with a shirt instead if it got too hot.

She filed off the bus with the group and followed along as they made their way down a sandy track, snaking in between slim gum trees, until they reached an opening. Through the trees Reyna saw a large body of silvery water filling the canyon between two craggy cliff faces. It was so majestic and unexpected. For a moment all she could do was stand still and try to take it all in.

"Over here, Reyna," Meryl called, breaking into her reverie.

She set her towel down on a sandy patch under a shady gum with Stacey and Meryl and sat, pulling her hat from her bag. The water's edge was less than a meter away. There were no waves, like at the beach or a big lake, just still, dark water glistening against the bright blue of the sky. It was late afternoon but the sun was still high, flooding the canyon with warmth and light. She glanced away as Zoe walked past, chatting animatedly with a group of people Reyna did not know.

"Zoe!" Meryl hollered, waving enthusiastically. Reyna winced. "Over here."

Reyna hid her frown. Meryl, it seemed, was intent on gathering them all together. Zoe broke away from the group she was with and joined them, spreading a large watermelon-shaped towel next to Stacey. Reyna nodded politely, determined to keep her distance.

She had been on the verge of making a giant fool out of herself when she had suggested a late-night swim with Zoe, and she had realised it not a moment too soon. When Jessica had turned up at Zoe's room, interrupting their plan, Reyna had only just escaped with her dignity intact. She had studiously avoided Zoe since, making sure to grab a seat at the back of the room for the remaining presentations, ordering meals in her room. It was easier that way. Of course, if she'd thought about it for a minute, she would have realised Zoe would be on this trip, but she had agreed to come at the last minute, with Meryl and Stacey convincing her she wouldn't want to miss out.

"I think I'm ready for a swim," Stacey said, rolling off her towel and shrugging out of her shirt. She was wearing a one-piece bathing suit with little shorts, her lean figure accentuated by the tight Lycra. In contrast, Meryl looked positively stocky, bounding off her towel and leaping over the short distance to the water's edge in shorts and an oversized T-shirt.

"Race you in," Meryl called, plunging her feet into the water. "Oh my god! It's freezing."

Stacey picked her way carefully down to the water as Meryl dove beneath the surface, coming up with a whoop. "It's heaven," Meryl called. "If heaven is an iceberg."

Reyna laughed, watching Meryl pretend to splash Stacey.

"Don't you splash me, Meryl Lions," Stacey warned. "Or you'll be finding a new room to sleep in tonight."

"Come on love, would I splash you?"

"Yes, you would. Now stop it."

Their voices echoed through the canyon, mixing with the chat of other groups similarly impressed with the icy cold temperature of the water.

Meryl scooped up a small handful of water and flicked it toward Stacey, who squealed and tried to jump out of the way, losing her footing as she did and tumbling into the water.

"Oh. My. God." She cried as she resurfaced, pushing the hair out of her face. "You are in big trouble now." Stacey took off after Meryl who was giving her very best impression of an Olympic freestyler as she powered toward the center of the water hole.

"They're brilliant," Zoe said. Reyna glanced over to see Zoe smiling softly at Meryl and Stacey.

"That they are," Reyna agreed.

"Shall we join them?"

Reyna hesitated. There were plenty of people in the water. It wasn't like she was specifically going swimming with Zoe. "Sure."

She slipped off her shirt and rolled it up, stuffing it into her hat. Her shoulders felt the intensity of the sun immediately and she hoped she wouldn't burn.

At the water's edge she dipped in a toe, shuddering at the temperature.

"It really is freezing," she said with a shiver.

"I know," Zoe replied, gasping as she strode into the water. "I'm a straight-in kind of girl though. Rip the bandage off quickly."

Reyna preferred to ease her way in, letting her body get used to the temperature of the water in stages. People around her laughed and splashed, enjoying the pure, crystalline oasis, surrounded by desert mountains and unbroken blue sky. Taking a deep breath, she slid under the surface, jerking back up with a gasp as the ice-cold water broke over her head.

"Want to swim across to the other side of the gorge?" Zoe asked. "I think it helps to stay warm if you keep moving."

Reyna paddled hard on the spot, trying to warm up. She could see groups of swimmers making their way down the length of the gorge to a patch of sunlight on the other side. "Is it far do you think?"

"Someone on the bus told me it's about ten minutes to swim across."

"Okay, let's do it."

They swam breaststroke slowly through the gorge, enjoying the way their voices echoed off the walls of the canyon, chatting lightly as they went. Their bodies quickly got used to the temperature, and Reyna forgot momentarily about the cold. She was just starting to tire when she realised the water had become shallow again, and she put her feet down and walked the last few meters.

The other side of the gorge was a slope of large granite rocks, soaking in the sunshine. Her skin freezing from the water, Reyna gratefully leant against one of the rocks, its heat permeating her skin and warming her body. Next to her, Zoe crawled up onto a large, flat, granite platform and stretched out.

"It's so warm," she moaned. "Now *this* is heaven. You should totally get up here. There's plenty of room."

It did look enticing. Around them, other groups were dotted amongst the rocks, basking in the sunshine. Reyna studied the rock, still shivering from the ice-cold swim. She found a handhold and pulled herself up until she was on top of the rock, careful not to bump Zoe as she stretched out. Heat prickled against her goose-pimpled skin from the rough rock.

"You're not wrong," Reyna mumbled, closing her eyes. "So divine." The light behind her eyelids was red from the beating sun. She shivered.

"You're still cold?" Zoe sat up, her voice concerned.

"I'm fine, just warming up slowly."

Zoe eased herself back down on the rock and slid closer to Reyna so that their arms touched. "Stay close," she murmured. "Body heat will help."

"Thanks," Reyna managed, her breath catching in her throat. She felt almost naked on top of the rock in just her bikini, Zoe's skin burning into her own. She shaded her eyes, turning her head to catch a glimpse of Zoe who was staring up at the never ending sky.

"We could be the only two humans on earth right here," Zoe said, turning her head to meet Reyna's gaze. They locked eyes for a moment. Reyna's pulse thumped in her neck, her gaze straying to Zoe's mouth. Time seemed to dissolve.

"You two look like a couple of iguanas," a gruff voice called up, breaking the spell of the moment. Reyna sat up, looking over the edge of the rock to see Meryl grinning at her from down below.

"You've got to try this," Reyna called back, her voice sounding far away to her own ears.

"We're going to swim back," Meryl said. "Catch you back on the other side. Don't miss the bus."

"Yeah, that would be a bugger," Zoe said, sitting back up. "I think we've still got a while, but maybe we'd better swim back soon too. Neither of us has a watch."

"But it will be so cold. I've only just warmed up. I can't go back in again."

"Uh, I don't think you have a choice. Unless you want to hike the whole way up the canyon and around, and that looks like it might take a while."

Reyna took in the steep canyon walls. "I'm not exactly dressed for that kind of hike."

Zoe's eyes raked over her body, leaving a trail of heat on Reyna's skin. "I don't know which would be worse, the bikini or the lack of shoes, but yeah, you're in no state for hiking."

Reyna shivered again, imagining herself trying to scramble and scrabble up the steep rocks. Not a good look.

"Still that cold?" Zoe asked and took Reyna's hands, rubbing them between her own. She blew on them softly, "that should warm you up."

"It has." Reyna said, her voice thick with desire.

Zoe looked up, catching the edge on Reyna's voice.

"Are you okay?" she asked, a line of concern sneaking between her eyebrows.

Reyna, resisting the urge to smooth it away, extracted her hands. "I'm good now." Zoe looked so alluring in the afternoon sun, the light shining behind her, creating a halo effect around her still damp hair. She looked younger, softer, her skin delectably smooth and supple. She had a tiny freckle on her upper lip that Reyna hadn't noticed before. She wanted to kiss it. A drop of water rolled down Zoe's neck, and Reyna followed it with her eyes as it trailed slowly across the arc of her chest and disappeared into her cleavage.

A volley of laughter down below reminded Reyna that they were not alone, and she looked away. What was this woman doing to her? Here she was, shamelessly lusting after one of her own employees, one who had just spent the last week in the arms of Jessica Myers, nonetheless. It was nothing short of embarrassing.

"We should probably get back," Reyna said, "if I can work out how to get down."

"Same way you got up. You just need to turn around. Watch." Zoe swung herself around effortlessly and shimmied down the rock.

Feeling far less graceful, Reyna followed suit, sliding down the rock and landing with a small thud. For some reason she felt ungainly around Zoe. What with the bike riding and mountain climbing, now adding in swimming and rock climbing, and she had probably had more physical activity this week than she'd had all year. Not that she was lazy, just time poor. It would be good to get into swimming again. She had been meaning to enrol Holden in swimming lessons now that the soccer season was ending. Perhaps she could do some laps while Holden was having his lesson.

Reyna followed Zoe back down to the edge, gingerly walking back into the water. "Oh god," she blew out. "I swear it's colder than it was before."

"Nothing for it," Zoe said with a grin. "We'll just have to power through. Come on."

"I forgot you're one of those extreme sports sadists," Reyna called as Zoe splashed into the water with a whoop.

The way back was quicker. They didn't stop to chat, swimming briskly through the canyon. The sun had sunk lower in the sky and the waterhole was now in shade, making the water seem icier and more remote. Looking up at the steep, rocky outcrops around her, Reyna marvelled at the untouched nature. Grasses grew out of narrow crevices, birds flew lazily overhead, thin openings in the rock hinted at caves, impossibly high up. She could imagine Australia's first people gathering here, traversing through the canyon when the waters were low, swimming and cooling off in the heat of the day.

Back on the other side they wrapped themselves in their towels and sat in a last patch of sunshine with the group who had drifted over to chat with Meryl and Stacey. Snacks were passed around and Reyna realised she was hungry for the first time all week. Her body felt alive, her skin soft and fresh from the water.

When the bus driver told them it was time to head back, Reyna was sad to leave. The place felt special, like a secret they had stumbled across. She knew rationally that this was a well-worn tourist spot, but in the dwindling sunlight, with nothing but the still water and the rugged canyon walls, she could believe for a moment that it was undiscovered.

She took one last look around, trying to memorise the beauty of the place.

"Pretty incredible isn't it?" Zoe asked, standing beside her.

"I almost wish we didn't have to leave."

"You can camp out here. That's something I'd like to do one day."

They turned to go with the rest of the group. "I'd like to take Holden camping," Reyna said as they made their way back up the sandy path to the bus. "He's never been."

"Never been camping at all?"

"No, I guess in England they didn't do that kind of thing much. The weather can be prohibitive, I suppose."

"I'm surprised you like camping," Zoe said. "I wouldn't have picked you for the sleeping outdoors type."

Reyna raised her eyebrows. "Well I'm no Bear Grylls but I definitely enjoy being out in nature, but I don't get a whole lot of opportunity to do it these days."

"We should go," Zoe said. "I mean, well," she smiled sheepishly. "Everyone should make time for camping. It's the best. I love cooking outdoors and going to sleep under the stars."

"Don't you sleep in a tent?"

"I have a swag."

They climbed onto the bus with the rest of the group and Zoe slid into the seat next to Reyna. Their knees touched and Reyna didn't move her leg away.

"Okay, so at the risk of sounding not outdoorsy," Reyna asked, "what is a swag?"

Zoe looked at her curiously. "You've never seen one? Well, they're all a bit different. Some are like a big canvas sleeping bag and some are like a mini tent that you can zip up over your head."

Reyna shuddered. "Don't you get claustrophobic?"

"I guess you could. Mine is one of the sleeping bag kinds so my head is always out."

"What if it rains?"

Zoe laughed. "You get wet! You can kind of snuggle down under the canvas and there's a flap you can pull over if things get really bad, but yeah, it's not great in the rain. If it looks like rain I tend to rig up a tarp overhead just in case."

"A regular MacGyver."

"Oh yes," Zoe snickered. "It's a shame you're no Bear Grylls. We'd make a good combination. Hey, will you be going to the party tonight?"

Reyna considered the question. She had previously decided to avoid the party and hide out in her room for the night, but in the afterglow of the afternoon, her resolve was weakening. "I might pop in. I'm on the early flight home tomorrow so I'm not up for a big night."

"I think we're all on that flight. There's only one flight a day to Melbourne."

"Are you going?"

"Yeah, but I think I'll need a nap first. It's been a big week."

"Lots of late nights?" Reyna asked, realising she was fishing for more. Would Zoe speak to her about Jessica?

"Late nights and early mornings. I haven't slept so well up here. There's so much to do and see, I didn't want to miss anything."

Or anyone, Reyna wanted to add, thinking about the morning she had spotted Zoe on the path after a night spent with

Jessica. But it wasn't her place to question Zoe. She rested her head back, watching the desert landscape rush past the window in a blur. She wished she could shake the tight feeling in her chest. Was it jealousy? She couldn't think about Zoe being with Jessica without the tightness creeping in. Her mind flashed back to Zoe's lips on hers. Had that meant nothing? She pushed the thoughts away in anger, frustrated with herself for caring. Zoe was young and free and single. That's the kind of thing people did at conferences. *You don't do that kind of thing at conferences.*

"Are you okay?" Zoe asked, interrupting her thoughts.

"Fine. Why?" Reyna's tone was clipped.

"You're frowning at the window like it's done something very wrong."

Reyna laughed, the tension easing in her chest. "I was just thinking about the early flight," she lied. "Lots to do this week."

"You must have a lot of your plate," Zoe sympathised. "I can't even begin to imagine what it must be like to be a CEO."

"It's like any job really. It's what you make it. It can be busy, rewarding, challenging, overwhelming, and exciting."

"I'm not sure I'd be up to the task."

"Maybe not right now, but if it was what you wanted, you could work your way toward it. It's just about developing the skill set. Is that the kind of thing you're aiming for in your career?"

"Actually no, I don't think I am," Zoe replied slowly. "After I graduated I just wanted to get a job and be the best financial adviser I could be."

"Well, from all accounts, it sounds like you're nailing that brief."

Zoe grinned. "Thanks. But lately I have been thinking I'd like to do more of the community action stuff."

"You've had a taste of it with your program."

"Exactly and I'd like to do more. I might look at doing some kind of volunteering in the future as well."

"I'd be happy to discuss how we could expand your program across the company, Zoe. If you're interested in doing more of this kind of work, you could look at bringing it to the national team."

"Wow." Zoe's eyes shone. "I would love to do that. I've been thinking of developing a training manual so that it can be implemented easily for the other sites."

"I'll have a chat with Thomus about assigning you some time to work on it. You should get started when we get back."

"That would be so great. Thank you! I've already started jotting down a plan if you'd like to see it?"

"Of course. It's my role to recognise and develop talent. Bring it to my office next week some time."

The bus pulled up in front of the hotel and the doors opened with a hiss.

"I have it here on my laptop if you want to take a look now."

"Oh sure," Reyna replied. "But didn't you want to get a rest in before the party?"

"I can sleep when I'm dead. This is way more exciting. Shall I bring it to your room?"

They joined the line of people filing off the bus.

"Sounds good. Give me ten minutes to get changed."

Back in her room Reyna peeled off her bathers, and threw on some underwear, forgoing a shower. Her skin still felt so fresh from the waterhole that she didn't want to wash it off. She ran a comb through her hair and twisted it into a knot at the nape of her neck. Should she dress for the party now? Did she even want to go? She was all at sea, floating on a raft of a hundred questions with no answers to be found. She was confused by her feelings for Zoe. The desire, the unmistakable flare of heat she felt every time she set eyes on her. It was starting to feel like more than just physical wanting. Sure, her body was definitely urging her into dangerous territory, but her heart was starting to get involved. She needed to be very careful. Thank god she was going home tomorrow and could put all this confusion behind her. She needed to focus on the facts. Holden needed her. Azoulay House needed her. Facts were facts.

She chose a pair of thin black leggings and a loose, oversized shirt with bird prints on it, fastening it at the waist with a belt. Then she turned a critical eye on her room, tidying up her suitcase and throwing her towel over the shower rail in the bathroom to dry. Suddenly she realised it was a mistake letting Zoe come to her room. It felt too personal. She had made that mistake once already. Perhaps she could cut her off at the path and suggest they look at her work over a cup of tea in the dining hall. That would be a far better arrangement. She grabbed her purse and room key and flung open the door, stepping out onto the path just as Zoe arrived at her door.

"I thought we could grab a cup of tea while we talk," Reyna said by way of greeting.

"Oh, damn, that would be good but my laptop is out of battery. I need to plug it in to show you the file. Should we just make a cuppa in your room while we talk?"

Reluctantly, Reyna let them back into her room, dropping her purse on the bed. She was immediately aware of how small the room felt.

"Power point?" Zoe waved her laptop cable glancing around the room for the nearest outlet.

"There's one under the desk." Reyna chose the armchair across the room by the window and sat down. If they were going to stay in her room she needed to put some space between them.

Zoe busied herself plugging in the laptop and turning it on. "Thanks for having a look at this. I'm really excited to see what you think," she said as she typed in her password, her back to Reyna. "I've broken it up into training modules for each week, so that the facilitator will know what key points to focus on at each session. It's not finished and I've just got a rough sketch, but you'll get the idea. I'm keen to see if you think it's enough of a manual for the other offices. Ah, here it is, I saved it in my email when I was working on it from home."

Zoe looked over her shoulder. "Do you want to come over here? It's just the cord won't reach for me to bring it over to you." Reyna realised she must look strange, sitting in a chair on the opposite side of the room and went to join Zoe at the desk.

For the next half an hour they looked over her work, discussing the structure of what she had put together.

"This is really very good, Zoe," Reyna said, impressed with the calibre of work she was seeing. It seemed no matter what Zoe turned her hand to she could produce star quality work.

"I mean, it's just a rough sketch," Zoe said, "but I think I'm on the right track."

"You're more than on the right track. You're blazing a whole new trail here. Well done." Reyna leaned forward. "I especially like this section." As she pointed to the screen Zoe's email flashed with the notification of a new message. *Jessica Myers.* Subject: *miss you already.*

"Oh." Zoe blushed, quickly closing the notification.

Reyna sat back in her chair, her mind warring with her heart. What did it matter what Jessica sent to Zoe. *It's none of my business. Absolutely none of my business.* "You really hit it off with Jessica, huh?" she asked, in spite of herself.

"What? Um, yeah I guess so. She's pretty..." Zoe seemed to be searching for the right word. "...fun."

"She's definitely the life of the party." Reyna pushed back her chair, wondering how to hint to Zoe that their meeting was done. She looked at her watch. "Speaking of parties. You'll probably want to go and get ready for tonight?"

"What about the tea?" Zoe said, closing the lid to her laptop slowly.

"The tea?"

"You mentioned we might have a cup of tea. Would you still...I mean, shall we?"

Reyna sighed. Was Zoe intent on torturing her? She just wanted to be by herself now, lick her wounds in private. It was bad enough lusting after one of her employees, but lusting over one of her employees who was dating the inimitable Jessica Myers? That was just life slapping her in the face.

"I could make it?" Zoe said, looking a question at Reyna.

"If you like." Reyna sat on the edge of the bed, kicking herself for not being firmer. Zoe found the kettle and filled it in the bathroom.

"Do you want Earl Grey, English Breakfast, or peppermint?" Zoe asked, flicking through the box of teas supplied by the hotel.

"I'll take the peppermint."

"Me too. Shall we share a bag?"

Reyna nodded. "Fine by me."

When the kettle clicked off, Zoe poured the steaming water into the mugs and dunked the bag a few times in each, tossing it expertly into the bin under the desk.

"Good shot," Reyna murmured.

"I'm not just an extreme sports sadist." She handed her a mug and gave her a lopsided smile. "I played basketball at uni for a bit. Cheers." She clinked her mug against Reyna's, sitting down next to her on the bed.

"So basketball, running, bike riding, and what else? Is there a sport you don't like?" Reyna said, searching for a neutral topic. Anything to take her mind off the fact that Zoe's thigh was inches away from her own. *Jessica Myers*. She's into Jessica. This is just work stuff.

"Golf," Zoe replied promptly. "I hate golf. I can't see the point of trying to get the world's tiniest ball into a hole a hundred miles away. Seems stupid to me."

Reyna laughed. "I'd never thought of it like that, not that I've really given golf much thought."

"I didn't sleep with Jessica, just so you know," Zoe blurted out suddenly, staring down at her tea.

Reyna started, her tea jolting dangerously in the mug. "Zoe, you don't have to tell me. It's absolutely none of my business what you do with your personal life." She took a sip of her scalding tea, attempting to quash the hope that was trying to get lift off inside her.

"I know. It's just…I didn't want you to think I came here just to muck about. I've taken this conference seriously and I've tried to make the most of every opportunity. And the stuff with Jessica…I don't know exactly what happened there."

"You certainly made the most of *that* opportunity," Reyna said, aware that her sarcasm sounded churlish.

"But that's just it," Zoe exclaimed. "I didn't." She stood and paced. "I didn't seek out Jessica and I have tried not to lead her on. For some reason she's taken a shine to me, but I don't feel the same way."

"You don't?"

"Not really, no." Zoe stopped pacing, looking helplessly at Reyna.

"Why not?" Reyna asked, her voice quiet.

"Because." Zoe took a step toward her. "Because all I can think about is you."

They gazed at each other, the air between them static with desire.

The Rule, Reyna. Don't forget The Rule. No complications with her employees. Feeling like she was floating above herself, Reyna stood, carefully placing her tea on the desk. She took Zoe's mug from her and placed it on the desk next to her own.

"I'm sorry," Zoe began, "I'll leave—"

Reyna took Zoe's hand in her own, interlacing their fingers, and Zoe stepped forward uncertainly. Reyna ran a thumb over Zoe's palm, her chest barely containing her breath.

"I want you too," she said simply, leaning in and claiming Zoe's mouth with her own.

Reyna was shocked by the intensity, the rush she felt as Zoe's thigh pressed between her legs, hands running the length of her spine. Heat razed through her body and she moaned, cupping her hands under Zoe's buttocks and pulling her in closer.

Zoe's mouth broke away from hers, kissing a trail down Reyna's neck, taking her earlobe into her mouth, sending shivers of delight across Reyna's skin.

"I want you so badly," Zoe murmured, kissing the line of skin under the collar of Reyna's shirt, tugging at the buttons, which popped open at her insistence. "Oh god. You are so beautiful." Her fingertips grazed the exposed skin, raising goosebumps on Reyna's chest. Zoe pushed the shirt from Reyna's shoulders and eased her bra off, letting it slip to the floor.

Reyna's breath caught, legs weak as Zoe dipped her head and covered her nipple, her mouth hot as her tongue flicked over the sensitive flesh. Reyna moaned again, calling Zoe's name.

"Is it okay?" Zoe asked, her mouth trailing kisses over to the other nipple. Reyna's knees buckled and Zoe caught her, arms around her waist.

"The bed," Reyna said urgently, tugging Zoe's shirt over her head.

They sank into the large bed, Zoe's hands in Reyna's hair, loosening it from the knot at her neck. Reyna traced Zoe's nipples, grazing the palm of her hand over the puckered skin. Zoe groaned, straddling Reyna's thigh, her jean shorts rough against Reyna's thin leggings. Reyna popped the button on Zoe's shorts and slid them down, her hand finding the heat between Zoe's legs, palm flat against the wet. Zoe pushed against her, crying out as Reyna slid her finger inside her, their mouths colliding for an urgent kiss.

Zoe rocked against Reyna's hand as she slid in and out of her slowly, the tension between them building unbearably. Zoe arched her back, her eyes closed, breasts straining forward. Reyna covered her nipple with her mouth, thinking she would explode as the desperate heat threatened to push her over the edge.

"I want to feel you too," Zoe whispered thickly, her pupils dilated as she looked into Reyna's eyes. Her hand reached down, pushing aside Reyna's leggings, the cool of her touch finding Reyna's throbbing, slick clitoris, running the length of it with the same rhythm Reyna was using inside her.

Reyna gasped, her hips rocking against Zoe's hand. They moved faster, sliding, stroking, bucking, mouths open to each other as their breathing became ragged, short, shallow.

"You're going to make me come," Reyna cried, burying her head in Zoe's shoulder as a wave of orgasm curled up from her toes and crashed over her body. At the same time Zoe clenched her hand, her eyes closed as she moaned, whispering Reyna's name over and over into her hair.

They fell against each other, Reyna's heart beating wildly in her chest as she tried to find her breath.

"Don't move," Zoe said. "Please don't move. I just want to hold you like this for a moment."

They lay against each other, intertwined in the sheets as their bodies stilled.

Shit, Reyna thought. So much for The Rule. She was really in trouble now. Zoe shifted in her arms, pulling the soft hotel sheet up over their exposed bodies as the sweat dried on their cooling skin. She wrapped an arm lazily around Reyna's waist and murmured into her ear.

"That was unexpected."

"You could say that," Reyna replied. Her inner voice berated her loudly. What on earth had she done. Her lack of control had just signed her up for a whole pile of awkwardness and pain at work. And not just her, Zoe as well. She had reneged on her responsibility to Zoe. As the boss, she should have been protecting Zoe from exactly this kind of behaviour from her superiors. Instead she had engaged in it herself.

Zoe's nipple grazed her own as Zoe shifted in her arms, igniting a spark that shot through the length of her body. She supressed a groan, wondering how to extricate herself from this exquisite nightmare. Zoe's hand traced a distracting path along her belly, causing a tightening in Reyna's abdomen. Her fingers delved lower, exploring the soft patch of hair between Reyna's legs, gently stroking the line of her pubic hair.

"Zoe I—" Reyna said brokenly, and then cried out as Zoe slid her fingers back into her wetness, filling her from the inside. Her hips bucked beneath Zoe's touch, responding of their own volition to the mounting pressure as Zoe's fingers rocked insistently inside her.

"I shouldn't—"

"Yes, you should," Zoe said, finding her mouth, her tongue sliding lightly against Reyna's with the same rhythm as her fingers.

Reyna knew resistance was useless as pleasure streaked through her body, her hips arching wildly as she climaxed, shuddering with aftershocks of pleasure as Zoe's mouth found her nipple.

Reyna sank back against the pillow, her breath ragged.

"You are so entirely beautiful," Zoe whispered, tracing the line of Reyna's jaw. Reyna studied the face before her, taking in the clear, bright eyes, the smooth, velvet skin, the enticing mouth turned toward her. Her chest ached, heavy with words she knew she couldn't speak.

"We should get up. You'll miss the party," Reyna said quietly, gently smoothing the hair away from Zoe's brow.

"I don't want to go to the party."

"It's your last night here. You'll regret it if you miss it."

"I'm exactly where I want to be thank you."

Reyna sighed, turning away to look up at the ceiling. An intricate pattern of rosettes had been carved in to the corners and she wondered stupidly why anyone would bother to go to so much trouble over a space where people seldom looked. She wanted Zoe to stay. She wanted to lie there, wrapped in her long, strong arms until daybreak. And then she would order breakfast and they could eat it on the bed, cossetted in the thick hotel robes, feeding each other morsels of fruit and drinking coffee. They would take a long hot shower (sorry Alice Springs water supply) and fall back into bed for one last heady moment before they dashed to the airport to get on the plane home. *Home. Holden.* Her reality hit her like an unexpected punch in the solar plexus and she sat up carefully, extricating herself from their embrace. She had made a commitment to Holden. One week away and she was already forgetting her responsibilities. Some parent she was.

"I've done you a disservice, Zoe," Reyna began, her voice sounding hollow to her own ears. A cold heavy stone seemed to have lodged itself in her chest, making it difficult to speak. "I should not have allowed this to happen. It was a mistake."

Zoe sat up beside her, pulling the bedsheet up to cover her exposed breasts. "Please don't say that. How could *this*..." She tipped Reyna's chin toward her and kissed her, their mouths hungry against each other. "...have been a mistake?" she finished, breathless as they broke off the kiss.

Reyna shook her head, mute with confusion.

"I just...oh god. Zoe, there are so many reasons this is wrong. I'm your boss, for one."

"It's not illegal."

"Yes, but it's not *right*. It's unethical of me to behave like this. Sleeping with you, well, it could damage your reputation, make it harder for you to get a promotion in the future, cause jealousy amongst your peers, distrust amongst management, the list goes on. There's a good reason these kinds of things are discouraged. Can you imagine what it would be like if people found out we had—"

"Surely we can work this out. If two consenting adults want to pursue a relationship it can't possibly matter if there's a work connection."

"But that's just it." Reyna forced herself to speak the words. "I don't want to pursue a relationship."

"You don't?" The hurt in Zoe's voice was palpable.

Reyna stared straight ahead, determined not to waver. "I don't. I can't."

"Why not?"

"It's just not possible for me. I have other commitments that preclude me from getting involved in anything else right now."

"Other commitments?"

"My nephew, Holden. I need to be available for him. I just don't have time to get involved with anything else." Reyna knew she sounded cold but it was for the best. "Look, why don't I have a shower while you gather your things."

Zoe was silent for a moment, her eyes turned away as she stared in front of her. And then she slipped out of the bed and retrieved her discarded clothing, putting it back on quickly. Reyna watched her from under heavy eyelids, biting her lip to keep from calling her back to the bed, back into her arms, back to the space where she could kiss away the pain etched on her face. She wanted to tell her she was so beautiful it hurt her chest. She wanted to speak words her heart hadn't served up in forever. She wanted to tell her, "Don't go. Stay here. Let's work it out." But she stayed silent, her lips sealed.

Fully clothed, Zoe unplugged her laptop, winding the cord carefully around the computer and hugged it to her chest.

"See you back in Melbourne then," she said finally.

Reyna met her eyes, startled to find them blank and unreadable.

"I'm sorry if I've hurt you, Zoe," she said, but Zoe didn't reply, letting herself out of the room with a quiet click of the door.

Damn it. Reyna balled her fists, feeling her nails bite into her palms. Her eyes welled, threatening to spill over. She looked around the room, through the blur of unshed tears. *Damn it, damn it, damn it.*

CHAPTER SEVENTEEN

Zoe (Saturday, two weeks later)

Thank god for spring, Zoe thought as she picked her way carefully down a slippery forest ravine, hearing Mel swear emphatically from in front on the trail. The weather was perfect. The sky was endless, not a cloud in sight, and a small breeze was cooling the back of her neck.

"You okay?" Zoe called without taking her eyes off the uneven ground. One misplaced step easily could send her tumbling down the steep incline in a blur of arms and legs.

"Yes. Stupid backpack is making me top heavy," Mel complained.

"Aren't you already top heavy?" Enid sang out with a giggle and then broke off abruptly as Mel allowed a small tree branch to slap its leaves back into her. "Oi!"

"Don't taunt me while I'm doing this, Enid," Mel growled. "How much farther is it anyway? Do you think we're still in the lead?"

Chiara, at the head of the group, stopped suddenly causing them all to bump up behind her. "I need to check the map again.

I think we were supposed to head around the hill when we got to about halfway down."

"Do you think this is halfway then?" asked Travis, his face dubious. "How can you tell halfway unless you're at the top or the bottom?"

"I've been counting the kilometres," Chiara reassured him. "This should be it. I actually think there's a little trail here." She pulled out the map and they gathered around, watching as she lined up her compass with the trail they were on and measured out the distance they had come.

"If my calculations are right…"

"And we very much hope they are," Mel groaned.

"Of course they're right," Enid said. "When has Chiara ever gone wrong?"

"I'd hate for this to be the first time. I don't want to be stuck out here getting eaten by bears tonight."

"Do we have bears in Australia?" Travis asked.

"We have Koala bears."

"Yeah, but they just eat leaves and stuff."

"Who knows what they do at night. Have you heard the way they growl?"

"Zip it, Mel," Zoe instructed. "Chiara, you were saying?"

"Look, this is where the trail should be." Her finger traced a line on the map. "And that should lead us to the final flag. From there we just have to make it back to base. I think most people will try to cut straight across the valley, but look at how steep those inclines are." They all examined the tightly bunched, wavy, blue contour lines on the map.

"So, what should we do?" Travis asked.

"I think we can follow the side of the hill and slip around the midline. It's longer in kilometres, but we won't have to go up or down which should save our legs."

"Let's do it," Zoe said. "Lead the way, Chiara."

They all fell into line behind Chiara as they picked their way across the barely visible bush track. If it wasn't for Chiara's exceptional orienteering skills, Zoe knew they would have been much further behind in this challenge. As it was they actually had a shot of winning the event.

Zoe breathed deeply, inhaling the sweet, eucalyptus-scented air, enjoying the warm patches of sunlight, filtering in through the trees. It was good to be outside again with her friends, free from the stresses of the last few weeks. The tall gum trees reminded her of Alice Springs, a sudden painful twinge gripping her heart. She wouldn't think about that now. She *couldn't* think about that now. She had wasted enough time breaking her heart over what had happened with Reyna in the small hours of the morning when she should have been sleeping. Dark rings around her eyes told a story of too many hours spent sitting in her kitchen drinking endless cups of tea.

They were moving faster now, jogging along the tiny path without talking, concentrating on their steps. Zoe could hear her friends breathing hard as they navigated the difficult path. She stretched out a hand and caught a bunch leaves, scrunching them up to hold under her nose for the aroma. Peppermint gum, she thought. They had mainly seen river gums in Alice. For the hundredth time she wondered if Reyna thought much about their encounter. They had barely seen each other over the last fortnight. Reyna had been locked away in her office, apparently having endless meetings. They had passed briefly in the hallway, Reyna stopping to ask in awkward, stilted tones how she was settling back in. Zoe had been torn between throwing her arms around Reyna, and giving her the cold shoulder. So instead she had found herself mumbling something vague and meaningless as she hurried away.

She thought back to the email she had received during the week and wondered again if it was worth considering. "I've had an email from Financial Literacy Australia," she announced as she carefully stepped over a fallen branch.

"Who?" Travis asked from behind her.

"They work with vulnerable community groups. Promoting financial literacy and health," Zoe replied, puffing a little as she spoke. "They've offered me a job."

"What?" Mel risked a look over her shoulder. "What kind of job?"

"Designing and implementing a program for schools."

"Zoe, that sounds amazing," Chiara called from the front.

"Wait, we need to talk about this properly," Mel said, stopping abruptly. Zoe skidded to a halt behind her, Travis putting his hands on her pack to steady himself. "Are you seriously considering this?"

"Yeah, I guess."

"Guys!" Enid called from along the path. "Zoe this is big news, but can we talk about it properly when we're back at the base. We need to discuss this when I can actually breathe!"

"Sure." Zoe gave Mel a nudge forward. "Keep up, Mel," she prodded.

"What! You just wait until I am not dying from exhaustion, Cavendish. I'm going to get you."

In the end they came in second place, a result Mel felt was definitely "none too shabby." As evening fell, they gathered around the campfire, balancing bowls of curry on their laps, eating by the firelight. Around them, similar groups clustered together, enjoying some well-earned rest after the day's orienteering race.

"So, Zoe," Mel said. "Tell us everything. What's the deal with this job offer?"

Zoe finished her mouthful. "I caught up with these guys in Alice Springs. They're called Financial Literacy Australia and they were interested in my seminar program. It turns out they want me to design a program to take into schools. They've got a grant to implement the program over the next five years and can offer me a proper salary and everything."

"Not like you get now, though," Mel guessed.

"Yeah, and only for five years," Chiara added.

"Five years is ages and who knows what else will come up during that time? And yeah, it's community sector-style salary, but that doesn't really bother me. I've got my mortgage all sorted with enough tucked away for a rainy day. I can easily afford to take a pay cut."

"Aren't we supposed to be aiming for pay raises in life?" Enid asked through a mouthful of curry. "And don't you love your job?"

"I *do* love my job, but maybe it's time to move on."

"Because of Reyna?" Mel probed. "You can't leave just because things went south with Reyna. That would not be cool."

"It's not because of Reyna. Well," Zoe caught herself, "not entirely because of Reyna. I won't lie. It is a factor, but you know how much I've enjoyed running my seminars. These guys are offering me an opportunity to upscale massively and implement a program for all Victorian school children."

"That's a lot of kids," Travis mused. "Do you have to teach them all?"

"Nope. They said I'd have my own team. I'd run some sessions, but I'd also be supervising the team to deliver the program according to the benchmarks I set. They also mentioned getting involved in some of their women's prison programs in the future, so I think there's lots of opportunity."

"Sounds pretty cool," Travis replied.

"Are you seriously thinking about taking this?" Mel asked.

"Yeah. Well, we're meeting up on Monday to go over the details. They asked me for a decision by the end of the week. Apparently, if I don't take it, they'll advertise."

"When does it start?"

"First of the month."

"But that's in three weeks!" Mel frowned heavily. "I'm not ready for that."

"Well, you might not have to be ready. I still have to meet up with them."

"It sounds like you've made up your mind."

"I haven't," Zoe said, knowing she pretty much already had. This offer was a godsend. No way could she stay working in the same building as Reyna after what they had experienced together. Her heart cracked into a million pieces every time she caught a glimpse of her across the office. She knew time would probably dull the pain, but why put herself through that when a great opportunity had presented itself just when she needed to get away?

"Just promise you'll talk to us before you make your final decision, okay?" Mel asked, taking a swig of her beer. "I don't want to be the last to know that my best friend is leaving."

"I promise."

She took the day off work on Monday, calling in sick. It wasn't exactly a lie. The knot of anxiety sitting in her stomach was making her feel nauseous and she had spent another restless night, fighting with the doona as she tried to court sleep.

At lunchtime, she took herself to the beach, strolling along the boardwalk as she licked a chocolate ice cream. Her meeting with Evie and Graeme had gone so well she was in no doubt about her choice. She would take the job. The salary they were offering her was much more than she had expected and would allow her to maintain the comforts she had become used to. Comforts mum never had, she reminded herself, shrugging off the thought angrily. She sat down on a bench and watched the waves. She was tired. Tired of beating herself up about her mum, tired of yearning for something that could not be, tired of dreaming about Reyna when she eventually fell into fitful sleep each night. It was a sort of torture, she decided. No need for waterboarding or whatever they did to people. Just make people fall in love.

Diligently, she pulled out her mobile phone and opened up the group chat she shared with her friends. *Interview went well. Job is amazing. I'm going to take it.*

Within minutes replies pinged back, congratulating her. Mel's made her smile. *Do they need a graphic designer?* Who knew? Maybe they would.

Next she opened up her email and sent a message to Evie and Graeme thanking them for their time today and accepting the position. Finally she created a message to Thomus, requesting a meeting with him first thing the following morning. He wouldn't wonder why she was accessing her emails when she was supposed to be off sick. He expected his staff to be contactable rain, hail, or shine.

The following morning she sat across from Thomus and handed him a typed copy of her resignation.

"What's this?" he asked, fingering the envelope without opening it.

"It's my resignation, Thomus," she said. "I want to thank you for the wonderful opportunities I've had here. I've loved working at Azoulay House and I'll be sad to move on, but I've had an offer I can't refuse."

"Going to Langley's?" he asked. "They offer big salaries my girl, but watch out. The culture is awful. You'll be working twenty-four-seven."

"Actually, with the greatest respect, I'm not 'your girl,' and I'm not going to Langley's. I'm moving to the community sector."

"The community sector," Thomus said, his mouth puckering around the word as if it tasted sour in his mouth. He gave a quick laugh. "Your bank balance won't thank you for that."

Zoe smiled. "I've been offered a significant opportunity to head up my own team with a more than generous remuneration package, so my bank balance will be fine, thanks." She rose from her chair, duty done. "I'm giving the required two-weeks' notice. Please let me know how you'd like me to prioritise my workload during the time I have left."

"Have you spoken to Reyna about this?"

"No," Zoe said quickly, her pulse jumping irrationally at the mention of Reyna's name. "I've come directly to you as my line manager."

"She'll be disappointed," he said with a scowl. "She invested a lot in you, taking you to FinCo."

Zoe felt a rush of guilt. She hadn't thought of that. But then again, Reyna had taken her to FinCo to present on a program she had developed and implemented for Azoulay House, on her own time. She would leave them with the intellectual property and they could continue to run the programs. That would have to do. "I'm sure I won't be the first bad investment Reyna's made in her life. It happens to us all occasionally. She'll get over it."

"You'll be wanting a reference from me."

"Thanks, Thomus. That would be great."

She left his stuffy office and returned to her desk where she managed to hide out for the rest of the day with few interruptions. She just needed to make it through the next fortnight and she would be free. It wasn't that she was running away, more like trying to slide out the side door unnoticed.

CHAPTER EIGHTEEN

Reyna (Thursday, a.m.)

Reyna stared at her computer screen in disbelief. Thomus's email was brief, just keeping her in the loop, letting her know that Zoe Cavendish had resigned. Would she like to join the morning tea for Zoe next week?

Morning tea? What the fuck? This was bad. She berated herself again for the poor choices she had made in Alice Springs. She had hoped the worst of it would be an awkwardness at work that would eventually dissipate. It seemed that her worst fears had been confirmed. She had stepped over the line and now Zoe clearly felt too uncomfortable to stay.

Reyna sat back in her chair, swivelling around to stare out the window. What a mess. She had tried to stay busy over the last few weeks, keeping out of Zoe's way, but obviously it had not been enough. Should she have tried to speak with her? Reassure her that it would all be okay? No doubt about it. She had failed in her duty as a manager in this situation, but she just hadn't been able to bring herself to have the conversation. If she was honest with herself, she wasn't sure she could be alone with

Zoe, worried she would lose her mind and scoop Zoe up into her arms and hold her tightly, kiss the worry lines away from her brow. But there was nothing for it now. Decency required her to act and she would just have to be strong.

Reyna swung her chair back around and picked up her phone, punching in Zoe's internal line. After the sixth ring Reyna was about to hang up when Zoe's voice came down the line.

"Hello?"

"Zoe, it's Reyna. Do you have a moment to come to my office?"

"Now?"

"If it's convenient."

"Okay, sure."

Reyna hung up the receiver and stood up to look out the window, restless as she waited for the knock on her door. When it came, she called, "Come in," and sat back down in her chair as Zoe entered the room.

Zoe, pale-faced and dark around her eyes in a way that left Reyna feeling uneasy, sat opposite her, hands folded over the notebook in her lap.

"Thanks for coming," Reyna said, feeling unsure of herself. Could she manage this? She gripped a pencil on the desk, opening her notebook out of habit just to stop herself from reaching across the desk. She wished she could erase the seriousness in Zoe's face, find a way to bring the sparkle back into her usually bright eyes.

"No problem. What can I do for you?" Zoe asked, her tone polite but cool.

"Thomus has been in touch. He tells me you've handed in your resignation."

"Yes."

"Zoe, I..." Reyna broke off. "You don't have to do this. We can work it out."

"I know. I'm not doing it because I *have* to. I've been offered an excellent opportunity. Too good to turn down."

"Really?"

Zoe's eyes narrowed. "Yes, really. I'm actually quite good at what I do."

"Oh, god, I didn't mean it that way, Zoe. I meant...I'm sorry. It came out wrong."

"That's okay."

"Do you mind me asking what?"

"Financial Literacy Australia has offered me a chance to develop an economic health and wellbeing program for schools. I start in a week and a half."

"That soon?"

"Yes. I did give my required two-weeks' notice," Zoe said primly.

Reyna blew out a frustrated sigh. This wasn't going well. "Of course. I'm sure you did. Look, is there any way I can change your mind? I don't—we don't—want to lose you at Azoulay House."

Zoe smiled grimly, her eyes refusing to participate in the activity. "Thank you, but my mind is made up. I've accepted the position. I think it will be a great move forward."

"It certainly sounds like the kind of thing you would excel at."

They gazed at each other across the expanse of Reyna's wide desk. An ocean couldn't have made them feel farther apart.

Reyna waited for Zoe to say something—anything—but she sat, resolutely quiet, as if biding her time until their meeting was over.

"So, there's nothing I can do to change your mind?"

"I wouldn't have thought so."

"But why do you have to leave? I get that this job sounds great, but you were running your own program here. Can't we give you more of that?"

"I don't *have* to leave. I want to leave."

"Why? Because of us?"

"What *us* are you referring to? You've been pretty clear that there is no us."

"I know, I mean..." Reyna looked away. "Zoe, I'm really trying here."

"Trying what? To get me to stay on as your *employee*?" Zoe spat out the word like it didn't belong in her mouth. "I don't really want that, Reyna."

"You don't?"

Zoe looked at her hands as if the answer were written in secret ink on her palm. "No. I want...I *wanted* you."

Reyna's breath caught in her chest. "It's not possible, Zoe. I explained that to you."

"Actually, you didn't. You told me you have too many commitments, whatever that means. But surely it's possible to make some room in your life if you really want to. People don't knock back something special because they have too many appointments."

"Is that how you think it is for me? Too many appointments?" Reyna felt a rush of frustration. "What do you think I should cut back on, Zoe? You tell me how to work it out. Should I renege on my duties to the firm and the three hundred and fifty employees I have across the nation? Or perhaps I should sideline my responsibility to my nephew whose parents died in a car crash nine months ago? What are your thoughts here, Zoe? Which *appointment* do I shift off so we can go out to dinner and hold hands in the evenings?"

Zoe paled. Pink spots stung her cheeks as if Reyna had slapped her. "Thank you for making it clearer. I hadn't fully appreciated your position."

Reyna ran a hand across her forehead, upset with herself for losing her cool. "I'm sorry if that sounded harsh. But my hands are tied."

"Got it," Zoe said, a muscle in her jaw flickering. "Is there anything else you need? If not, I'll get back to my desk. I've got quite a bit to finish up before my last day."

Reyna took a shaky breath, trying to calm her racing pulse. "I hope you'll change your mind, but if you don't, I wish you all the best, Zoe," she said, finally. "If there's ever anything I can do for you, please don't hesitate to be in touch."

Zoe looked like she was going to say something but changed her mind, nodding instead. She rose from the chair, hugging her notebook to her chest and hurried out of the room.

Reyna put her head on the desk, thankful for the tinted windows that meant she had ultimate privacy. For a moment she let herself forget she was the CEO of a national firm and cried like a girl with a broken heart.

Zoe's farewell morning tea was excruciating. Reyna gave the required speech about how much Zoe had brought to the firm and how sorely she would be missed, allowing herself to mean the words in a way she realised she had probably never done before. She smiled heartily and clapped along with the group as Thomus presented Zoe with a voucher from the team for an adventure travel store, and a potted plant, "so she wouldn't forget them as long as she kept it alive." Zoe gave a pretty speech about how great the team was and how much she had valued all the opportunities she had had with Azoulay House. She didn't meet Reyna's eyes, her gaze sweeping past her as she thanked everyone and wished them all the best. Zoe put a little stack of cards at the end of the table and invited everyone to grab a copy of her new email address if they should wish to contact her in the future. Reyna found herself tucking the card into her suit pocket as she edged away from the gathering.

She left work early that day, stopping at the school to pick up Holden before heading for home. She didn't want to see Zoe leave the building. Her building. That would be too much. Somehow she had kidded herself into believing something would change at the eleventh hour. They would sort things out and Zoe would stay. She had them working together into the future, perhaps until Holden was older, more settled, and then they'd see what might lie between them. Fantasy, she realised as she parked the car in the driveway and followed Holden into the house. That had been pure fantasy.

"Do you have homework to do this afternoon?" Reyna asked as she made her way to the kitchen.

"Yeah. Maths." He dumped his bag on the floor and pulled out a thick folder. "I hate maths."

"You hate it? That's a strong word."

"It's stupid. It's hard and I don't get it."

"I can understand that. How about we have a chocolate milk and look it over together? I'm actually pretty okay at maths, but don't ask me to spell anything. I'm useless at that."

"Are you? But how do you manage to be the boss if you're a crap speller?"

"Spellcheck, my friend. Good ol' spellcheck."

"We're not allowed to use spellcheck." Holden pursed his lips. "We should be able to if you do."

"I think they want you to try to learn it first," Reyna answered with a laugh. "I just was a dunce at it."

"But you're good at maths?"

"Not just good, pretty damn good. Crack open your book. I'll get the chocolate milk."

They sat up at the kitchen table going over his homework problems, Reyna taking him methodically through the principles of each question in a patient and easy way that allowed him to grasp the underlying concepts. Under her tutelage he began to understand how to work out the problems for himself.

"Correct again," she said, nudging him with her elbow. "At this rate you'll be moving on to advanced calculus before you know it."

"Thanks, Aunty Rey." He stretched his little arms above his head with a yawn. "It makes sense when you explain it to me. I wish you could be my teacher. Hopefully we don't have to do the advanced cactus stuff. This is enough for me."

She ruffled his hair, feeling a flash of guilt that she wasn't around in the afternoons more often to help him with his homework. "Why don't you have a play before dinner? I'm going to make some spaghetti."

"Yes!" he crowed, jumping down from the table and making a grab for a couple of his Lego figures on the couch. "Bolognaise?"

"The pretend bolognaise."

"Tastes real enough to me."

She watched him slide around on the floor, battling his Lego people with intense sound effects. If only Zoe could see this. She would understand how important it was that Reyna not stuff this up. How could she have made any other choice? He needed her, and he needed her here.

On Saturday afternoon it stormed so hard it was if the sky was trying to shake something loose. Reyna could commiserate. She and Holden hunkered down in the living room, snuggled into doonas, reading (comics for him, a report from HR for her) and eating popcorn. The thunder was so intense they looked at each other in awe with every boom and crack. The windows rattled and the corrugated roof sang with the sound of the relentless rain. When her mobile rang she wondered for a moment if she should answer it. She had heard somewhere that you weren't supposed to use your mobile during a storm, but she couldn't remember why so she answered it anyway, seeing Samira's name on the display.

"Are you guys getting this?" Samira asked excitedly. "What a wild storm, hey?"

"I know! I was worried the windows might actually blow out."

"The rain radar says most of it will have passed over in the next half an hour. The boys want to know if Holden wants to come around and get muddy with them when it's calmed down?"

"I'm sure he would love that. Hang on I'll ask him." Reyna smiled at Holden who was looking at her expectantly.

"What?" he asked.

She put her hand over the receiver. "Jessie and Gid want to know if you want to go and jump around in puddles with them when the storm has passed."

"Yes!" he cried, untangling himself from his doona and jumping off the couch. "Let's go."

"Not right now, darling. We need to wait for the storm to pass." Reyna directed her conversation back to Samira. "That's a definite yes."

"Okay, come over when it's safe to drive. The boys can make mudpies out in the yard and we can have tea. John's making scones."

"Yum. He is so Martha Stewart."

"I know! I'm so glad I married him right now," Samira said with a laugh and rang off.

Holden bounced over to the window, pressing his nose against the glass as he stared out at the storm. "I think it's mostly stopped now," he said as a flash of lightning made him jump back from the window with a start. "Woah! That was massive! Maybe not." He gave her a sheepish grin.

"Why don't you go pack a bag with a change of clothes and a towel so we're ready to go when the storm passes. I'm sure it won't be too long. When they're violent like this, they usually move pretty quickly. We can look at the radar together and watch it moving if you like."

The sky was still dripping with tendrils of grey cloud as they pulled up at Samira and John's house. The road was awash with pools of rain and Holden had to leap from the car, over the rushing gutter and onto the sodden nature strip.

Samira threw open the door, kissing them both and ushering Holden straight through the house into the backyard, where the boys were already up to their elbows in mud. "Get on out there," she said, but Holden needed no encouragement, running out into the yard with a joyful whoop.

"And now we drink tea and eat scones," Samira said, leading Reyna into the kitchen.

The kitchen was warm and smelled of freshly baked, floury goodness. John's legs were sticking out from under the kitchen sink and Reyna could hear banging and swearing.

"You all right there, John?" she called out.

"Changing... the... seal," he grunted. "Bloody annoying."

"Need a hand?"

He wriggled out from the under the sink and raised his eyebrows at her. "You any good with plumbing?"

"No," she admitted with a grin. "But I could pass you something."

He growled something incoherent and shuffled back under the sink.

"Ignore him. He'll work it out. He's playing house god today," Samira said. "He does cooking *and* repairs. Tea?"

"Yes please."

Reyna settled on a stool at the bench as Samira made them a pot of tea and popped a load of scones into a bamboo basket. "Voilà," she said with a smile as she arranged the condiments in front of them at the kitchen bench and sat across from Reyna. "You joining us, John?"

"Done!" he cried as he emerged from under the sink, wrench in hand and a smudge of something black across the tip of his nose.

Samira snorted and Reyna giggled as he waggled his eyebrows at them. "What is it? Why you laugh, oh cruel sirens?"

"Come here, husband." Samira grabbed a cloth and wiped the smudge clean. "Now you are presentable."

"Reyna," John said, kissing her on the cheek and squeezing her shoulder. "You look ravishing but thin. And tired. Eat scones."

From the backyard there were yells of delight, and Reyna looked out the window to see Holden swinging from the Hills Hoist as Jessie and Gideon pelted him with mud. "They're having fun," she said with a wry smile.

"We can chuck them in the bath afterward. You'll never know the difference."

"Oh, I don't care. He's loving it. That's what counts."

"Are you loving it?" Samira asked, through a mouthful of scone.

"What do you mean?"

"Like John said. You look tired. Sad. What's going on?"

"Great, so you're both basically saying I look haggard. Gee thanks, guys."

"No," Samira protested, swatting her with a napkin. "You just don't seem entirely yourself."

"Work is...work."

"Problems?" John asked, pouring himself a beer. "The minions not behaving themselves?"

"More like the boss isn't behaving herself."

"What? What does that mean."

Reyna took a deep breath and told them everything that had happened up in Alice Springs, ending with Zoe's resignation.

"So I basically cost her her career and lost a star employee in one fell swoop," she finished, taking a small sip of her tea. She caught a look passing between them.

"Sounds big," John said, taking a swig of his beer.

"It sounds," Samira said carefully, "as if Zoe has chosen to move on for a good reason."

"Yeah, because she couldn't work with me anymore."

"Don't you think the new job is suited to her? From all you've said, I get the impression this is a good move for her."

"I do. I just feel bad. Maybe if I hadn't behaved so unethically she wouldn't have been tempted to leave."

John didn't look convinced. "And it's a loss for your business?"

"Yes."

"Not for yourself at all?"

"What's that supposed mean?"

"It means, that it sounds like you *like* this woman."

"Of course I like her."

Samira cut in. "I think John's trying to ask if you have feelings for Zoe. As in, did you want more from your…encounter?"

Reyna sighed deeply. She spread her hands helplessly, looking back out the window. "How can I?"

Nobody said anything.

Reyna transferred her gaze to her teacup, staring at the milky brew. "It's like I told Zoe. There's no room in my life for a relationship. I've committed to raising Holden, and I have a business to run."

"So that's it for you, huh?" John asked, spreading jam thickly over a scone. "Single forever."

Reyna shrugged. "At least for the next few years. Until Holden gets a bit more independent."

"Reyna, it's possible to do both, you know. You get a babysitter and go out for a drink while the kid's asleep. You grab a coffee when the kid is having a play date with friends. Sometimes kids even have sleepovers. People have children *and* relationships all the time," Samira said, her brow wrinkling. "I just don't get why you can't."

"Because those are the times when I'm trying to catch up on all the work from my firm. When Holden is playing, I'm working."

"Is that how you want it to be forever?"

"I don't know." She hadn't thought about that before. Was it possible to change the way her business was set up so that less burden sat on her shoulders? Should she be micromanaging less and would she even want to do that?

"Can you get some more support at work, spread the love around a bit more? Perhaps you don't need to have your finger on every pulse. I mean," Samira took a bite of her scone, speaking through crumbs, "maybe let people do their jobs a bit more independently?"

"Maybe. I'd need to think about it. The firm has grown so organically I guess I hadn't noticed how large it's become."

"I'm not saying you should quit your job so you can start dating, but maybe it's possible to restructure things and change your approach so that you at least have the option of a life if you should ever want one. You've never been good at prioritising relationships, but you at least used to have some time for that stuff."

"Before the firm got so large."

"Exactly. Is this what you want? A life where you're married to your firm, rather than a warm and loving partner to help you raise your child?"

"God." Reyna's mind boggled at the thought. It was too intense. "I'm not looking to get married, and I'm really only just coming to terms with the idea that I'm raising a child as it is. Cut me some slack here, guys."

John patted her on the back reassuringly. "Have another scone. They're a good pairing with an existential crisis."

That night after she had checked on Holden and settled the doona under his chin, she faced the mountain of unfinished paperwork on her desk and her inbox with over a hundred unread emails. For the first time, perhaps ever, she felt uninspired. Unbidden, an image of Zoe's face, laughing as they cycled with no hands down the road in the early morning, came to mind. Reyna loved how joyful she was, how she seemed to embrace life, lighting up her surrounds with her infectious energy. She closed the lid of her laptop and walked away from her desk, her heart heavy. She no longer felt like working.

It would be good to have someone to share these burdens with, she thought as she poured herself a finger of scotch and went to sit on the couch. She didn't even have a good book to read, she realised, suddenly aware that all her spare moments were filled with work decisions and activity. There was always something to be done, something to be signed off on. When she had first started the firm it was small, boutique, just her and a few choice employees to service a select few clients. As their reputation had grown, so had the number of her employees, matching the demand with the service. It had seemed natural to set up around the country. In this technological day and age there was no issue working for clients in other locations, and gradually she had begun to set up her satellite offices as the profile of the firm grew.

But when had she ever decided to do it like this, she wondered? Here she was, sitting at the top of her own empire, nursing a lukewarm attitude and a badly bruised heart. She had an HR department now and payroll; she had IT and accounts, and a group of middle managers, but she didn't have a general manager, someone to oversee everyone and report back to her as CEO. Should she be looking for a deputy? Or a board of directors. It was suddenly clear to her that she needed some other kind of management structure to spread the load, because as it stood, she was it—kit and caboodle. It was time to change but it would be hard. She enjoyed the control, everything had to be signed off by her and no rogue decisions or alternative pathways would be taken by managers with differences of opinion. It would take a lot of trust to take a step back and bring in an extra tier of management to ease the burden on her.

Perhaps she should just sell the firm, she mused, sipping her drink slowly and flicking randomly through channels on her rarely watched TV. Financially, she was already set up for life. Everything she did from here on in was just a bonus. But she really did enjoy the work her firm did, and if she wasn't running Azoulay House, she knew she would gravitate toward doing the same sort of work all over again. She would just have to start from scratch, which would mean more work. No, she didn't want to sell. But Samira's voice rang in her head. Did she want to be *married* to her firm? *No way*, her body cried out in protest, reminding her of Zoe's hands on her skin, Zoe's mouth against hers, Zoe's warmth and humour and attention, directed straight at Reyna, wanting to hear, to understand, to know. She had spent so long on her own, holding herself aloof at the top of her castle that she had forgotten how desperately beautiful it was to be seen, truly seen by another. She longed to pick up the phone and call Zoe, to tell her she had been wrong, to suggest a walk by the river or a coffee by the park. Zoe would like those kinds of places and Reyna felt an awakening inside her, a drive to get outside and see the world that she was missing, locked up in her office all the time. She had been getting out and about much more with Holden, and her focus had definitely begun to shift, but with Zoe it was as if a fire had been lit inside her and no amount of internal dousing would put it out.

She thought about the card she had pocketed at Zoe's farewell. It would be so simple to pick up her phone and send a simple email, not too confrontational like, *Best wishes for the new job*. But did Zoe even want to hear from her now? There was no mistaking the coldness between them. She had barely glanced at Reyna at her farewell, and Reyna couldn't blame her for that. She had been ruthless in her office, cutting Zoe off in no uncertain terms.

Her heart twisted painfully, recalling the look on Zoe's face as she had left Reyna's office. It was unlikely Zoe would ever want to have anything to do with her. She had lost her job and been rejected in one move. Reyna was probably the last person she wanted to hear from.

Maybe she could consider a restructure, but what was the point of creating a whole bunch of extra time now that she had alienated the person she wanted to spend it with? Holden, she reminded herself. If she cut back on her work obligations she could rely on her parents a bit less, she could pick him up from school more often. They could do his maths homework together. She owed it to her sister and brother-in-law to give their son the attention he deserved. Sarit, whose only son was her whole world, would have desperately wanted her to do that. With a heavy heart she knew it was too late to fix things with Zoe, but maybe down the line there was the possibility that she would meet someone.

There was so much to consider with a business restructure. Her head swam trying to imagine where to begin. You don't have to do everything yourself, she reminded herself, switching off the TV and going to fetch her laptop. There were people to help with this sort of thing. She returned to the couch, her hands hovering over the keys. What was the name of that specialist firm who had tried to headhunt her for a board of directors last year? They did exactly this kind of thing. It came to her in a flash: Macintyre & Claud. She typed it into her search engine and clicked on their website, scanning their content. They looked excellent at face value and she remembered the woman she had dealt with, Linda Macintyre, had been extremely professional in her communication. Before she could second-guess herself, she clicked on their contact button and sent through a meeting invitation. At the very least, it was worth a discussion.

CHAPTER NINETEEN

Zoe (One month later, Monday, a.m.)

Zoe used the laser pointer to direct the room's attention to the list of bullet points she was displaying on her slideshow. "As you can see here, we have five Key Performance Indicators. If we meet these KPIs, we will be well on our way to maximising coverage and delivery outcomes for the program. According to the Department of Education's directive, we're rolling out the program across the regions in this formation." She flicked to the next slide. "In line with this, we now have a timeline for the inner South-East incursions, with fifty primary schools signed up to complete the program over the next term. Our first schools start their programs next week."

She paused, looking around the table at the group. The faces of her new team looked back at her expectantly, reflecting her enthusiasm and dedication to the project. She had been able to handpick them from the current staff pool and recruit a few new members to the team as well. Evie and Graeme sat at the head of the table, each taking notes.

"Now that each of us has our timetable of schools, and the finalised program map, we're ready to go. Any questions?" Zoe asked, completing the slide show.

"None from me," Graeme said. "I'm impressed. You guys have moved this along with superhuman effort. I'll admit I didn't expect to see anything get off the ground before the end of the year."

Zoe acknowledged the compliment with a nod. She had been working around the clock to get the new program up and running as quickly as possible, driving herself harder than she ever had before. Every spare moment on weekends and evenings had been dedicated to the work, leaving little space in her mind for thinking about anything else. Or anyone. Her friends were starting to complain, calling her out on her new and boring "all work, no play" attitude, but she had promised them it was just until she got the new program up and running. In truth, tired as she was, it suited her to lose herself in this work. At night when she finally tumbled into bed she dreamed of Alice Springs, of tantalising kisses, of Reyna's touch on her burning skin, waking in a tangle of sheets with her pulse jumping wildly. But during the day there was thankfully little room in her brain for thoughts of Reyna. "No time like the present," she replied.

"Yes," Evie agreed. "The fact that we'll have data before Christmas is actually quite astonishing. This goes way beyond our expectations. Congratulations to you all."

"The team has worked exceptionally hard," Zoe said, knowing her team, anxious to impress her, had probably been working much harder than they would have expected to. A mixture of wry smiles and nods came back at her from around the room. "But now that we have our material and a schedule, we can all take a breath and focus on the fun part—educating the kids." Not that she intended to take a breath. She had signed up to do some of the school incursions, but she would also be building the next term's schedule and gathering the data for review and assessment as they went along. She had plenty to fill her plate.

"Right," Graeme said with a grin, snapping his notebook shut. "Go team!"

"You can't hide from us forever you know," Mel said, sounding hurt on the phone. "You haven't even seen my new haircut. I look amazing and my best friend doesn't even know it."

Zoe laughed. "I'm sorry, I just really want to finish this work tonight before the first incursions roll out. It would be good for the team to have this info before they head out in the morning."

"Good or essential?"

"Well, you know, I think it would be helpful."

"In other words, you've become a work-obsessed recluse and we should just give up hope of ever seeing you again."

"No," Zoe protested. "It's not like that. We'll get together soon, I promise. Just let me get this off the ground first, okay?"

"It's just dinner. One hour at La Travoletta. You need to eat."

"Actually, I've got some leftovers that I should finish. Next week, I swear."

She rang off, feeling guilty for avoiding her friends. She checked her watch. Six p.m. If she skipped dinner, she could go for a quick run instead and then get back to work. The team didn't really need another email from her, but she hoped they would find it helpful and it would keep her busy for the evening. With a sudden flash of understanding she realised this was probably what it was like for Reyna, only a hundred times more involved given the size of Azoulay House. Nights filled with work, weekends spent compiling data and answering emails in preparation for the week to come. It was a strangely comforting thought.

As she stepped out of the shower an hour later, she was surprised to hear her doorbell chime. Perhaps it was one of her neighbours, she thought, quickly throwing on a tracksuit. They didn't often drop over but occasionally they popped in to give each other news of happenings in the building.

"Who is it?" she called before she unchained the door. Was that whispering she could hear?

"Delivery," a low, gravelly voice called from the other side of the door.

"Of what?" she rejoined, feeling suspicious.

"Ummmm, pizza!" Mel's voice replied. "Open the door Zoe. The food's getting cold."

She threw open the door to find her friends squeezed together on her landing holding three steaming boxes of pizza and as many bottles of wine.

"Wha—"

"This is an intervention," Mel said, impervious to her protests as she pushed past Zoe into the apartment.

"Yeah," said Enid, balancing the pizza boxes in her arms, following behind Zoe. "Now let's eat. I'm starving."

"Sorry," Chiara mouthed as she scooted in behind Enid.

"At least we have wine," Travis added.

Zoe followed them to her kitchen and watched as they bustled around with plates and glasses, dumping the pizza boxes onto her coffee table and settling onto her couch. She was torn between frustration that her plans for the evening had been derailed and an overwhelming desire to burst into tears at the sight of her friends.

Giving up, she grabbed a plate and pulled up an oversized floor cushion.

"Thanks, you guys," she said as Travis slid a piece of pizza onto her plate and Enid handed her a glass of wine.

"We couldn't leave you to rot away in this hellhole," Mel said, wiping her hands on a napkin. "Enough is enough."

"It's hardly a hellhole and I wouldn't say I'm exactly rotting away."

"Near enough," Enid mumbled, fighting with a string of cheese that stretched between her mouth and her pizza. "You haven't been out in forever. Yikes, so stringy!"

"So, what's the deal Zoe," Travis asked. "Why are you hiding out?"

"I'm not. I'm just working. You know how it is. New job, lots of responsibilities. I really want to do well."

"Yeah, but there's working and then there's *working*," Travis insisted. "You seem to have taken working to a whole new level. You even missed the beach relay comps. We've done that as a team for five years straight!"

"I know. I'm sorry you guys. I just couldn't face it."

"Hey, we've found you a perfect match," Enid chirped. "So you're going to need to make some time in this ridiculous schedule to go on a date."

"No," Zoe shook her head vehemently. "Absolutely not. I'm done with dating."

"What do you mean done? You can't be done." Enid raised her eyebrows incredulously. "You're still vaguely young. You might live for another fifty years. You can't be *done* now!"

"Fifty? I hope I've got more time left than that. But whatever, I am done."

"Zoe. There is life after Reyna, you know?"

"Thank you, Enid," Zoe replied stiffly. "This has nothing to do with Reyna." Even saying her name out loud left a sting in her mouth. She knew there was a reason she had been hiding away.

"Okay, okay, don't get your knickers in a knot."

"Hey," Chiara interrupted. "Regardless of all that stuff, we need to spend some time together. We've hardly seen each other for months now. What with you, and Mel…" She trailed off.

Zoe looked sharply at Mel, taking in her new spiky black hair for the first time. She had gone from Madonna to Mel & Kim. "What do you mean. Where have you been, Mel?"

"If you'd been around in the last month, you'd have noticed that Mel's hardly been around as well," Enid said. "It's as if you both disappeared off the face of the earth."

Mel suddenly jumped up from the couch. "Just grabbing some more napkins," she called, disappearing into the kitchen.

"You can't run away from us in here, Mel," Enid called. "We can still see you. Zoe's apartment is way too tiny to hide."

"Oi!" Zoe protested. "But yes, come back here, Mel, and explain."

Mel stuck her head around the kitchen wall. "Fine." She returned to the couch with a handful of napkins.

"So?" Zoe prodded.

"First tell us why you're never going to date again."

She sighed deeply. "What can I say? You all know what's going on for me. I broke my dysfunctional heart over a woman who barely knew I existed, and now I have to hide away and lick my wounds for the rest of my life. Case closed. There's no mystery here. But where have you been?"

"Okay, okay," Mel held up her hands. "I've been seeing someone."

"Why the big secret?" Zoe asked.

"I wasn't sure you'd be pleased."

"Why? Who is it?"

"Her name is Sasha."

"Sasha?" Zoe wrinkled her brow in confusion. The name was familiar.

"When do we get to meet her?" Chiara asked.

"Tell us about her," Travis added. "What does she do? How did you meet her?"

"I, uh, well," Mel stuttered, unusually tongue-tied. "She works with computers. We met—"

"At work!" Zoe said, understanding suddenly dawning on her. "It's Sasha from IT! You're dating someone from the IT department! Mel, how could you?"

"She's not like the rest of them," Mel said quickly. "She's smart and really funny and sweet. She's actually been really helpful at work too."

"Well she could have tried to be some of those things when I was working there."

"Shut up, Zoe. She's actually really great."

"Sorry," Zoe said, realising she sounded mean. "If you like her, that's all there is to it."

"I do. She's pretty great." Mel's face broke into a shy smile. "I think this might actually be something."

"Wow." It was a bit of a shift to get her head around the idea that Mel was dating someone from the department that they had always professed to loathe, but if Mel was happy, that was all that counted. Realisation suddenly dawned on Zoe. "Wait, is that why you were so cagey a few months ago when I asked you if you were seeing someone at work?"

"Yeah." Mel looked sheepish.

"But why didn't you just say?"

"I dunno. It took us a bit to get our shit together. I wasn't sure if it was going to work. I kind of slept with her on a whim after we both worked late one night and ended up going for a drink, but I felt a bit weird about it. Luckily she was persistent, in a good way."

Mel grinned again and Zoe said, "Ew," before she could stop herself. "Sorry. Just getting used to the idea, that's all."

"No worries. I know you're going to love her when you get to know her. She really is loads of fun. In fact, I was hoping we could all get together this weekend."

"I don't think I can," Zoe said reflexively, but Mel cut her off.

"Please. This is really important to me." Mel's eyes were surprisingly serious.

It was impossible to refuse. "Fine."

"Great. Everybody in then? Dinner at La Travoletta on Saturday, seven p.m. Sharp."

"You're the one who's usually late, Mel," Travis said with a grin.

La Travoletta's was crowded, even for a Saturday night. In recognition of their group's long-standing patronage, the restaurant had reserved a table for them in a secluded alcove that sheltered them from most of the noise.

"Ever been here before?" Travis asked a nervous-looking Sasha who looked strange to Zoe in her crisp jeans and faded denim shirt. Zoe had been used to seeing her at work in a pair of neat black trousers and an Azoulay House-branded polo shirt. Casual Sasha was a bit disconcerting.

"Nope," Sasha answered with a shy smile. "It's my first time." Zoe couldn't believe the difference. So far Sasha had been open and engaging, had shook Zoe's hand politely and asked her how her new position was going. It was a whole different side of the standoffish, unhelpful IT girl Zoe had previously avoided like the plague.

"You'll love it here," Travis said. "The pizza is so good it's practically an institution."

A waiter approached their table, and then seeing the familiar group, called out a hearty greeting. "Ciao, friends. Same as usual?"

"Hi Rocco," Mel said. "We have one more tonight. Can you bring us an extra pizza?"

"Sure thing. Coming right up, ladies."

Sasha's eyebrows rose, looking pointedly at Travis. "Ladies?"

"It's cool," Mel reassured her. "Our running team's name back at uni was The Girls. It kind of stuck. We always reserve our table under that name so they're in on the joke. Trav doesn't mind."

"Right." Sasha gave another smile, this one with a nervous showing of teeth.

Enid poured out a round of drinks and they peppered Sasha with questions while they waited for their food.

"Enough, enough," Mel finally cried. "Poor Sasha. You'd think it was the first time you lot had ever met another human being. Oh thank god, the food's here."

Two waiters approached with their food, expertly shuffling around the drinks and cutlery to make room on the table. Sasha looked on in amusement as Mel took a piece of pizza and began to heap pasta on top of it.

"I've seen her do this before," Sasha said to Zoe. "It's the strangest form of carb loading I've ever seen."

"Too right," Zoe agreed. "Grosses me out."

"Hey, what's not to like?" Mel protested. "Pizza, good. Pasta, good. Pizza topped with pasta, double good."

"The restaurant actually made her a pasta pizza for her last birthday," Chiara told Sasha. "It looked hideous but she loved it."

"Yes I did, and I'm still waiting for them to put it on the menu. I keep telling them it'll be a total hit."

"So Sasha," Enid said, ignoring Mel's furious look. "How long have you worked at Azoulay House?"

"I've been onboard since the early days," Sasha replied, using her knife and fork to cut up her pizza, which amused Zoe who was using her hands to funnel a slice of Margherita into her mouth. "Reyna needed a secure platform for her web presence in order to facilitate an intranet to transfer sensitive client data. A small team of us came on line not long after she started the firm."

"Sounds complicated," Enid said. "And you've been there ever since?"

"Yeah, almost seven years now. It'll be strange when the new structure kicks in. Reyna's always been such a hands-on boss."

Zoe paused, her pizza slice halfway to her mouth. "What new structure?"

Mel, eyes wide, shot Sasha a quick headshake but while Zoe noticed, Sasha did not appear to.

"Oh, didn't Mel tell you?" Sasha went on. "Reyna has decided to restructure the firm. She's going to bring on a General Manager and take a step back from the day-to-day running of the business. She's also looking for a board of directors. It will mean a big change to the way the business runs. She won't be nearly so involved in the intricacies, which is probably good. She has way too much on her plate."

"How do you know this?" Zoe asked, catching a frown from Mel. "Sorry, just wondering," she added.

"I run the IT structure. She's had me add in functionality for a General Manager and the board. I think she's looking to get it all happening ASAP."

"So, Reyna will have less to do?"

"Oh, far less. I don't really know the ins and outs of what she's going to do in terms of her own position, but yeah, she might actually get her weekends back, poor lady. She's been working round the clock for at least the last seven years."

"You wouldn't catch me working like that. I'm all about the holidays and the weekends. Speaking of, who's up for a kayaking-camping adventure this summer?" Mel said, with an obvious attempt to shift the conversation away from Reyna and Azoulay House. "We haven't done one in ages. We could make our way around the peninsula?"

Zoe's mind raced, tuning out as the group discussed the logistics of such a trip, nodding and smiling along with the rest, but thinking of Reyna. Why had she suddenly decided to free up her schedule? Zoe felt a burning bitterness which she tried to push away. Reyna hadn't been willing to do that for her. What could have happened now to make her suddenly change her tune?

CHAPTER TWENTY

Reyna (Thursday, p.m.)

Reyna looked at her watch. With a start she realised it was almost three. If she didn't leave now, she'd be late to pick up Holden from school. She switched off her laptop and stowed it in her briefcase, scooping her notebook and mobile phone into her handbag.

"Nikki," she said, popping her head around her assistant's door. "I'm heading out. I'll be online later tonight to finalise the Sydney briefs, so can you make sure they're collated before they go in the folder?"

"Sure," her assistant replied with the bright smile she reserved for any request from Reyna. Reyna had seen her responding to other people's enquiries with a much less enthusiastic demeanour. "Are you in the office tomorrow?"

"No, I'll be working offsite. Get me on the mobile if you need me."

"No worries. Have a great weekend, Reyna."

"You too," Reyna called over her shoulder, already heading down the corridor.

Thankfully traffic was light and she slid into a parking space behind the school in record time. She would just get there before the bell if she moved fast. Whenever possible she liked to be waiting outside his classroom with the other parents when the bell rang, and she knew her parents did this when they picked him up too. If she didn't quite make it in time, he would go and play on the monkey bars with some other kids until she arrived, but she imagined it was nice for him to see a friendly face waiting for him.

Reyna hurried through the leafy school grounds, smiling at a few parents she recognised as she made her way to Holden's classroom. She really didn't know enough of them, but that would all change when her new restructure came in to play.

She thought back to her conversation with Linda Macintyre that morning. Linda had a selection of candidates for the General Manager position, ready for Reyna to review. If she liked the look of any of them on paper, she could progress to the interview stage. Linda had emailed the list to Reyna with their respective résumés, and Reyna looked forward to going over them tonight. Now that she had decided on the change, it couldn't come quickly enough. She just needed to hold on for a little longer. Patience, she reminded herself, coming to a halt outside Holden's classroom just as the bell rang. She still had the board of directors to select. But at least she could feel movement, a sense that she was on the cusp of a big change.

She hung back as children streamed out of the classrooms, keeping her eyes peeled for Holden. When his classroom seemed to have emptied but he still hadn't appeared, she felt a tug of anxiety. She hoped he hadn't been hurt and ended up in the sick bay. Usually they called her if there was an issue.

And then he was there, standing on the steps of the classroom, chatting earnestly with somebody who was hidden by the doorway. As Holden took a step backward the person he was speaking with moved forward into the light and Reyna found herself looking up at the slim figure of Zoe Cavendish, her light brown hair swept up in the familiar butterfly clip. As if in answer to Reyna's confusion, Holden suddenly looked over at her, pointing and waving. Zoe, apparently following his direction, looked over to where Reyna was standing, shielding her eyes from the sun with her hand.

"Aunty Rey," Holden called, cantering down the steps toward her. "Look! She used to work for you."

Reyna's head spun as Zoe followed Holden over to where she was standing.

"Hello," Zoe said simply, a polite smile in place. "Small world."

Reyna blinked, words stuck in her throat. Her mind was at sea. Zoe looked pale, a slightly haunted look behind her smile. "What are you—" Reyna began, but Holden jumped in, dancing around her excitedly.

"Zoe's been in this week doing the money program with us. I told her my aunty was good with money and how you have your own money house and everything, and she said she used to work for you! Isn't that so cool?"

"Holden was keen for us to say hello," Zoe added.

"Can I go and play on the monkey bars for a bit before we leave? I'm learning a new trick and I want to practise it."

"Sure." Reyna ruffled his hair, catching his bag as he shrugged it off his shoulders and raced over to the playground. "You're here with your new job?" Reyna asked, feeling stupidly slow. It was if someone had erased all the words from her mind and left her with an empty canvas.

"That's right. We're doing the schools in the southern region first. This is actually my first school."

"And you're here."

"I'm here."

"How's it going then? The job, I mean. Is it everything you hoped it would be?"

"And more." Zoe hugged her arms around herself, as if she was cold, even though the sun was shining brightly.

"Well that's great." Reyna found herself glancing over to the playground to check on Holden.

"I'd better let you go," Zoe said, following her look.

"No, I... He'd be happy doing that for hours. I just like to keep him in my line of sight. In case he breaks something." Reyna gave a self-conscious smile. "I'm not one of those helicopter parents or anything, but you should see the way he throws his body around. It's as if he thinks he's made of rubber."

"I know what you mean. This is the first time I've ever really spent time with kids, and they're pretty full on. Awesome, though. I love the crazy questions they come up with. One kid asked me to help him work out how long it would take for him to save his first million from his paper-round."

"Aiming high! I like it. I'm pretty sure I had similar thoughts as a child."

"Definitely one to watch," Zoe replied with a grin.

"So you're loving it then?" Reyna asked, allowing her eyes to finally connect with Zoe's. A jolt ran through her and she quickly looked away again, returning her gaze to the playground.

"I am. I have a great team and everyone's worked really hard to get the program up and running."

There was a pause while they both watched Holden dangle precariously from the monkey bars by one leg. Reyna sucked in her breath.

"It must be hard to watch him do that kind of stuff and not try to stop him," Zoe said.

"It is. I can't think how many times I've wished I could ask my sister how she would handle things, but of course..."

"You can't," Zoe finished.

"I can't."

"I hear there are some changes afoot at Azoulay House. It sounds like you've been pretty busy yourself over the last month."

Five weeks. But who's counting. "I have," she agreed. "I'm restructuring."

"That's great," Zoe said, her voice sounding far away.

Reyna turned to look at her again, catching and holding her gaze. "I hadn't realised how tied I was to my work until, well...what happened with us. I realised I wanted things to be different."

"You did?"

"Zoe," a voice from behind them called out. They both turned around to see Holden's classroom teacher standing at the top of the stairs. "I need to lock up the classroom in a sec, got a staff meeting to get to. Are you right to come and pack down your stuff?"

"Of course, I'll come straight up," Zoe replied and turned back to Reyna. "Holden is a great kid. I'm glad I got to meet him like this. Everything makes more sense now. Nice to see you, Reyna. Take care."

"And you," Reyna managed, as Zoe turned and jogged up the steps. Reyna wished she could call her back, but what was there to say? Nothing in her world had changed. Yet, she reminded herself. It wouldn't be long now.

"Aunty Rey," Holden cried from the monkey bars, causing her to turn in alarm. "Look at me." He was balancing on one foot at the top of the rungs, arms out in the air.

Her breath caught in her throat. "Nice one," she replied, fighting her instinct to tell him it wasn't safe, to warn him that he might hurt himself. "Hop down now, darling, we're going home."

They listened to the radio in the car, Holden singing along to the pop songs he knew in his sweet falsetto. Reyna giggled to herself, listening to him squeak out the high notes. When they got home, Holden raced for the kitchen.

"Can we make pancakes for afternoon tea? Sometimes I used to make them with Mum after school and she let me have syrup on them."

"She did? You've never mentioned that." Reyna was always torn between trying to re-create the things that Sarit and her husband had done with Holden and then thinking that was a terrible idea. "Do you think you would remember the recipe?"

He shrugged. "Sure. It's pretty simple. I think it was just flour and milk and eggs. And syrup. Do we have syrup?"

She rummaged through the fridge and retrieved an almost full bottle of maple syrup. "That's a yes on the syrup. Let's do this."

Under his careful direction they mixed up the pancake batter, spooning it into a sizzling pan and flipping them when they bubbled. When they had a small stack made they set them on the kitchen table and began to eat them.

"I like to roll mine up like this," Holden said, struggling to roll the pancake into a cigar shape without tipping out all the syrup. Reyna followed suit.

"So tell me about what you've been doing with Zoe at school. What's the program like?"

"It's pretty cool, actually," Holden said, nabbing another pancake and tipping a healthy slug of syrup over the top of it. "They're teaching us how to budget for things and how to save and stuff. I think I'd like to save up for my own goalie gloves for soccer next year."

"That's a great idea. I guess we haven't really discussed pocket money. What did your mum and dad do about pocket money?"

"They used to give me five dollars a week, but I had a big list of chores I had to do to get it. Maybe we could do the same here but without the chores?" He looked at her with large, hopeful eyes.

She shook her head with a grin. "I think the chores part sounds kind of important. People don't usually just give you money for no reason."

He sighed deeply and focused on rolling up his next pancake. "Okay, that's what they said. I can do the chores."

"And what else have you done in the money program?"

"It's mostly maths, which is weird 'cause usually I hate maths, but Zoe is a fun teacher and it doesn't feel like maths when she does it. And we're doing the difference between need and want, like how you *need* food but you *want* lollies, even though they're food as well, and how to split your money up so you have enough for the need stuff."

"Wow. Big stuff."

"Yeah, I think she's coming back tomorrow too. I can tell you what she says if you like. Do you know how to budget?"

Reyna suppressed a smile. "I do. That's something I'm pretty good at."

"I thought it would be. Because of your money house. How much money do you actually have at the house?"

"You mean Azoulay House?"

"Mmm, hmm," he mumbled through a mouthful.

"We don't actually keep money at my work. It's more like we help other people work out what to do with theirs."

"Like what Zoe is doing with us!"

"Exactly."

"Did she do that at your work too?"

"She did."

"Why did she leave?"

"I guess…she wanted to try something different."

"But it sounds exactly the same! Were you sad when she left?"

"I was."

Holden nodded, his eyes serious. "It's the worst when people leave. Aren't you the boss? You should have just told her not to."

"I wish I could have," she replied, watching him scoop the last mouthful of pancake up into his mouth and wipe his hands on his trousers. His mop of curly black hair bounced around his head, his creamy olive skin and dark eyes a picture of childhood. "But it doesn't work that way."

"Did you at least tell her you would be sad if she left?"

Reyna pursed her lips. "I don't think I really did, no."

His brow wrinkled in confusion. "But why not? Maybe she would have stayed if you'd told her you wanted her to."

Reyna was saved from answering when her mobile phone suddenly broke into the latest pop song from across the room. She raised an eyebrow and he grinned. "I changed your ringtone to something cooler."

She grabbed it, Samira's name lighting up the screen.

"Hiya."

"Hi, Rey. The boys want to know if Holden would like to come for a sleepover on Friday night and come with us on Saturday to the adventure playground in Mount Martha? We're heading out first thing Saturday morning so we'll be gone most of the day. I know you're pretty busy with work so I thought you might be happy for a bit of time to yourself?"

"Sure, let me just check with Holdy." Reyna waved the phone at him. "Jessie and Gideon are inviting you to sleep over tomorrow night and then spend the day with them at the adventure playground in Mount Martha. Would you like to—"

"Yes, yes, yes!" Holden jumped up from the table doing a little victory dance.

"No surprise, it's a yes," Reyna said with a laugh into the phone.

"Excellent. Pack him some trousers. They have a zip line there and the boys tell me if you're wearing shorts you get a wedgie."

"Right. Will do. When shall I bring him?"

"The boys have karate straight after school, so how about just before dinner? They've begged for pizza and a movie and we gave in."

"Sounds great," Reyna said. "See you tomorrow."

They rang off and Reyna filled Holden in on the plan.

He tipped up his plate, licking it clean of syrup and making happy noises. "Dad and I went on a massive zip line once," he said. "Jessie and Gideon are right. You do get a wedgie if you're wearing shorts."

The next day as Reyna dropped Holden at school, she looked anxiously around for Zoe. His questions had spun around in her mind throughout the night, as she tossed and turned in bed. Why hadn't she told Zoe how she felt about her? Maybe they could have worked it out together. By morning she had decided that if she saw Zoe when she was dropping Holden off for school, it would be a sign. She would tell her everything—how she couldn't stop thinking about her, how she ached for her, how she had never been touched, emotionally or physically that way in her life. *If* she saw her.

She kept her eyes peeled, nearly tripping over a small boy who had stopped to tie his laces in the middle of the path but didn't catch so much as a glimpse of her. Holden had thought Zoe would be back in their classroom today, but her sinking heart told her Zoe had probably moved on to the next school.

And who knew? Zoe had probably moved on to the next relationship. Having given Zoe no indication of her feelings, she was bound to have written her off as a crazy ex-boss, glad to be as far away from Azoulay House and its CEO as possible.

As Reyna left the schoolyard, she couldn't help but scan the grounds one last hopeful time, but there was no sign of the slim, athletic figure. She had missed her chance.

Her day dragged. A quick glance through the résumés Linda had sent her last night had yielded two potential candidates for the General Manager position, but now she had to wait for Linda to contact them and set up the interviews for her. She had an awe-inspiring list of potential names for her board of directors, but after she sent Linda the names that particularly resonated with her, there was again nothing to do but wait to hear back. She tried to focus on the Sydney briefs, but her mind constantly flicked back to the colour of Zoe's eyes, the feel of her mouth, the heat of her skin, the taut line of her belly. Reyna finally gave up, shutting her laptop and heading out of the house for a walk.

With an hour to spare before she was due to pick up Holden, and a fresh spring day unfurled before her, she decided to take a roundabout walk to the school, putting in her headphones to listen to music. It was a rare treat to have this kind of time to herself, but the heaviness in her heart made it difficult to enjoy. Come on, she urged herself, trying to buck up her spirits. When did she ever get to just wander about in the sunshine? She and Holden hardly ever had the chance to walk home from school, even though it was only a twenty-minute walk, because Reyna never had the time to walk there in the first place to pick him up. But things would be different next year, she thought, inhaling the scent of plum blossom on the air. Things were going to change.

She reached the school with half an hour to spare and found a seat at a picnic bench in a patch of sunshine near the front gate. Switching to a podcast, she tried to relax on the bench, closing her eyes as she listened to a women's business podcast she enjoyed but seldom had time for. She smiled to herself as the presenter made the point that most people listening to her show would either be too tired to take on board the advice or too busy. She usually fell into both of those categories. She would pay for her lack of industry over the weekend, but knowing that Holden would be off with the boys meant she had an entire extra day up her sleeve to catch up, and she forced herself not to worry.

A tap on her shoulder caused her to start, her eyes flying open as she spun around.

"Hi," Zoe said, standing before her with a nervous smile.

Reyna pulled the earbuds from her ears and stood. "I thought you had gone."

Zoe's face tightened, a hurt look crossing her eyes.

"I didn't mean it like that," Reyna said quickly, putting her hand on Zoe's arm. "I was worried I wouldn't see you. I hoped I would."

"You did?"

"Yes." She dropped her hand from Zoe's sleeve, suddenly unsure of herself. "I wanted to talk to you. I..." Reyna cursed as the bell rang. She shook her head. "I have to go and get Holden."

"Of course. It was good to see you. I'm glad we got to say bye."

"It doesn't have to be goodbye," Reyna said, before she could stop herself.

Zoe narrowed her eyes. "It doesn't?"

"Have dinner with me tonight."

Zoe looked at her incredulously. "I'm sorry, you want *me* to have dinner with you tonight?"

"Yes. Please. If you're free? Holden is staying at a friend's house, so we could go out or you could come to my place."

"Come to your *place*?"

"If you'd like to."

They stared at each other for a moment, until Reyna became aware of the stream of children pouring out of the classrooms. "I really have to get Holden," she repeated.

"Okay."

"Okay?"

"Okay, I'll have dinner with you tonight," Zoe said hesitantly.

"Good." Reyna kissed Zoe softly on the cheek. "Come for seven. I'll text you the address."

When the doorbell rang at seven thirty, Reyna was in the middle of changing her outfit for the fourth time and wondering if Zoe was actually coming. She had initially decided on a pair of casual slacks and a soft, velvet shirt, changing to something a little more formal when she realised that might not have looked very keen. She then worried her outfit was far too businesslike and boring, changing into a cocktail dress, which, at the last minute, she had determined to be horridly suggestive, discarding it in a crumpled pile as she flicked through her wardrobe in despair. Hurriedly shrugging back on the first outfit, Reyna padded to the door as the bell rang again, barefoot and tucking in her shirt.

She opened the door to a nervous-looking Zoe, dressed in a simple blue dress and holding a bottle of wine.

"Come in," Reyna said, ushering her inside. "We're having Indian."

"You know how to cook Indian? That's impressive," Zoe said, following Reyna down the hallway, and then stopped clearly taking in the array of takeaway containers Reyna had spread across the kitchen table.

"I definitely don't know how to cook Indian, but I remember you said you liked it when we were in Alice Springs, so I got a bit of everything."

Zoe laughed. "You didn't have to do that."

"I think I did. My cooking skills aren't exactly up to date standard."

"So this is a date?" Zoe looked at her from under her eyelashes and Reyna felt her heart skip in her chest.

"I hope so," she replied softly and took Zoe's hand. Reyna intertwined their fingers, tugging Zoe gently toward her. "In fact, I'm hoping it will be the first of many. If you'd like that."

Zoe's brown eyes were hesitant. "This is a bit of a change to your tune, Reyna."

"I know. There's a lot to talk about. But these last five weeks have been…hard. I've tried to just get on with things, but all

I could think about was you. I told myself it would pass, but everywhere I looked, everything I did, every place I turned, I saw your face. I felt your eyes on me. I heard your voice in my head. When I saw you at the school yesterday, it was as if the sun had finally come out after five weeks of darkness. I know my life is pretty crazy right now, but I'm making some changes so that it doesn't have to be this way forever. And if you're still interested, I'd like to see where things could go for us."

It was a long speech and Reyna waited for Zoe to say something, searching her eyes for a response. Finally, Zoe stepped forward, caressing Reyna's cheek with the back of her fingers.

"I'd like that too," she said and grazed her lips against Reyna's.

Reyna shivered, pulling Zoe in close, wrapping her arms around her waist. "So can we do some more of this then?" she asked, claiming Zoe's mouth with her own and deepening the kiss. When they broke off, Zoe smiled coyly and shook her head.

"Food's going cold."

"It's better that way," Reyna replied, kissing her again.

In the morning they sat on a bench in Reyna's backyard, drinking tea and eating toast in the soft yellow sunshine.

"We didn't do quite as much talking last night as we probably should have," Zoe said, taking Reyna's hand.

"No," Reyna agreed, wrapping her arm around Zoe's shoulder and nibbling her ear. Her heart felt light and happy in a way she wasn't sure she had ever experienced before. She was almost giddy with joy and relief. "Do you have plans today? We could do some more…talking?" she said with a coy smile.

"Oh yes," Zoe said, snuggling in closer under Reyna's arm. "We definitely need to do more *talking*."

Reyna caught Zoe's eyes with her own, feeling suddenly serious. "Things might be a bit tricky at first, Zoe, until I've got the business under control, but if you're willing to stick with me, things are going to be different. I'll have more free time on my hands. Hopefully I'll just be working like a normal person, maybe even nine to five."

Zoe gasped in mock horror. "No! Nine to five? For Reyna Azoulay? That's unheard of."

Reyna looked sheepish. "I think I can do that. I really want to for Holden's sake as well."

"Speaking of," Zoe said, turning her gaze to the garden as she took in the soccer nets and cubby house. "Will this be a problem for him?"

"No," Reyna replied. "He really liked you. He's always known I'm gay. Gay old Aunty Rey," she said with a grin. "You could meet him properly if you'd like to stay for dinner tonight?"

"Hmm, but that would mean we'd have to spend all day together." Zoe narrowed her eyes. "Don't you have work to do?"

"I do," Reyna admitted, "but I can try to catch up tomorrow."

"You know what? I also have some work to do. If you have a spare computer lying around here we could both squeeze in a little work at some point today."

"Ooo, I can't decide if you're a dream come true or a terrible enabler," Reyna said, nuzzling her face into Zoe's neck. "But you smell like a dream come true, so I'm going with that one. Does that mean you'll stay for dinner?"

"I will."

Bella Books, Inc.

Women. Books. Even Better Together.

P.O. Box 10543
Tallahassee, FL 32302

Phone: 800-729-4992
www.bellabooks.com